THE NOTORIOU

BY

ANTONY PELLY

"The whole art of war consists in getting at what is on the other side of the hill."
   Arthur Wellesley, Duke of Wellington

SCOTLAND, 1746

"God Almighty! Keep them from the house, child."

The redcoats came across the hilltop. It was so unexpected that the clansman lying watching the track into the glen was unaware that they were there behind and above him. There were about ten of them, under a sergeant. They were tired, bored and lethargic. Long fruitless days struggling across barren hills searching for the will o' the wisp Prince Charles Edward - 'Bonnie Prince Charlie' - had long since lost its appeal.

The girl in the farmyard below was the first to notice them, working their way slowly down the steep hill towards the farm. She was in the hard packed dirt area in front of the house, perfecting her sword dance with two sticks in place of swords. She did not stop, but called urgently towards the house:-

"There's redcoats coming down the brae."

A face appeared briefly at the doorway and was gone.

"God Almighty. Keep them from the house, child. Keep them occupied, by all we hold dear."

She did not answer, but stooped and adjusted the sticks a little. She looked up, seeming to see the soldiers for the first time. She waved to them. One or two waved back. She stood watching them as they reached the bottom of the hill and made towards the farm.

"Have ye come to see me dance?" She called to them,

and laughed. "Watch."

She was graceful as a young deer, beautiful in her dance. Her feet flew between the sticks. Her body seemed weightless.

"See," she said, pausing in her dance. "D'ye like it?"

The soldiers stood at the farm gate, uncertain. A dangerous moment. With a bad sergeant the men might have raped her, raped her and killed her.

"That's a pretty dance you're doing," said the sergeant. "Go on."

She laughed again. She lifted her arms above her head and sprang into the dance, leaping and twirling round the sticks. Abruptly, she stopped.

"Do ye want a drink? I'm thirsty."

A bucket of clear burn water stood at the farmhouse door. She plunged the dipper in and took a mouthful, then held the dipper out towards the soldiers. They pushed the gate open and shuffled into the yard.

"Thanks, lass. Where's your mam and da?"

"They're away on the hill, the both of them, searching our beasties. They're gone, our beasties."

The soldiers exchanged glances. Every head of stock they could lay hands on had been rounded up. Since their victory over Bonnie Prince Charlie at Culloden the army had devastated the Highlands with a savage brutality. They passed the dipper round between themselves.

"There's nae a soul here but me the day. They'll be back come dark if ye want to wait for them."

The sergeant walked to the open door. He leaned his hands on the jambs and bent forward into the gloom.

"All right, lads. Let's go. Thanks for the drink, lass."

She smiled at them as they filed out through the gate and set off down the track out of the glen.

The girl reset the sticks, and fell to her dancing again.

"They're gone," she called into the house.

Slowly, circumspectly, the two men came to the door. They stood back in the darkness of the interior.

"Dear mother of God, but that was close. You've saved our lives, Jean. You're the bravest girl in Scotland. Let me never have as close a shave as that again. You've the coolest head in Scotland, Jean. I never saw such coolness, nor such courage.

"If all my people were as brave as you - aye, and as cool, - we'd have taken the kingdom, so help me God. I'd be on my throne. I'd not be running through the glens like a hunted hare. Damn Murray and all his faint hearts....

"Jean, child, I can never thank you for this. See, I have nothing now, but when I come back and claim my kingdom you shall have your reward. You shall sit at my side when I am crowned. Hear me, Neil. If ever, - ever, - I say, - you or your kin are in peril, Jean, if ever you are in need - you or your kin - come to me and I will not disappoint you. Do you hear me, Neil? She's saved our lives. We owe this girl the greatest debt that any man can owe."

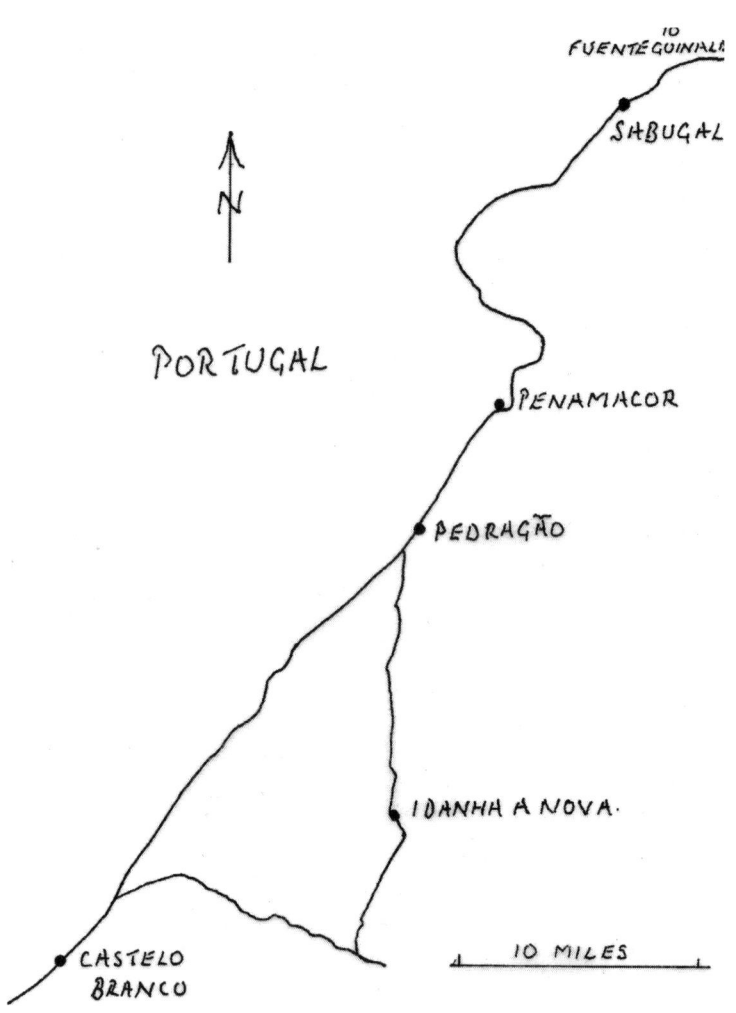

Chapter I

IDANHA A NOVA, PORTUGAL. APRIL 1812.

They always had to be careful in Portugal

What constitutes a spy? Truth to tell, Colquhoun Grant was never entirely comfortable with the question. In Lord Wellington's eyes he was an 'exploring officer' or, an ever more frequent description, an 'intelligence officer.'

To the French he was a spy - 'the notorious Grant,' with a price on his head big enough to set some peasant up for life - if the French paid it, of course, and didn't shoot the betrayer or hang him for his treachery.

The French would execute him on the spot if they captured him.

But what does constitute a spy?

Before and during a battle the spyglass is as valuable a weapon as any musket or cannon. To know how the enemy intends to manoeuvre, where he is massing his force, where his main attack is going to come, that is the information that wins battles. Nobody calls that spying. It is the vital gathering of knowledge that is essential to win the day.

How many times had Lord Wellington been heard to say with pride that the French had no idea of his movements, whereas he knew what they were about almost before they did. True, most of the information came from the Spanish or Portuguese, volunteered or paid for, but the English exploring officers gave him the most vital information because their training and military knowledge enabled them to evaluate what they saw.

Lord Wellington's whole strategy was founded on information. With five French armies in Spain, as there were, against his one small English army, Lord Wellington would have been unable to lift a finger had he not known exactly what the French were up to. Without a constant stream of information he could never have survived in the Peninsular for the four years that the war had lasted so far.

And always there was the one vital unanswered question, the possibility beyond all others for which Lord Wellington needed the earliest information: would Napoleon come back to Spain to lead his armies in person, unite them, and, no shadow of doubt, outnumber the English army so decisively that no amount of good generaling could defeat him? And if he did come back, when would it be?

Because if that happened, and Lord Wellington was taken unawares, it would be the end.

The English would be driven out, annihilated even, perhaps. Lord Wellington would be disgraced. Probably the Government would fall. Napoleon's hold on Europe would be complete and unshakeable. But it could only happen if Lord Wellington failed to get information of Napoleon's approach. And that would not happen as long as the constant stream of intelligence continued to pour into his

Headquarters.

There was a fine line between gathering intelligence and spying. Colquhoun considered that he never quite crossed it. Always he wore his uniform, his conspicuous red coat with its major's insignia and its green facings of the 11th Regiment of Foot, often under a cloak, to be sure, but always he went about openly as an officer of Lord Wellington's army.

There was no question that it was not spying when he sat his horse on some hilltop and trained his spyglass on the French. Then, it was up to them to retaliate, as they invariably did, and up to him to outride them and escape - as he invariably did. How many times had they spotted him watching them? How many times had they unlimbered a light gun, the nimble gunners taking no more than a few seconds to get a round off at him. How many times had they sent a troop of light cavalry pellmell up the hill to get him? Always he had out ridden them.

It was almost a game. He had laughed at them as he galloped off, jumping anything in his path, secure in the knowledge that he could out run anything the French could put against him.

He was not quite so sure when it was a matter of hiding and watching them unobserved. But then it was really up to their cavalry scouts and outriders to sweep the country efficiently and prevent him getting so close to them. Not that the patrols strayed far from the main body of the army if they could help it. The guerrillas hanging on their flanks were far too terrifying a threat for even the bravest of the French, courageous and bold soldiers as they were.

Anyway, Colquhoun enjoyed the life. Somewhat serious minded, a highland Scot, he had more acquaintances than friends among his brother officers in the 11th Foot and was more than happy to be on detachment from the routine of regimental life.

He liked the Spanish: they liked him. He trusted them: they trusted him. He felt entirely safe amongst them. They had saved him from capture many times. Leon, the Spaniard who rode with him, part servant, mostly companion, he trusted with his life.

The Portuguese he was not so sure about. There was always a possibility that they might betray him. Portugal had never risen against the French in the totally committed, passionate way that Spain had. But their country had not suffered to quite the same extent as had Spain. They were perhaps not so passionate a people. The Spanish would never betray him for money. The Portuguese just might.

And here he and León were, back in Portugal, for the third time, as it were.

Twice before the French had invaded Portugal, and twice been driven out by Lord Wellington.

This third incursion, Colquhoun was sure, was nothing more than a diversion, possibly ordered directly by an out of touch Napoleon in Paris, possibly simply to try to divert Lord Wellington's attention from Badajoz, just over the border into Spain a hundred and fifty miles to the South, - which city he was currently besieging, - and possibly in the hope that they could re-supply themselves by finding and looting English supply depots.

Most likely Marshal Marmont, who had been commanding Napoleon's Army of Portugal for a year now, was far too good a general to have made this third incursion unless he had been specifically ordered to do so. His army had only two weeks' rations. It would be impossible for them to live off the land at this time of the year - April - and if they had not achieved whatever it was they had set out to do before their food ran out, they would have to retreat back into Spain.

Well, the two weeks were up.

Marmont's army had achieved nothing.

They were beginning to starve. All the supply depots in their path had been burned. They were going back, retreating back into Spain, there was no doubt of it.

Colquhoun and León had been shadowing them the whole time.

This morning at the Portuguese town of Castelo Branco they had made contact with the Hussars of the King's German Legion who formed the cavalry screen of Lord Wellington's army. Colquhoun had passed on all his information and in exchange had learned that the town of Badajoz had fallen and Lord Wellington was now moving seven divisions of his army North to confront Marshal Marmont.

Colquhoun's information was vital.

Marmont only had three divisions - three divisions against seven, if only Lord Wellington could catch him.

The atrocious April weather was going to hamper Marmont's retreat. All the rivers were so swollen as to be impassable. Of course, it was the same for both armies. Both would be floundering in the mud, both soaked for days on end, both hungry, both exhausted: but if Lord Wellington could catch Marmont before he had a chance to cross the river Agueda and find sanctuary in Spain, there could only be one result.

Marshal Marmont's Army of Portugal would cease to exist.

The afternoon was more like Scotland than Portugal.

Remorseless freezing rain poured from a leaden sky. Clouds drifted round the tops of the hills. Water dripped from hats, cloaks and boots. It ran in rivulets down the necks, flanks and legs of their horses, whose breath steamed in the chill air.

Not that Colquhoun particularly minded, or even noticed it. His childhood in the far North of Scotland, let alone soldiering in the Iberian Peninsula, had inured him to hardship, be it heat, cold, hunger or fever. He was too well pleased with the day's work, and the way things were going, to mind about the weather.

Riding a few paces behind Colquhoun, León was hating every moment of the afternoon. He was not feeling well. His hot Spanish blood loathed the rain and longed for the sun. It was Portuguese rain, too: somehow worse than Spanish rain.

León never felt comfortable in Portugal. He neither liked nor trusted the Portuguese. Not that there was anything unusual in that. The Portuguese neither liked nor trusted the Spanish. In a surly sort of way. They had none of the fire and passion of the Spanish. Portugal had not risen against the French in fanatical loathing of the invaders as had the Spanish. They just wanted to get on with their lives - unless, of course, they were in the direct path of the French army, in which case they suffered just as badly as did the Spanish, and, he had to admit, reacted in the same way. But otherwise, they just wanted the French to go away.

Grudgingly, León also had to admit that the Portuguese army, fighting with the English, was not altogether useless. But that was only because they had English officers training them and kicking them on. They were not naturally good fighters: not like the Spanish.

And he always suspected that the Portuguese might betray them for money - something that would be unthinkable to a Spaniard.

They always had to be careful in Portugal.

Like now.

Major Grant - known to the Spanish as *Granto Bueno* - wanted to spend the night in a Portuguese village close to the retreating French - Idanha a Nova, - a poor sort of a place on a steep hillside. Who knows who might be watching them and hurrying off to betray them to the French for some money reward.

If the afternoon had not been so wretched, if he had been feeling better and had not been so utterly miserable in this never ending rain León would have persuaded *Granto Bueno* to spend the night in the open. He had never felt so cold and tired and wet.

They had, after all, been more or less in the saddle for over two weeks without any rest or shelter, watching the French army all the time, always on their guard, always having to stay alert, always hungry. It was no wonder he felt exhausted. *Granto Bueno* was probably right. They would have to take the risk and get dry under cover.

At least they had food. The German Hussars had filled their saddle bags. He groaned. If only the rain would stop.

Colquhoun heard the groan and skewed round in his saddle.

"Not far to go now, *amigo*. We'll get you under cover and some food in your belly. You'll feel better tomorrow."

They crested the hill. The track led down in front of them, corkscrewing back and forth down to a river in the valley below. The river was angry, swollen twenty yards wider than it would normally be at the shallow crossing area, writhed in mist and spray and rain.

'Don't think I'd like to take that on without knowing what I was doing,' thought Colquhoun, 'nor without a horse like this.'

The key to his success. Lord Wellington ensured that he

always had the best horses in the whole army, money no object, thoroughbred crossed Irish draft, usually, strong, hardy, intelligent, and fast.

Cautiously Colquhoun eased the horse into the swirling water. It snorted and pawed the shallows, nose down, testing the water, then slowly moved forward into the flood. The strength of the current pressed against them. A false step and man and horse would be swept away. The water was half way up his boots, the far bank blurred in the mist and rain. Behind him, León's horse reluctantly followed Colquhoun's lead and slowly, carefully, the horses picked their way across and out onto the far bank.

The track led uphill through the rock and scrub, a mile, maybe two and they would reach Idanha a Nova. The track widened a little, and they rode abreast.

"Go on ahead, León, and see if the coast's clear. I don't think they could be there, but you never know."

The French rearguard, so far as Colquhoun knew, was on the main road - if you could call the rutted track by such a grand name - several miles to the West, struggling hungrily and as fast as they could in this rain back towards the Portuguese town of Sabugal and the comparative safety of numbers in joining up with Marshal Marmont's main force. It was unlikely, especially on a day like this, that they would come foraging so far from their line of march.

But you never knew.

And you never took the chance.

The early evening was gloomy enough outside. Inside the church it was almost dark.

Colquhoun stood just inside the door, waiting for his eyes to adjust. One or two votive candles did nothing but emphasise the surrounding gloom. It was empty - no, there was a little black bundle of a woman kneeling rapt in prayer.

No danger there. The rain dripping from his cloak was forming a considerable puddle even in the short time he had been there.

He shivered involuntarily and stepped forward.

The woman was praying desperately to the Blessed Virgin, explaining that the cow had died. She had driven it off when she heard the French were coming but what with the hurry and the steep ground and the cow so close to calving perhaps it had eaten something it shouldn't but whatever the reason it had died calving and the calf dead inside her. Without milk from the cow and meat from the calf she had lost they didn't have food to keep themselves through the lean months of spring until the crops could be harvested and unless the Virgin would intervene they would starve. And then the French had robbed her, too - not a week ago, the Godless plunderers, stealing whatever they could lay their hands on, God rot their souls in Hell for all eternity. But, thank the Lord, they hadn't found everything. She had been cunning. She had hidden a little so carelessly that the French found it easily, and thought her a stupid old woman and had laughed at her, God rot them, and thought they had been clever and gone off jeering at her. But she had had the last laugh, because they hadn't found her proper hiding place - not that there was much in it, the Blessed Virgin must understand. So there was a little left, - the Blessed Virgin must know the whole truth, but she must intervene to help them, please God, oh, please God. If the French should come again…..

At first she was not aware that a man had entered the church, and ignored the footsteps up the aisle beside her.

Then the holy father appeared, - a thief himself, God forgive her for saying so, but he was, because he demanded tax from her, and why should she pay him who did no work himself - he came hurrying from his private room behind the altar towards the footsteps.

She heard him say:

"*Granto.*" And then:

" I was half expecting you."

Granto?

The footsteps said:

"Are we safe here?"

"Yes. They're at Pedrogão. They came last week, but they won't come back. They're in a hurry to get back North."

That must be the French, God curse them.

"Thank God. León is about done in. We must stay here the night."

León?

León and *Granto?*

Granto? The one the French called 'the notorious spy?' With a price on his head? And León? That was his Spanish companion. The Spanish had no place in Portugal. The French were offering good money for them. Enough to buy many cows. Could it be that the Blessed Virgin had heard her plea?

Her heart started to pump and she shrank down lower on her knees.

"Somewhere with a proper hot fire would be most welcome, padre. It's been a bleak day with the rain."

"Yes, yes, of course. Let's think...."

If she peeped between her fingers she could just make out the footsteps - muddy, spurred boots below the skirt of a muddy, dripping, long cloak, and a hand holding a soaking soldier's hat wrapped in oilskin.....

Footsteps was saying:

"That's a handsome thought, but even for warm quarters such as that I can't take the risk. It's too dangerous. If they surprised us down here, we'd not have a chance. We must stay up on the plateau….."

Of course she couldn't go, but her son could, the useless oaf. Pedrogão, the padre said. Not too far. 'Blessed Virgin, you have heard my prayer. Blessed Virgin, I hail you as the Mother of all Goodness. Thank you, thank you. You have delivered them into my hand. You have saved us. Blessed Virgin, I thank you. I thank you.'

They brought the Portuguese peasant straight to the commanding officer of the 27^e *Ligne*, the regiment on rearguard duty. The officer was no fool. He sent for the Lieutenant who had commanded the foraging party in Idanha a Nova not a week ago. The Lieutenant was no fool either. He was a seasoned revolutionary soldier with many years experience in the ranks before he had won his commission.

"*Mon Colonel*, if Major Grant has been foolish enough to lodge in Idanha a Nova, he is ours for the taking."

"How so?"

"The village is right on the edge of the high plateau - falling off it, you would say. The land falls steeply from the plateau. The village is built on the East slope, and the fall is steep. It's tucked in under the high ground - you hardly can see it until you drop into it from the plateau. It's even steeper to the South - impassable that side. A few men at the bottom on the East could see anyone escaping that way. And better still, a kilometre onto the plateau, to the West, there's a good hill with a rock pinnacle that gives a clear view of anything that moves up out of the village. It's steep on the village side, but an easy climb from the back. Put a lookout up there and presuming we come from the North the only way he could possibly go would be South West - back towards Castelo Branco, which is probably what he would do anyway. A good detachment of dragoons there would plug that gap."

"How many men would you need?"

"Are you sending me, *mon Colonel*?"

"Yes."

"Then give me every man you can spare and it will be my honour to bring Major Grant back to you, dead or alive, as you wish."

"Oh, bring him alive. A trophy like that must be seen, and paraded. He can go on his own legs to the Marshal. He wouldn't thank us for a half rotten corpse and a good public execution for this *sacré* English spy will concentrate the minds of these *sacré* peasants."

"Then give me every man you can spare, *mon Colonel*, and every horse."

And if the Lieutenant failed it would not be the Colonel's fault. Grant had got away so often that it was almost inevitable he would do so again. Like a ghost, he would probably vanish. But if the Lieutenant should succeed, why then the honour would still be his. And what an honour!

They spent the night in a hovel on the edge of the village, where the steep road up from the square passes the little convent. Only a few more hovels - farmhouses, to be charitable - and the village ended and gave way to the stone walled fields and plots on the edge of the plateau where the villagers grew their crops and grazed their livestock.

They stabled the horses at ground level with the pig and livestock and dogs, and climbed the ladder to the upper floor where a miserable fire filled the whole space with a choking smoke. At least it might keep the fleas at bay.

The black garbed woman tending the cooking pot was suspicious. The man was silent. But their son was in the army, fighting to free them from the French, and the English were the only ones who might get rid of the hated invaders, so they indicated to Colquhoun and Leon to come to the fire and warm themselves.

To their surprise *Granto*, the English one, who the Spanish called *Granto Bueno* - *Granto* the good, - spoke Portuguese as well as they did. They could understand everything he said.

He apologised for having to be there, for putting them in danger, and produced some silver to pay for his lodging. He shared his bread with them, and some meat taken from his saddle bag. He asked them about their farm, and seemed to understand the difficulties of their lives. When they told him about their son he was full of praise for the bravery of the boy, and said how well the Portuguese army carried itself, and how bravely they stood and fought the French.

In the end, they were proud that the holy father had chosen them to lodge *Granto*. Their standing in the village would go up. They would be respected. It would be a proud thing to say they knew *Granto* and had sheltered him. They were welcome, both of them, even though the other one, - who seemed too tired to do anything but eat a quick mouthful and then fall asleep - was a Spaniard, and therefore not to be trusted.

But asleep, and in the company of such a man as *Granto*, surely even a Spaniard was acceptable.

They spent a miserable night. To Colquhoun's concern, León lay curled up shivering. He wondered if the Spaniard had caught a fever from the dreadful weather and whether he might have to leave him here. It should be safe enough. The advance guard of Lord Wellington's army would be here tomorrow or the next day. The French would not come back this way. He begged a blanket from the old woman and draped it over Leon. It seemed to help. León stopped shivering and fell deeply asleep.

Colquhoun at first slept fitfully, then heavily. They were half poisoned by the smoke from the fire. He had meant to wake in the small hours before dawn and vanish into the hills, but he slept on in a troubled sleep, instinct warning him to wake up, his body and mind too leaden to respond. León slept like one dead.

Frantic knocking on the door below jerked everyone awake.

A voice, desperate in its urgency, was shouting:

"Danger - Danger. The French are here, searching the village. They know *Granto* is here. They're calling for him by name. They're searching every house, hundreds of them. Go. Get *Granto* out. They're surrounding the village. Go this instant before they get here."

Colquhoun was on his feet at the first knock.

He kicked León awake, threw the saddle bags through the hatch and slid down the ladder after them. The noise had frightened the horses. They were straining at their head collars, showing the whites of their eyes, clattering back and forth against the rope that tied them. He cursed that they had not left them saddled after rubbing them dry last night.

"Easy, easy." He made his voice soft and comforting. "Easy now, easy."

And as they quieted at the sound he called urgently. "I hear you. Go" to the unseen voice outside the door.

The knocking stopped: running footsteps faded down the

street.

Colquhoun flung first his own and then León's saddles onto the horses, soothing them with his voice, cursing silently as he searched for the bridles in the dark stable, calling urgently "Come on, León, come on!" as León tumbled down the ladder. He adjusted his saddle, girthed up and swung the animal round to the door.

"Ready, León?"

A bleary "Yes" and León was beside him.

"When I open the door vault on and ride like hell for the high ground. Don't stop for anything or anyone."

León nodded. He looked like death.

"Go!"

Colquhoun pulled the door open and the horse outside in one movement. He was mounted almost before they had cleared the stable door.

The morning was barely light, the rain still sluicing down. Water was streaming down the street.

Colquhoun put spurs to the horse. It bounded forward.

A French soldier appeared in the road in front of him. The man looked stricken, paralysed by the sudden galloping horse. He had marched all day yesterday and half the night. He had waited shivering in the pelting rain through the small hours as his officers sent men off to block the roads. He was numb with cold and fatigue. He was hungry. He was in no mood for heroics. He sprang out of the roadway as fast as his aching body could spring, and the two horses rushed past him and out of the village.

They did not get far.

French dragoons were coming up the road towards them.

Their yell of triumph alerted Colquhoun before he saw them. Without pause he turned the horse and jumped the stone wall beside the road into the nearest field.

Now it was anyone's game in the mass of fields and little paths and stone enclosures that stretched for quarter of a mile to a fringe of small oak trees and the scrub and jumbled rock of the hill beyond.

To his left, if he could reach it, the hill fell away to a saddle. If he could get over it before the dragoons he could outride them and lose them in the wild scrub country beyond.

He jumped a stream and another wall, sure that León's horse would follow his lead, and swerved onto a path that surely led to the saddle.

"Come on, León. Come on."

Peering up, he saw two dragoons coming down towards him through the trees from the saddle. One of them was shouting to men he could not see.

To the North, then, was the only hope.

The dragoons were no match for them. They had been mounted all night. They and their horses were exhausted.

León was trailing yards behind Colquhoun as he reached the oak trees. He pulled up and for the first time realised that they were watched from the hill above them. He had been unaware of it, but now he heard the shouted voices.

The French had soldiers up there.

He felt quick admiration for the officer who had laid this trap, quick anger at himself for falling into it.

From the shouts there must have been twenty or more of them, strung out along the top, several on the rock pinnacle that commanded the view of everything below them. They had spotted Colquhoun's red coat through the gloom of the morning almost as soon as he cleared the village. Without his enveloping cloak, which he now realised he had left in the hovel in the rush to get out, his uniform - red coat, white breeches - was a beacon to his pursuers.

The stunted oak trees were giving way to impenetrable scrub in a jumble of rock. The horses stumbled. The urgent shouts from above were being answered from somewhere close by.

Infantrymen must be closing in on them across the fields.

Colquhoun dismounted. The horses could help them no further.

"Come on, León. Come on!"

León joined him. He looked ghastly. He was gasping for breath.

Maybe they could find somewhere to hide in the rocks.

León was behind him again, ten yards or more as Colquhoun fought his way through the bush.

There was a shot, and a cry.

He stopped and turned. León was staggering like a drunk, collapsing. Behind him, Colquhoun could see the blue coated Frenchman and the still smoking musket. Another blue coat appeared. Colquhoun saw the musket come up to the man's shoulder. León was no more than five yards from him.

"No!"

He saw the man's eyes swivel from León to him, saw the look in them and the smile, saw them turn back to León, the light in them, and then the face disappeared behind the smoke of the musket shot. León was thrown forward onto the rocks.

"No!"

León was still alive - just. He looked up at Colquhoun with a baffled, blank look, perhaps knowing him, perhaps already too far gone. A boot sent Colquhoun sprawling as he tried to lift León's head. Another shot. León's body shuddered and was still. There were several blue coats there now, a third smoking musket, three or four pointing at him.

He did not move. An officer appeared, drawn sword in his hand.

"Sir, you are my prisoner."

"You've killed him. Why did you kill him?"

The officer shrugged, glanced contemptuously at León's body.

"Who is he? Your servant? A peasant."

"The truest patriot who ever lived."

"A patriot, pah! Do I have the honour of addressing Major Grant?"

"I am Major Grant, yes."

Colquhoun hardly heard the cheering and the shouts of triumph as soldiers came running to the spot. He was looking down at León whose blood was mingling with the rain and running dark onto the rocks.

"Goodbye, *amigo*. You have served your country well."

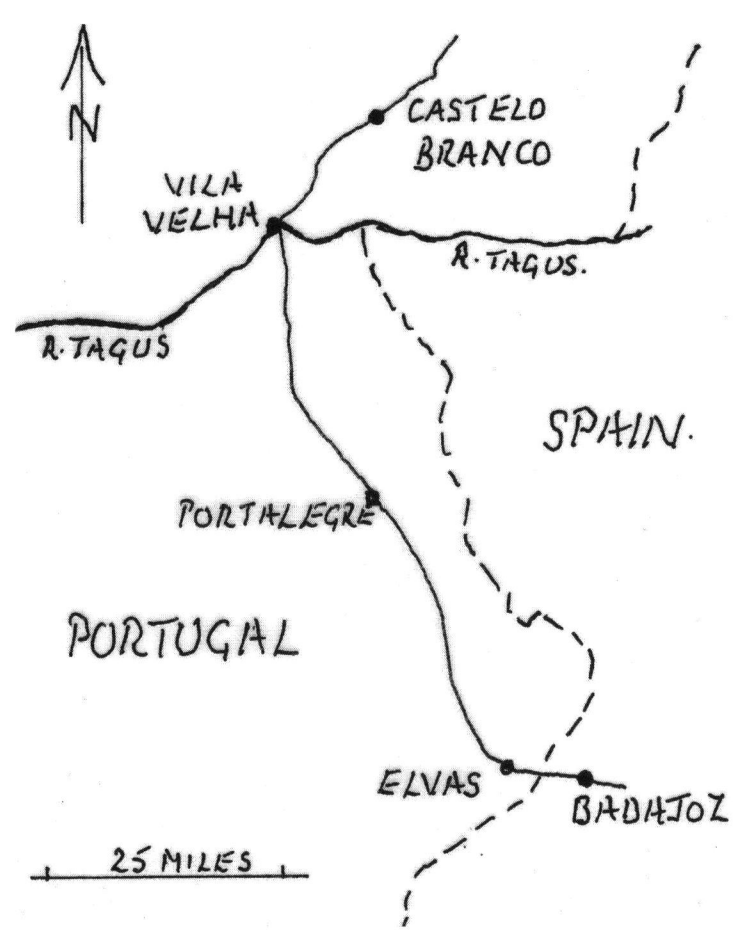

Chapter 2

SABUGAL, PORTUGAL

"The small difference of the colour of your coat."

Having caught their quarry, the French seemed to lose their nerve. In other circumstances they might well have burnt the village in reprisal for sheltering Colquhoun, raped, mutilated and killed every inhabitant they could lay hands on. They had done so with less provocation throughout Spain and Portugal.

Perhaps they could hardly believe their luck in capturing a will o' the wisp, and feared he might vanish before they could parade him to their commanders. Perhaps they feared that the German Hussars could not be far behind Colquhoun, and that if overtaken by them in the open miles from any help the dragoons would quickly be overwhelmed and then they would be cut down to a man. Perhaps even they feared that Milor Wellington and the whole English army were just over the horizon.

Whatever the reason, they were in a hurry to be off.

Colquhoun was temporarily reunited with his horse. The saddle bags had gone. His pistols, of course, were gone. His money was gone. His spyglass had gone. His sword and sword belt were taken. His cloak he had left behind in the hovel. His bicorne was lost.

Most alarmingly, though, most ominously, his leather

bound notebook, in which he recorded all his information about the movements and strengths of the French army, had been pulled triumphantly out of the saddle bags by the French officer.

In it Colquhoun had recorded the make-up of the whole Army of Portugal from the corps and divisions and their component regiments to the names of their officers from general down to commanding officers and sometimes, where he had been able to get the information, to the names of officers commanding companies.

It listed cantonments and their fortifications, artillery strengths and dispositions, the movement of supplies and the wounded, orders of march, detachments of units, the depredations of an army living off an alien land, - anything and everything that Colquhoun had seen and noted as he had watched and shadowed the French army.

If anything was going to hang him, it would be the notebook.

The officer thumbed through its pages, whistled several times in astonishment, stowed it safely in his tunic and looked significantly at Colquhoun. It was a look which boded ill.

The rain did not stop.

León's body was ignored. Colquhoun hoped that the villagers would come when they were gone and bury him. The rain was washing the blood away. There was a puzzled look on León's face. For the first time in many, many years Colquhoun wanted to weep. Whether for León or for his stupidity in getting captured he did not know. Probably both. He tried to set his face into an impassive mask, to ignore his captors.

They tied his hands in front of him and his legs under the belly of the horse. The dragoons surrounded him, a sergeant of dragoons took his reins, the infantry formed up - there were two companies of them, well over a hundred men, Colquhoun's practiced eye automatically recorded - and without ado they set off back to rejoin the French rearguard.

Colquhoun did not remember much of the ride into captivity.
His captors splashed grimly heads down through the mud and rain. They kicked their exhausted horses on as though the whole English army was at their heels. Empty bellied and dog tired themselves from their sleepless night they were obviously now if not afraid at least apprehensive that they might be caught by the German Hussars.
The rain beat down incessantly.
Colquhoun rode numbly in their midst, in shock, shivering uncontrollably.

His escort changed when they caught up with the French rearguard at the little town of Pedrogão. The dragoons handed him over to a contingent of hussars. No one offered him food or drink. He was too proud and too numb to ask. The hussars were too wet and in too great a hurry to treat him other than as baggage.
They set off northwards immediately.
The road was clogged with the rearguard soldiers. Mud-covered artillerymen cursed as they manhandled guns and gun teams in the rutted tracks. Wagons and caissons, not many, but enough to block the road, lurched and swayed as their swearing drivers flogged the miserable animals trying to pull them. Everywhere the infantry marched, sullenly, soaked to the skin, cold, hungry, empty handed from their

raid into Portugal. Flaring arguments and shouted threats did nothing to clear the way.

There was an urgency in their progress, though, an apprehension that the English might catch them before they could reach the safety of Marshal Marmont's main force.

The hussars pushed their way through. They passed Penamacor with its castle perched high over the road and swung round up the far side of the valley behind the town onto the high cold plateau.

Colquhoun stopped shivering. The numbness was beginning to wear off. He was hungry now, and thirsty despite the rain. He sucked the moisture from his sleeve: it tasted salty and muddy. He wished he had his cloak, though the hussars surrounding him were little better protected from the rain than he was.

They hurried onwards in a mist of sweaty steam.

Colquhoun had first-hand experience of captivity. Aged eighteen, on his first military adventure - an abortive raid on Ostend fourteen years ago, - his whole regiment had been taken prisoner, and had existed in some discomfort for the best part of a year until they had been exchanged. He had used his time then to good avail to learn fluent French and had had the comradeship of his fellow officers. Even so, it had been a miserable time.

This would be different. It was a bitter, bitter blow. Deep down he had thought that he could always outrun and outwit the French, that this would never really happen. But it had, and Leon was dead, shot like a dog. Leon who had been the best of companions, totally trustworthy, totally reliable.

At the very least, he could expect rough handling and

close confinement.

If indeed he was still alive in twenty four hours time.

Why, Colquhoun wondered, had they not shot him then and there?

Perhaps because they looked on him as a spy, a dangerous spy, and spies usually ended up on a rope. Perhaps they wanted to hang him publicly as an example. Perhaps they wanted to interrogate him. Perhaps they simply wanted to parade him alive to the Marshal - there would always be a shadow of doubt that he really was dead if no one had seen his body.

Or would they acknowledge that an officer in uniform is not a spy? Unlikely. Worse than unlikely. They had been calling him a notorious spy for months. He had a price on his head. A good one, at that. No, beyond a doubt they would treat him as a spy.

How quickly would they hang him? If they kept him prisoner even for a few days the chances must be good that Lord Wellington's seven divisions would catch up with the French and force them to battle. If he could survive that long, if he could argue his case strongly enough for them to accord him a court martial, then they might forget him once they realised they were facing overwhelming odds. Maybe he would be able to slip away.

Colquhoun wondered whether Marmont knew that Lord Wellington was so close on his heels with more than twice the number of men.

Of course the rain, the mud, the swollen rivers, the almost impassable tracks - they were the same for both armies, but the chances must be high that Lord Wellington's well fed troops would catch up with Marmont's hungry and demoralised men.

Yes, if they didn't hang him straight away the chances

were more than even that this captivity would last for a few days only.

Somewhere on the Spanish border the two armies must meet.

The outcome was inevitable.

He would be free within days.

The road led on interminably, though in happier times he would hardly have noticed a journey of twenty or thirty miles. The hussars were not disposed to talk to him, nor he to them. They were simply in a hurry to get to wherever they were taking him, and, no doubt, to get rid of him. Colquhoun imagined it would be the town of Sabugal where Marshal Marmont was regrouping his army before retreating back into Spain.

And at last, at long last, the road started to slope down into the river valley and eventually they could look across the river to the town and five towered castle of Sabugal on the far bank.

There were soldiers everywhere, wherever Colquhoun looked. Marmont's three divisions must all be there, camping miserably in the rain, all those who could not cram into any habitable house in the town.

They crossed the bridge and rode up the hill round the curtain wall of the castle into the square. It was packed with men, so crowded they had to dismount by the castle gate. Every sort of rough shelter had been erected so that the place looked like the worst slum of London or Paris, an impression heightened by the state of most of the houses Colquhoun could see. Some were roofless. Nearly all had windows and doors missing, torn off, no doubt, to fuel the soldiers' camp fires. The scattered remains of wrecked furniture told the same story. Wood smoke from a hundred sullen fires hung low in the air. The square reeked of smoke, wet wool, sweat and suffering humanity.

On foot, the hussars pulled Colquhoun through the crowd. Except to curse them for barging through, no one paid them the slightest attention.

The hussars made for the largest house in the square, - apparently not vandalised - where they were clearly expected. Four soldiers with fixed bayonets appeared, arranged themselves round Colquhoun and he was led inside. There was a brief exchange with an officer, and Colquhoun was marched into a crowded room.

Seated behind a table across the room Colquhoun recognised the ample figure of General de la Martinière, Marshal Marmont's Chief of Staff.

Not the best of auguries.

De la Martinière was notorious for his explosive temper and hatred of the English. He looked up at Colquhoun, stared at him malevolently for a moment, then pointedly went on reading the papers on the table.

Covertly, Colquhoun took in the room. Several clerks were writing at small tables at the side of the room. An *aide de campe* stood behind the General. Four staff officers were studying a map spread out on another table. They all ignored him. Everything was wet: the smell of soaked, unwashed men was overpowering.

Water dripped from Colquhoun and puddled round him on the floor.

He watched de la Martinière. The General's face was getting redder. His breathing was getting louder. He seemed to be puffing himself up, almost bobbing up and down in his chair. Suddenly he slammed the papers down on the table and erupted to his feet.

"You piece of English shit. You son of a syphilitic whore. You red coated turd. You despicable spy. Well, we've got you now. What have you got to say for yourself, you arsehole, before I hang you."

"I am no spy, General. I have always worn my uniform. I have always moved openly."

"You lying hound, you son of a whore. You're a spy. The rope's too good for you, but, by God, I'll hang you from the tallest tree before the day is out."

"You cannot hang me, sir. I am a prisoner of war. Under the rules of war…"

"The rules of war, you dog. Who are you to dare to speak of the rules of war? There are no rules for a spy except the rope."

"I am not a spy, General. As a man of honour.…"

"Honour, you arsehole! Don't speak to me of honour, you spy. Your dirty trade has no honour. I'll hang you like the dog you are. What were you doing at Idanha a Nova?"

Colquhoun was silent.

"What were you doing there, arsehole? Spying! That's what. Spying like the miserable cur that you are."

Colquhoun said nothing.

"Lost your tongue, have you? Answer me, you dog. You'll lose a deal more than that before today is out. You'll pay me for your vile trade, by God you will."

He came round the table glaring at Colquhoun, dancing with fury in front of him.

Colquhoun stared back.

Without warning de la Martinière lashed out open handed and hit Colquhoun across the mouth. Two handed, he grabbed Colquhoun's jacket. He pulled him forward, at the same time sweeping his right leg behind Colquhoun's knees and pushing him violently backwards. Hands tied and off balance Colquhoun crashed to the floor. Immediately de la Martinière started kicking him, shouting insults with every kick.

Colquhoun drew himself into a ball, shielding his head, taking most of the blows on his forearms. Growing up with six elder brothers he had learned very early in life how to protect himself.

"Rules of war, you dog" – de la Martinière aimed a kick at Colquhoun's ribs - "I can do anything" - another kick - "anything" - another kick - "that I want" - another kick - "to an arsehole like you."

One of the officers stepped forward and took the General's arm, pulling him away.

Colquhoun lay without moving. With a final kick aimed at Colquhoun's head de la Martinière allowed himself to be led back to the table.

One of the staff officers came across to Colquhoun and helped him to his feet.

"A thousand pardons, Monsieur," he said quietly. "When you are dealing with a pig this sort of thing happens."

"Take the turd away. Get it out of here. Get him out."

Colquhoun was bundled out of the house, back across the square into the castle. The inner courtyard was small, crowded with single storey buildings so close there was hardly room to walk between them. Colquhoun was thrust into a tiny stone room. He had time to take in that it was empty of any furnishing whilst they cut the rope tying his hands and then the door was slammed shut and he was in total darkness.

He could taste blood on his lip and his mouth felt swollen. He was well bruised by de la Martinière's attack, in some considerable pain, but so far as he could tell, no bones were broken. He rubbed his wrists to get the circulation going again and sat down with his back against the cold stone wall.

He wondered how long it would be before they took him out and hanged him. He wished they would feed him before they did so. His stomach was gnawing with hunger. He guessed it must be about three o'clock in the afternoon. He could just faintly make out the outline of the doorway. Otherwise he was in complete darkness.

He pulled his boots off and emptied the water out of them.

The door bolt was drawn back. Colquhoun squinted into the sudden light. A young sub lieutenant of dragoons stood in the doorway.

"Major Grant? Would you care to accompany me, sir? My apologies for the quarters they have assigned you. My word, but you do look a mess, sir. If you would follow me, we must try to give you a bit of a brush up."

If he had not been so wet and cold and bruised and above all so hungry Colquhoun would have been almost amused. Presumably his hanging was to be something of an occasion. He must be looking his best for it. It would have been easier on a full stomach. He sighed, and followed the officer out of the castle.

They picked their way across the square. The rain had eased off. The crowded soldiers seemed less miserable. Colquhoun supposed that they had eaten their *soupe*, wherever they had managed to get it. Probably ration wagons had come in from Spain. They headed down a street on the far side of the square, under an old stone archway and into a second square fringed with fair sized houses. The dragoon led him to the largest. Two sentries came to attention on the door as they went in. They went upstairs to a bedroom crowded with makeshift camp beds. An orderly appeared.

"Here," said the dragoon, "Make him look a bit respectable."

The orderly shook his head and made a clucking noise. He looked Colquhoun up and down disapprovingly.

"*Mon Dieu*," he said. "What can sir have been up to? Sir is in need of a wash and a shave."

He invited Colquhoun to take his jacket off, clucked again at the sorry, sodden state of it, and, whilst Colquhoun busied himself with a jug of cold water at a wash basin, disappeared with it for some minutes, returning with it held reverently, brushed and looking at least like a uniform coat. He held it out rather proudly to Colquhoun, disappeared briefly again and came back with a bowl of hot water on a tray which held an array of soap, razors and towels.

"Sit down here, sir."

He wrapped a towel round the dubious Colquhoun's neck. Colquhoun was not at all sure that he liked the prospect of a French soldier holding a cut-throat razor to his throat, but he need not have worried. With great care and a continuous chorus of clucking noises of encouragement either to himself or to Colquhoun - he was not sure which it was - the orderly shaved him and proceeded to comb his hair.

The dragoon pulled a watch from his waistcoat and studied it.

"Time to go down, sir."

So he was scheduled to hang at four o'clock, perhaps. Well, show them how a Highlander could die. The shave had done wonders for him. He felt half human again. He buttoned his jacket, thanked the orderly and followed the officer back down the stairs.

They crossed the hallway. The dragoon opened a door and motioned for Colquhoun to enter.

The room was full of French officers, all with glasses in their hands. There was a fireplace with a chimney - a rarity in Portugal - with a fine bright fire blazing in it. The buzz of conversation stopped. They all turned to look at him.

He recognized some - most - of the faces. Through his spyglass he had seen them riding with the Marshal, hurrying along a column to deliver an order, shouting, swearing, pointing, joking, gesticulating - the Marshal's staff.

A colonel in the uniform of the *Chasseurs à Cheval* stepped forward.

"Major Grant? We are honoured to meet you face to face at last, sir."

There was a burst of friendly laughter.

"Colonel Richemont, sir, at your service. Allow me to introduce you."

To a man, the officers shook his hand, as though he was a newly joined member of their mess. Someone gave him a glass of wine with:

"Come and stand by the fire here, major. You look like you need warming up."

They gathered round him in a babble of questions.

"How did they catch you?"

"Where is Milor Wellington?"

"Is he coming north?"

"How many divisions has he got with him?"

"How many men did you lose at Badajoz?"

"How far behind us is Milor?"

"What state are the roads in South of the Tagus?"

"Is your flying bridge still there. We heard it had been burned and Milor cannot cross."

"My dear fellow, let me fill your glass. Not too bad a wine for this Godforsaken country, is it?"

The warmth and the wine on his empty stomach were making his head swim. 'Careful. Careful,' he kept saying to himself. 'For God's sake, man, be careful and think. Think.'

"Poor fellow's done in. That pig beat him up."

"You'll feel better when you've had something to eat."

And at that moment an orderly threw open an interconnecting door, and announced that dinner was served.

They took him through, showing him to a place at the top of the table, to the right of the empty chair at the head. Colonel Richemont took the place opposite him. They stood at their places. A door across the room was held open by a liveried footman. Marshal Marmont strode in, resplendent in a uniform coat heavily encrusted with gold embroidery, silk breeches and buckled shoes. A handsome man, fine featured, only six years older than Colquhoun, a personal friend of Napoleon since his earliest days in the artillery, whose meteoric career had earned him a Marshalate four years previously.

"Ah, Major Grant. We meet at last. You will do us the honour of dining with us. We have all waited many months for this opportunity of seeing you face to face. We will have much to talk about. Pray be seated, gentlemen."

With a scraping of chairs the company sat down.

"What have we got this afternoon? Ah, that looks good"

And so it did, to Grant's famished eyes. A large ham, a goose, legs of mutton. Side dishes. What smelled like new baked bread. Grant had not seen such a meal in months. Evidently, as he had heard tell, the Marshal did not believe in starving himself whatever his men might or might not be eating.

"Well, Major Grant, have you heard of the exploits of Colonel Richemont here. No? No, you were otherwise occupied, of course. Two days ago, at Guarda, Colonel Richemont collected fifty or so *Chasseurs* and put the Portuguese army, four or five thousand of them, completely to rout. He captured five of their flags and took eight hundred prisoners. Not bad for fifty men, eh? Gave me a problem, though. Who on earth wants eight hundred Portuguese prisoners?"

There was a general laugh around the table. Colonel Richemont managed to look self deprecating, pleased and proud. His gesture was very Gallic:-

"Old men and boys. Militia. They threw down their arms at the sight of us and scattered like birds. We could not kill such *canaille*. It was simply a matter of rounding up as many as we could."

"It was gallantly done, Richemont, and the Emperor shall hear of it. Even so, I would rather have you in my grasp, sir," - he turned to Colquhoun - " than ten thousand Portuguese prisoners. I feel a lot more comfortable with you in here than having you hanging round my flanks with your spyglass. I have been a great admirer of your resourcefulness, you know, and your bravery. I regret that your servant was killed in this morning's affair. Come, Major, enjoy your dinner."

Despite his swollen, bloodied lips and bruised body the food tasted delicious, the goose particularly so. Colquhoun ate ravenously. A footman was constantly at his elbow, refilling his glass whenever he took a sip from it.

All the time the Marshal was watching him covertly, disguising it in easy banter with his staff. At some moment a trap would be sprung.

Of course, the Marshal had invited him to dinner to get

information out of him. But with every mouthful Colquhoun felt stronger, more confident that he could cope. How much of Lord Wellington's movements did Marmont know about? Did he know that seven divisions were hard on his heels?

Interrogation in whatever form it came was a game that two could play. He let his eyes glaze over and slurred his speech as he refused another refill of his glass.

"You have given us a lot of trouble, you know, Major Grant. I have been aware that you have been close to us ever since we left Ciudad Rodrigo. You have been a thorn that I am very glad to have removed from my flesh. You had presumably made contact with the German Hussars yesterday?"

"I was on my way to do that."

"Is that so? Have you heard then that Badajoz has fallen to Milor?"

"Yes, I'd heard that from the Portuguese."

"From the Portuguese? Really? You surprise me. They say that Milor lost ten thousand men in the assault."

Marmont was watching him intently.

"Your information -" Colquhoun broke off, looked concerned, confused, at a loss what to answer. He avoided the Marshal's gaze, embarrassed, looked at his plate, picked up a piece of bread and rolled it into a ball. -"Your information, sir, surely it must be inaccurate."

He saw the gleam of satisfaction in the Marshal's eyes.

"Well, that's what they say. And Marshal Soult is on his way up from Andalucía, so they say. Had you heard that? No? Come, come, surely that is common knowledge. You had not heard? The Portuguese had not told you? You amaze me. Milor Wellington may be in a lot of trouble, I think. Half his army gone, and Marshal Soult on his heels."

"I know… Well, no, I don't know… Again, sir, your information is better than mine."

"Hmm, yet I hear that Milor is even now on the left bank of the Tagus. But you knew that, of course."

Again, the intense watching of his face.

"No. That is…That I cannot say, sir."

"The Portuguese did not tell you? How remiss of them."

"Well…"

"With how many men, Major? Two divisions? He could hardly risk more with Marshal Soult at his back."

"No, indeed he cannot. He's had to leave…. Well, no, he couldn't… Well, that is, I suppose he couldn't. But…"

"But what, Major?"

"No, no, I don't know."

"I expect he wants to see me off out of Portugal. Follow me back to Ciudad Rodrigo, perhaps?"

"I'm sure he'd wish to, but…"

"Yes?"

"Well, in this rain, and with Marshal Soult…"

Colquhoun broke off. He shrugged his shoulders.

"You will know better than me, sir."

"Perhaps, Major Grant. Perhaps not."

Colquhoun looked woodenly back at the Marshal then dropped his eyes again. After a while the Marshal looked away. "Hmm," he said. Abruptly, he threw his napkin down, and stood up. All the company rose with him. He nodded at Colquhoun and strode out of the room.

They took Colquhoun back to the stone cell in the castle. No officer escort for the return across the square. Four soldiers with fixed bayonets marched him back. He was so exhausted and so full of the Marshal's food and wine that he curled up and slept for several hours.

When he awoke his body had stiffened again and throbbed with pain from de la Martinière's beating. There was no further chance of sleep. The cell was too cramped and the floor too inhospitable. It seemed a very long time before he could make out the faint outline of the doorway.

He was desperate to relieve himself. He banged on the door. Silence. He banged again. Someone, somewhere close yelled:

"Stop that bloody noise or I'll smash your fucking head in."

Probably an NCO. Probably no idle threat. He gave it up, tried to gauge which way, if any, the floor sloped, and relieved himself in what he guessed was the lowest corner.

He tried doing some exercises to get his blood going, but the space was too small to swing his arms and the ceiling too low. He tried running on the spot. It helped a bit, but it seemed a very long time before he heard voices outside and the bolt scraping as it was drawn back. The door swung open.

A sergeant peered in at him.

"Out."

Four soldiers with fixed bayonets were crowded into the cramped space outside. They were grim faced. His heart sank. He had seen impassive faces like this too many times as prisoners were led out to face the lash or the gallows. He wondered whether they would hang him or shoot him. He hoped it would be a firing squad. Quicker, cleaner, a more honourable way to go. He straightened his red coat and squared his shoulders.

The rain was beating down again from the leaden sky.

He judged it must be about eight o'clock. There was no sign of an improvised gallows or firing squad, no silent hollow square of soldiers waiting to watch him die.

Sabugal's square was a lot emptier than it had been last night. The infantry would be on its way back to Ciudad Rodrigo. No time, perhaps, to be wasted on the execution of the enemy spy.

To his surprise he was led across the square, through the old archway and back to the Marshal's headquarters. He was glad of the walk to ease his aching body.

Two of the staff officers he had met the previous evening were in the anteroom. The atmosphere was businesslike: the cordiality of yesterday's meeting had vanished. One of the officers tapped on the dining room door, disappeared for a minute and then reappeared.

Colquhoun was ushered in.

The room, which last night had been welcoming, was transformed. The table was now covered with maps and papers. Clerks were working in a huddle at the far end, watched by a knot of *aides de campe*. The atmosphere was tense. Marshal Marmont sat again at the head of the table. Beside him stood a glowering General de la Martinière, eyes blazing with malice at Colquhoun, evidently in a scarcely controlled fury.

"Major Grant." Marmont came straight to the point. "I cannot spare you much time this morning, but you are causing me a certain moral problem. General de la Martinière is in no doubt that you should be shot forthwith as a spy. This notebook that I have here" - to Colquhoun's consternation he picked up a leather bound notebook that Colquhoun instantly recognised -"sets out details of my army's dispositions in great detail. Accurate detail, Major. Remarkably accurate detail. The undoubted work of a spy.

General de la Martinière argues that all that separates you from a spy is that red rag that you are wearing - the small difference of the colour of your coat."

"What you call the colour of my coat is the uniform of the British army, Marshal. I have always worn my uniform. I have always moved openly as an officer of Lord Wellington's army. Whenever you have seen me you have always seen a British officer in uniform. I am no spy, Marshal."

"General de la Martinière does not think so. Many of my men do not think so. I am not sure that I can answer for your treatment as a prisoner. You understand me, Major? In this case the rules of honour and of gentlemanly conduct are, to say the least of it, blurred. But I respect you, Major, as a brave man. In your way, perhaps, an honourable one. So we have a dilemma. Are you a spy? Or are you an honourable prisoner of war? What are we to do with you?" He spread his hands in a very Gallic gesture of bewilderment, then raised a forefinger and pointed it in the air.

"Give me your parole, Major Grant. Give me your word of honour as an officer and a gentleman that you will take no further part in any way in this war and I will give you the benefit of the doubt and treat you as an officer and gentleman. I will guarantee you that no harm will come to you at the hands of my army in Portugal or Spain.

"Unless I am exchanged?"

Marmont shrugged his shoulders.

"Of course."

"And if I don't?"

Again Marshal Marmont shrugged his shoulders eloquently and spread his hands, fingers extended.

"I regret, Major, that I am a busy man. If I do not have

your parole I must hand you over to General de la Martinière."

Colquhoun glanced at the General. From the expression in his eyes there was little doubt that he would either be swinging from a rope or shot within the hour.

"But reflect, Major," the Marshal went on, "you are out of the war now. Whatever you decide, you can do nothing more for Milor Wellington. Choose life, Major, and perhaps in happier times we will share a glass of wine together as friends. I have had a great respect for you, albeit cursing you as a confounded nuisance, since first I came to this God forsaken part of the world and got embroiled in this cruellest and most dishonourable of wars. I would not wish to have the blood of a gallant officer on my hands."

It could only be a matter of days before Lord Wellington caught up with the French.

Seven well fed divisions to Marmont's starving three - maybe four if he got back to Ciudad Rodrigo in a hurry.

A British victory was certain. Rescue was certain.

If there was any taint of dishonour in such a rescue Lord Wellington would certainly send a captured French officer back and wipe the slate clean.

"Very well, Marshal. You may have my parole."

Marmont looked searchingly at him for a minute, then picked up a paper from the table.

"General de la Martinière has thoughtfully prepared a form of parole for your signature."

He read out:-

> "I, the undersigned, Colquhoun Grant, Major in the 11th Regiment of the English infantry, taken prisoner of war by the French army on the 16th April 1812, undertake on my parole of

honour not to seek to escape or to remove myself from the place of my captivity without permission, and not to pass any intelligence to the English army and its allies: in fact not to depart in any way from the duties which an officer prisoner of war on parole is honour bound to perform; and not to serve against the French army and its allies until I have been exchanged, rank for rank."

He threw the paper back onto the table.

"Are you prepared in honour to sign this undertaking, Major Grant?"

He looked searchingly at Colquhoun.

"You fully understand its meaning? You undertake in honour to play no further part at all in this war? Ever... Yes, yes, until you are exchanged, of course....Very well."

He looked almost disappointed, Colquhoun thought, as though he would have expected Colquhoun to have chosen death before this pusillanimous surrender.

"General de la Martinière will witness your signature. Then, General, there can be no misunderstanding."

He clicked his fingers towards the clerks, one of whom hurried forward with a pen.

He watched as Colquhoun signed, motioned for de la Martinière to sign as witness, and as he did so, said:

"General, you have your answer. You will, of course, honour this document. As for you, Major, it is fortunate for you that you have chosen this option. Had you not General de la Martinière would have hanged you this morning on a gallows twenty foot high."

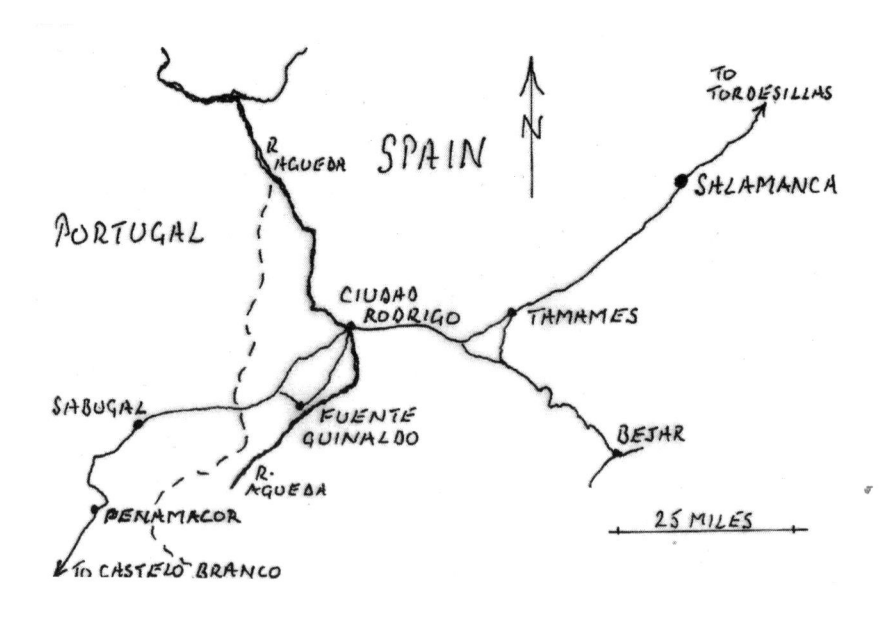

Chapter 3

SALAMANCA, SPAIN

"Tell him the Wild Geese flew early this year."

So General de la Martinière would not be permitted to hang him.

Thank God for the Marshal's intervention.

Marmont raised a hand in a gesture of dismissal and picked up a paper from the table. One of the *aides de campe* stepped forward and motioned for Colquhoun to follow him. They went back to the anteroom.

The aide said "A lucky escape, Major." He smiled. "Personally, I have always thought it unworthy to call you a spy. I have had nothing but admiration for your boldness. It took a certain amount of persuasion from us to get the Marshal to intervene. General de la Martinière was all for hanging you this morning, just as the Marshal said. I should make sure you never come across him again. A cup of coffee? Let me see what I can do."

Colquhoun wondered what would happen now. As a paroled officer he should have a reasonable amount of freedom of movement. He assumed that he would be 'sent to the rear' which in this case would be Ciudad Rodrigo or Salamanca, and then dispatched off back to France to await exchange.

The trick was going to be to delay being moved for a day or two, until Lord Wellington's seven divisions could overtake Marmont and bring him to battle.

There was also the possibility, presuming Lord Wellington knew by now of his capture, that negotiations could have been started for his exchange and might be concluded within a day or two.

He did not have to wait long to find out. The young officer of dragoons who had escorted him the previous evening appeared in the anteroom. The aide bowed and disappeared. The dragoon greeted Colquhoun affably:

"Good morning, sir. I am to be your escort, me, that is, and Lieutenant Montford. I'm Sub-Lieutenant Leveque, by the way, Charles Leveque. We have no horses, you see, so we're not much use to the cavalry at the moment."

An interesting piece of information - or it would have been had Colquhoun not given his parole.

"What happened to your horses?"

"Oh, we've lost a terrible lot. Not enough food and this terrible weather. They've been dying like flies. Our whole squadron is dismounted. They took the ones that were still alive to make up another squadron."

"I see. But I have given my parole. Surely I don't need an escort?"

"General de la Martinière's orders, I'm afraid, sir. One of us is to be with you at all times, night and day. If you would step this way, sir."

Leveque led the way back into the castle square - which Colquhoun noted was now almost empty of troops - to a house adjacent to de la Martinière's headquarters. He led the way up two flights of stairs. A dragoon stood smoking his pipe at the head of the stairway. His carbine was propped up against the wall. He and Leveque nodded to each other.

"Here we are, Dutoit. It's this room, isn't it? You have the key?"

The dragoon nodded. To Colquhoun's irrational irritation he did not remove the pipe from his mouth.

"Well, this is it," said Leveque. The room was at the back of the house. It had been a bedroom, as the smashed remains of two large beds testified. It had obviously been very recently vacated by a substantial number of Marshal Marmont's soldiers. It stank - of wet clothes, mud, unwashed bodies, sweat, blood, urine, shit and tobacco smoke.

Apart from the broken beds the only furnishings were a small table and a chair, but somehow the room managed to look filthy and chaotic. A heap of bloody bandages in one corner suggested that it might have been used as a first aid post or hospital. Colquhoun imagined that the French, as so often happened, had smashed the beds out of pure malice when they left. They were probably running in fleas anyway.

The dragoon shut the door behind them as they stood taking in the desolation of the room. Behind them, the key turned in the lock.

There was a lengthy silence.

"I say," said Leveque. Further words seemed to fail him.

"There must be a mistake. I have given my parole. I am not a close confinement prisoner."

"Oh, no, that's right enough, sir, I'm afraid. General de la Martinière's orders. But, I say, this isn't very nice. Dutoit! Dutoit!"

The key turned in the lock again. The pipe smoking Dutoit opened the door and blew an insolent mouthful of smoke into the room.

"Are you sure it's this room?"

Dutoit nodded. A man of few words.

"Well." Leveque was at a loss for words again. "Well. Well, find us another chair, there's a good fellow." The door closed again. "I've got a pack of cards. I thought we could pass the time with them."

Colquhoun declined Leveque's offer. It was little over twenty four hours since he had been captured. He felt physically and emotionally drained, suddenly overwhelmed with exhaustion. Sleep was an all overriding necessity. The smashed beds offered no comfort. He sank down against the wall, first sitting, then slipping onto the floor. Wearily he closed his eyes.

When Colquhoun awoke Leveque was sitting disconsolately at the table, staring out of the window into the broken window of a deserted looking house four yards away across the street. His head was propped on both hands. His playing cards were scattered on the table in front of him He turned round and smiled:

"I say, sir, you must have been all in. You've slept for hours. D'you see, I got Dutoit to find you a blanket. I do hope you feel better. There's some *soupe* for you here. Afraid it's got cold. And some bread. This is a terribly boring job, you know."

Colquhoun groaned, and went back to sleep.

The room was Colquhoun's prison for the best part of two days. Young Leveque thankfully went off duty in the evening, to be replaced by a taciturn Lieutenant Montford. He arrived with a bedding roll which he placed under the window. He made himself comfortable in it, and lay without speaking with his hands clasped behind his head until the light faded. Colquhoun was thankful for the silence. The affable Leveque was like a large friendly puppy. Not what Colquhoun needed in his present mood.

He alternated between gloom and anger - at himself for getting captured, at the death of León, for which he felt responsible, whether he should have given his parole, whether he should have refused and damned them and gone honourably to de la Martinière's gallows, but chiefly because he had been tricked.

By all the rules of war, a paroled officer should not be treated as a prisoner and locked under escort and guard in a stinking bare room. They had his word of honour that until he was exchanged he would take no further part in the war. They did not trust him to keep it. His honour was deeply impugned, and it hurt.

And all the time he was listening, hoping to catch the first sounds of the call to arms that he prayed would come at any moment as Lord Wellington's army caught up with Marmont's.

From Leveque he learned, although it was obvious from the rain still intermittently pouring outside, that all the rivers were in spate, and impassable. Until they went down Marmont would not be able to get back to safety across the river Agueda at Ciudad Rodrigo. Once across Marmont could defend the river line with its steep banks and swift flowing water and laugh at Lord Wellington, whatever the imbalance in troop numbers. But until then he was trapped.

It was the perfect situation for Lord Wellington.

But, of course, the rivers were equally flooded for both armies. Perhaps the English could not get across the river Tagus at the flying bridge at VilhaVelha. Perhaps the boats had been swept away. At best, the roads must be well nigh impassable.

Before it was light on the third morning he was summoned from his captivity by a strong squad of line infantry commanded by a hard faced sergeant. They put him in the middle of the squad and set off Eastwards towards the Spanish border.

Most of Marmont's army must have marched this way already.

Sabugal was deserted. The road was deep in liquid mud, heavily rutted and strewn with the debris of a retreating army. All Colquhoun carried was the blanket Leveque had found him, but, used to horseback, he found the going hard and felt admiration for the French soldiers who were weighed down with packs and weapons but seemed to take the appalling condition of the road in their stride.

The rain had stopped. Dawn brought a spectacular sunrise. Within minutes the whole world was steaming and the whole squad was pouring sweat.

They crossed the unmarked border and reached the Spanish village of Fuenteguinaldo by midday. Marmont's army was camped all around the village on the high open plain. Soldiers crowded in every building. Colquhoun knew the village well. It had been Lord Wellington's Headquarters the year before, and the English army had spread out across the plain around just as Marmont's did now.

If Colquhoun had hoped for better treatment here he was mistaken.

They locked him in a first floor room, an officer locked in with him and a guard on the door. A different officer appeared with every change of shift. But to a man they were friendly and apologetic. Word had got around that Colquhoun had given his parole. They admired him as a brave and resourceful adversary. They considered it a slight both on their personal honour and on the honour of the French army that Colquhoun was held in close confinement.

As a result they tried to make his captivity as easy as they could. They made sure he was fed, that he had a bed and could wash.

And they confronted de la Martinière and somehow got him to agree to allow Colquhoun to exercise in the square beside the great central church that dominates the village.

Lord Wellington's headquarters had been in the handsome two storey house to the South of the square, the same house that Marmont was occupying. But there the parallel ended.

Then, the Spanish inhabitants had gone unmolested about their business. There had been a little local market daily in the square. There had been scant sign in the village of the army's presence. Just a few staff officers strolling around: there had been a small guard on Wellington's headquarters: a few dispatch riders: the occasional sight of Lord Wellington himself, simply dressed, walking in the square.

Now the Spanish had vanished, some probably to the hills in the distance, most of them probably keeping a very low profile in shuttered rooms. The headquarters house was alive with staff officers in their brilliant uniforms, with nodding plumes and glittering orders, the square crowded and jumbled with the wagons of Marmont's personal staff, his cooks and valets, his baggage. And everywhere were clusters of soldiers sitting round their fires, the air heavy with wood smoke.

Because they disapproved of his confinement his escorts told him openly whatever they themselves knew of what was going on.

On the 18th April - two days after his capture - the flood waters had broken Marmont's flying bridge at La Caridad on the river Agueda, some miles upstream from Ciudad Rodrigo, cutting off his retreat.

For three days it had been impossible to repair it.

Marmont was getting anxious that three divisions of the English might be closing in on him.

Food was in short supply.

They had lost most of their horses.

Marmont had sent his artillery miles upstream to cross the Agueda at Villarubia.

Marmont suspected that it was a deliberately spread rumour that the English were approaching. He knew that two English divisions had left Portalegre. They were probably held up on the Tagus.

The flood waters were going down. The rivers would be fordable.

Food was desperately short.

The rivers were fordable at last. One of the divisions - commanded by General Sarrut - was moving out. The whole of the rest of the army would be following the next day.

Colquhoun's heart at first rose with every morsel of information and then sank as the scales seemed to tip from Lord Wellington's to Marmont's advantage.

There was no call to arms - no galloping messenger tearing up to Marmont's headquarters shouting that the English were coming, no distant sound of gunfire to herald Lord Wellington's approach. The atrocious weather must have held up the English army to such an extent that if they did not appear now Marmont was going to slip out of the trap.

There was only one gleam of hope. On the third morning his escort suggested that he might like to see the church.

"It has one of finest reredos in Spain," he said. "The full height of the church, equivalent to five storeys high, painted woodwork done by Lucas Mitata in the late fifteen hundreds. And still as bright and as beautiful as the day he painted it. You must see it."

Colquhoun had seen the reredos many times. His Scottish soul baulked at the images and paintings and the statues in Spanish churches. But the local priest was one of the many of his cloth who acted as eyes and ears for the English, gave Colquhoun shelter and passed his messages onwards. To date he had not seen the priest, and imagined he must be keeping out of the way of the French. The offer to go into the church was too good an opportunity to miss.

Together Colquhoun and his escort stood in front of the altar and gazed up at the magnificently painted scenes from the Gospels. A voice behind them said:

"It's uniquely beautiful, isn't it?"

Colquhoun's heart leaped. They both turned round. The black cassocked priest was standing just behind them. Neither gave any sign of recognition. For a few minutes the priest explained the woodcarved scenes. Then he bowed, looked Colquhoun squarely in the eye, said *"Vaya con Dios"* - go with God, the benediction he had always given Colquhoun on parting, and glided away. Colquhoun left the church certain that if Lord Wellington did not already know of his whereabouts within a very short time the information would be passed to him. Not much help, but better than nothing.

After four days at Fuenteguinaldo, in bright hot sunlight which mocked the misery of the recent rains, the infantry escort squad appeared and Colquhoun was marched off with them Eastwards to the Agueda, across the river, past Ciudad Rodrigo, and, as fast as they could travel, through the vast open plain lands back to Salamanca.

Colquhoun did not know it. Marshal Marmont did not

immediately know it, but twenty four hours after the French army left Fuenteguinaldo six of the seven divisions of the English army had reached the area. Had the Agueda remained impassable for one day longer Wellington would have caught him. Colquhoun would have been freed.

Once they had crossed the River Agueda at Ciudad Rodrigo Colquhoun knew that he had lost any chance of being rescued.

The city of Ciudad Rodrigo had been besieged and taken by Lord Wellington three months ago and was now held by the Spanish but Colquhoun was sure that Lord Wellington would not risk an attack across the river, still angry and swollen, still a formidable barrier to advancing troops. And at Ciudad Rodrigo Marmont joined forces with his fourth division which, nominally besieging the town, had been watching his back on the sortie into Portugal.

Colquhoun's escort wasted no time. The road was relatively good. Two more gruelling days marching brought them into sight of Salamanca's cathedral. They crossed the great Roman bridge and entered the city as the sun began to sink and the heat to go out of the day.

As he had trudged along Colquhoun had returned again and again to the giving of his parole and the dishonouring of it by de la Martinière - indeed by Marmont, since he must be aware that Colquhoun was being treated as a prisoner. If they dishonoured it, should he be bound by it? Would he be justified in trying to escape? Would he be justified in passing any information he could back to Lord Wellington if the chance arose? Should he withdraw the parole? That would be the honourable way, but he had a very fair idea that if he did so he would be swinging from a rope in very short order. That, at least, was not an option.

In a way, the question was taken from him.

They confined him in a second floor room overlooking the central courtyard in the Convento de San Roman in Salamanca. The convent was heavily occupied by the French army. A light infantry unit was billeted there, soldiers, - Colquhoun automatically noted, - of the *4th Régiment d'Infanterie Légère* of General Sarrut's 4e Division, seasoned troops who had taken part in every engagement of the war. Colquhoun had often seen them in action. He had a very healthy respect for them.

As the night came down the dark uniformed soldiers clustered round their fires in the courtyard and filled it with a constant tide of comings and goings. Smoke from their fires hung over the courtyard. Voices, laughter, occasional shouts, singing - all the comfortable noises of an encampment at night drifted up to Colquhoun's window. Escape would be out of the question.

Of the original inhabitants - monks, Colquhoun supposed, - there was no sign. As before, an officer was locked into the room with him, and an armed guard was posted outside the door. At least the room had a bed.

He was barely awake the next morning when the door was unlocked and a tall, elderly, dignified figure in a priest's black cassock stood on the threshold.

"May I speak with your prisoner?" the visitor addressed himself to the escort.

"But of course, father."

The officer politely excused himself, and left the room.

"Major Grant? I am Patrick Curtis."

"Doctor Curtis?"

"Be careful, my son."

The priest spoke quietly, with a warning glance at the

door.

Colquhoun grimaced, angry. Such an elementary mistake.

"I heard that they had an English officer here, held under dubious circumstances. I thought you might need some comfort."

Doctor Curtis smiled, a charming conspiratorial smile that went well with a lilting Irish brogue.

Doctor Curtis. Don Patricio Cortes to the Spanish. Rector of the Irish College in Salamanca for over thirty years. A man of seventy two, though he looked no more than sixty, courteous, quiet spoken, a man of effortless authority, a man who treated everyone the same, from king to peasant, as equals and all worthy of his time and friendship.

The man, moreover, who ran the most comprehensive spy network in Spain right under the unsuspecting noses of the French.

Both men knew exactly who the other was. They had never met before, Colquhoun deeming it too dangerous to enter Salamanca, and Doctor Curtis deeming it unwise to draw attention to himself by leaving the city. But, via intermediaries, they had been in contact for over a year.

By unspoken consent, they moved to the window, the furthest point from the door, and stood looking down at the early morning activity in the courtyard.

"Is this safe for you to come here?"

"Any man is entitled to spiritual comfort when oppressed."

"Don't put yourself in danger on my behalf, Don Patricio."

"They say that you have given your parole. It does not look like it."

"I have. But they don't trust me - at least, de la Martinière doesn't. Nor, I must suppose, does Marmont. I was fortunate not to be hanged out of hand. But they treat me as a prisoner. I have complained to every officer of my escort every day. They just shrug their shoulders and apologise. Orders, they say. Deeply regrettable. Not their doing. I'm sure it's not. All my escort officers have behaved honourably as gentlemen."

"De la Martinière is a most unattractive man, I fear. He hates the English profoundly. Marmont, of course, is less straightforward, a much more complex character. But I have found that his intentions are usually honourable. I will ask him for an audience and put your case. Does Lord Wellington know you are here?"

"I believe he will. I saw the padre at Fuenteguinaldo. He will have told Lord Wellington of my circumstances. But I beg that you do not put yourself in any danger on my behalf."

"I would do the same for anyone who is mistreated. I think we can expect a request for your exchange to arrive very shortly. Today, perhaps. We will look out for it - it is not difficult. A flag of truce is there for all to see."

"I do not think that Marmont will agree it. He has no wish to see me on the loose again. As I say, de la Martinière was all for hanging me out of hand. I think they will impose a condition that I take no further part in the war in Spain. They may not agree to an exchange until I have been sent back to France. Maybe if they agree an exchange at all it will be on condition that I return to England."

"Yes, I agree. Your capture has been a great relief to the French army."

"And what use will I be to Lord Wellington if they do impose such conditions?"

They were silent for a minute.

"As a priest, Don Patricio, am I bound by my parole when they ignore it?"

A long silence.

"This is the cruellest and most horrible of wars. Its cause is vile. Its execution is vile. I am not even sure that the concept of honour is alive in Spain any more - except, perhaps, that it binds the conduct of officer to officer. Perhaps it places some small limits on the horrors that are occurring every day. No, I think that God will forgive you in any action you can take to shorten the war. I do not think He will judge you. In these terrible circumstances if they do not act honourably to you, I see no moral reason why you should act honourably to them."

Colquhoun digested this in silence for a while.

"I hate even to contemplate this. It goes against everything I believe in."

"Of course it does. But I believe God will understand. Surely anything that helps to defeat the French must be acceptable in His sight."

Colquhoun was silent, gazing down on the activity in the courtyard below. At length he nodded.

"I hope you are right, father. I feel that I am in danger of imperilling my immortal soul if I break my word."

"Again, my son, of course you do, and it would not be right that you should think otherwise. But the circumstances are so strange and unnatural that normal rules of behaviour do not - cannot - apply. If it will help you, in God's name I will pardon you here and now for the breaking of your parole. In God's name, I believe it is right that you should do so."

Again, Colquhoun nodded.

"Then pardon me, Don Patricio, though my heart may never again be easy in the matter, and send a message to

Lord Wellington that Marmont has lost most of his horse. Possibly fifteen hundred head. Food is short. He will not be able to concentrate his army again for some time."

Father Curtis laughed.

"Ah, excellent. That accords exactly with my own observations. Lord Wellington shall have this intelligence immediately. As to your parole, in the name of God I pardon and absolve you for any and all acts that you may consider as breaking your parole."

Briefly, he made the sign of the cross in Colquhoun's direction.

"There, now. Are there any comforts I can bring you to make your confinement more bearable?"

"My boots are worn through. If I am to be sent back to France on foot I will surely need some new ones. And I would dearly love a razor and some soap."

"I will see what I can do. It will give me a valid reason to visit you again tomorrow. I will bring you a greatcoat, too. The nights are still cold."

Colquhoun's first visitor the following day was not, however, Doctor Curtis.

Authoritative footsteps and a sharp word of command announced the new arrival. Colquhoun was standing at the window looking down into the courtyard, wondering for the umpteenth time whether he should have given his parole and, having done so, should have broken it by passing information to Doctor Curtis, despite the priest's assurance that God would forgive him. Whatever God might think about it, it was an uncomfortable feeling, a sort of unclean thing to do. He was not at all sure that his God had such a cavalier attitude to the forgiveness of sins, nor that he approved of the easy remission of sins that the Catholic

Church found so convenient. His God was not so accommodating. He felt frustrated, miserable and angry.

Automatically, he watched the soldiers below. From their activity he felt certain that they were preparing to move out. He wondered where to, and whether he could find out and pass the information on to Lord Wellington. He smiled to himself. Parole or no, old habits die hard.

He turned to face the door, keeping his back to the window so that whoever came in would be looking into the light and unable to see his features.

Colquhoun's escort for the day was a young Lieutenant of Dragoons - no doubt horseless - who had evidently been up all night on some energetic bedroom enterprise. He had appeared looking happily exhausted, apologised for the necessity of his presence, asked if he might borrow the bed, and had thrown himself onto it and fallen heavily asleep within seconds with a serene smile on his face.

The sharp command and the jangle of the key in the lock brought the dragoon to his feet with impressive speed - an involuntary reaction, honed, no doubt, by years of practice.

The door opened. The sentry stood back to attention.

A Light Infantry officer stepped in. He glanced briefly at the dragoon, sized him up in a second, and jerked his head marginally. The dragoon saluted and hurried out, pulling the door too behind him.

They stood looking at each other.

"Major Grant?"

"Yes."

"Major Magaud. *4ᵉ Régiment d'Infanterie Légère.*"

His face was hideously scarred. One scar ran slanting from his forehead down across his nose - smashed by the blow and deeply furrowed - and down his cheek to his chin. A second wound must have taken off the bottom of his left ear and broken his cheekbone. Its scar ran horizontally across his left cheek and vanished into a heavy grey moustache.

Had he known it, he needed no introduction. Colquhoun had heard of him, had his name recorded in his notebook, and had seen Major Magaud's unforgettable face not three weeks ago on the road into Portugal.

He must have been about fifty, Colquhoun thought, a grizzled warrior, one of the thousands of French revolutionary officers who had led their men dauntlessly across Europe for twenty years, inspiring them to victory by their extraordinary courage.

Instinctively, Colquhoun felt drawn to him.

Major Magaud's dark uniform was faded and stained. He was powerfully built, and strong, despite his age. He carried a leather bag on his left hip, slung across his body from his right shoulder. His left hand seemed to rest on the bag. It drew Colquhoun's eye. Magaud saw his glance. Their eyes met. The hand was wooden, fashioned half clenched.

"I am ordered to escort you to Bayonne. We leave tomorrow at first light. In honour I must inform you that if you attempt to escape, if you show the slightest irregularity in your conduct, I am ordered to shoot you immediately and without question. If there is any attempt to rescue you the guerrillas may fire the first shot, but I shall fire the second. You understand me? If they attack us, you are a dead man on the spot."

"Major, I have given my parole. I am not a prisoner."

Magaud shrugged.

"Those are my orders. I deplore them. I apologise for them. But I shall carry them out without hesitation if need arises. Evidently General de la Martinière does not trust you. Indeed, he considers that you are a spy and should have been hanged."

"And you, sir? Do you consider I am a spy?"

Again, a shrug.

"I have always worn my uniform. I have always acted openly. Your whole army knows it. Why do you treat me like this?"

"Those are my orders. As one officer to another I must in honour inform you of them." Major Magaud looked squarely at Colquhoun. He had seen death a thousand - scores of thousands of times. He had killed more men than he could remember, seen horrors, no doubt carried out atrocities no human should even contemplate. One more would not give him sleepless nights, be the victim never so gallant, never so worthy of his respect. Those were his orders. Without question, he would obey them.

"Then I must thank you, sir, for this information. I understand that you are under orders in this matter. I have given my parole. I shall give you no cause to carry out this order."

Magaud nodded.

"We understand each other, then. But, come, Major. We will be travelling companions for three weeks. I have seen you several times already, though never yet close enough to shoot you. I have always admired your courage and your audacity. We will have much to talk about on the march, I hope."

He skewed the shoulder bag in front of his body. He reached into it with his right hand and brought out a large flask and two battered tin mugs.

"We will drink a glass together, no? Here, hold this mug. We've both drunk from ruder things than these, I'm sure. Here's to travelling companions, then, and a safe march back to France."

'So that', thought Colquhoun, 'temporarily answers that.'

Magaud would treat him more or less as a paroled officer so long as Colquhoun behaved as one and they were not attacked by the guerrillas. Correctly, then, he would behave while in Magaud's charge.

And afterwards? When they reached France? That would have to depend.

Doctor Curtis arrived shortly after Magaud had gone. The dragoon escort excused himself and left the room.

"Don Patricio, I am glad to see you. I hoped you would come today. I have just been told that I am to leave tomorrow for France."

"Ah. That is bad news. An officer came in under flag of truce yesterday. 'T'is a pound to a penny he carried the request for your exchange."

"They have no intention of exchanging me in Spain."

"No, it seems not. Lord Wellington has put out an offer of two thousand dollars for your return alive."

"Then I am a dead man. I am to be escorted - if that's the right word - by Major Magaud of the 4e Léger. He is under orders to shoot me immediately if any attempt is made to rescue me."

"Ah. Is he now?"

Doctor Curtis contemplated this in silence, looking down at the activity in the courtyard below.

"Yes. Some three hundred of the 4e Léger - the fellows down in the courtyard there - are leaving Salamanca tomorrow. Magaud's men. They are a very good unit: but you will know that already from past encounters."

"Yes, I do indeed. I have a great respect for them. I think

any rescue attempt would be wasted effort anyway if they are moving in that strength. It would be enough to see off any guerrilla attack."

"I agree. In which case I must immediately ensure that word has reached his Lordship and our Spanish friends that they must leave your convoy alone. One wonders why they have been recalled to France. It cannot be merely to escort you. There are rumours of a big campaign this summer in Northern Europe. I suspect they may be true and that the *4ᵉ Léger* are to join it. You will find out soon enough once you join them. Here, I have brought you some things."

He unslung a battered leather bag from his shoulder. An old cloak was draped over it.

"I thought the older and more battered the better. They are less likely to take a fancy to these things and relieve you of them. And best on reflection not to bring a French greatcoat. You don't want to be shot at as a Frenchman wearing one, nor do you want to wear any French uniform and give anyone the excuse to call you a spy. I have put a razor and some soap in the bag, and some biscuit. Oh, and shoes. Spanish. And a bandana. The sun is hot now. Again, best not to wear anything French."

"Thank you. They will make a great difference. You are very kind. I do hope you are not risking yourself doing all this."

"I do not think so. But I confess I am deeply troubled by your treatment. Assuming the flag of truce yesterday was a request for your exchange Marmont has no valid reason for its refusal. I fear they may have no intention of sending you to join your compatriot paroled officers at Verdun. I fear they may divert you to some confinement in Paris where they can watch you and be sure you are no threat to them. I will try everything I can to find out what Marmont is planning, and to pass the information to you. Do not expect miracles, though. He is hardly likely to advertise his intentions and I may indeed be mistaken. More likely he simply wishes you out of Spain.

"Nor do I think it will be easy to contact you. Your escort are the best of the French army and will guard you closely. Whatever they are planning for you, however, you will have to pass through Orleans. The road branches there, either to Verdun where they will hold you pending your exchange or on to Paris. If there has been no message from me - or indeed if you need help - when you reach Orléans find your way to the Sainte Croix cathedral. Ask there for Father O'Shea. He is as committed to our cause as I am. Tell him the Wild Geese flew early this year. Then he will know you are a friend of mine. You can trust him with your life. He will have other contacts for you if need be."

"Father O'Shea? What on earth is an Irishman doing in a French cathedral?"

"Oh, he's French right enough. They pronounce it Auchay. His great grandfather, I think it was, was one of the Wild Geese -You know, the Irishmen who fled to France after the battle of the Boyne. His family has been in France for over a hundred years. But there has always been a strong Jacobite tradition with them and although the last claimant - Cardinal Henry - died two or three years ago, the tradition lives on. They are Royalists, and, of course, the clergy in France had a very difficult time in the Revolution. They live in hope of a Bourbon restoration. They are no lovers of the Emperor."

"I see. I shall have something in common with him. My family was Jacobite. Nearly all the highlanders were. We were at Culloden. My mother helped Prince Charles Edward escape the English army when he was hiding out after the battle. I have always felt it a trifle ironic that I fight for the English, but it's all a long time ago now."

"No more ironic than with me, an Irish Catholic passing information to the English army in Spain. I love Spain and the Spanish. It broke my heart when Napoleon marched in. He raped this country. I had to do something about it. Something to help. Politics, as they say, make strange bedfellows."

"Yes."

They were silent for a while, watching the French soldiers in the courtyard below.

"Does Lord Wellington know that these *4ᵉ Léger* men are going back to France? Every little bit of information is a help."

"Not yet. I only heard yesterday evening. But I will send him the information today telling him that you go with them and stressing particularly that if he wishes to see you alive again the guerrillas must leave them alone. I will put the word out with my own people too, of course. Immediately. But a good thing to have it endorsed by Lord Wellington"

"Do you know anything about Magaud?"

"Not specifically. He will be a good officer, I imagine. An elderly man, is he not? No nonsense, I imagine."

"Mmm. I would think not."

"I fear that I must go. Too long a visit will raise suspicions. Major Grant, I hope we may meet again in happier circumstances. Perhaps when you have driven Napoleon and all his works out of the country."

"Thank you, Don Patricio. Your coming has been a godsend to me."

"That is what I am here for. *Vaya con Dios.*"

"*Vaya con Dios,* padre."

They shook hands. Colquhoun watched the tall figure

cross the courtyard below him and felt a sense of loss. The dragoon reappeared. The day wore on slowly.

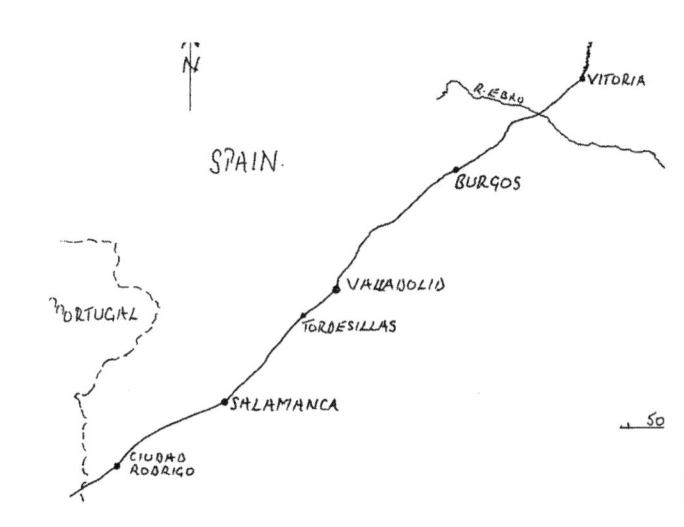

Chapter 4

BAYONNE, FRANCE

She moved among the soldiers, offering her wares. She did not look at Colquhoun but she was working her way towards him, no doubt of it.

Again, they came for Colquhoun before dawn. The soldiers of the *4ᵉ Léger* were already formed up in the courtyard. They put him in the middle of a strong platoon under the command of a young *sous officier* who wore two pistols holstered on his belt. Major Magaud, who appeared briefly to inspect the platoon, was also, Colquhoun noted wryly, carrying two similarly holstered pistols. He fervently hoped word had reached the guerrillas to leave the convoy alone.

So far as he could see, there was no horse drawn transport. Magaud and the *sous officier* both carried packs. He imagined it was endorsement that Marmont had lost most of his horse and a desire to travel at maximum speed.

The *sous officier* pointed out Colquhoun's battered pack to Magaud.

"Open it."

Magaud looked at the razor, opened it, looked at Colquhoun in the colourless light of the early dawn, looked again at the razor, shrugged, and tossed it back into the bag. A small gesture, but an encouraging one.

At about the same time that the column was marching out of Salamanca Marshal Marmont sent for Doctor Curtis. He wasted no time on civilities.

"You twice visited Major Grant. Why?"

"The Holy Catholic religion which you and I, Marshal, both profess, enjoins us to succour the distressed, to visit the sick and the prisoner and to administer comfort and consolation to them."

"Bullshit. What business had you with him? You had some purpose, I know it. What did he tell you? What information did he give you?"

"Why should he give me any information? Information about what, Marshal?"

"Don't play tricks with me, father. He is not of our religion. He is a heretic, a Protestant."

"We are both Christians, Marshal. We both follow the precepts of our Saviour, and he is my countryman."

"Hah. You lie, priest. He's a Scotchman and you're an Irishman. The Scotch and the Irish hate each other. You were up to some mischief, I know it. It is material to the interests of the Emperor that I should know what he has told you. Tell me here and now what I know the Scotchman has confided in you."

"If you know what Major Grant has, as you put it, confided in me, you have no need to ask me. He has confided in me, if that is the correct way to describe it, that he gave you his parole and that you do not honour it."

"Major Grant's parole is no concern of yours. What has he told you? Unless you tell me I will have you imprisoned."

"Prison holds no terrors for me, Marshal. I cannot tell you what I do not know. I visited Major Grant because he was in distress. He has given you his parole, yet you treat him as a prisoner. He does not understand why. His honour is compromised. Why do you treat him thus?"

"Do you question me, priest? Do you dare to question me?"

"I do, Marshal. In the name of God and of human decency. A prisoner who gives his parole should be treated honourably. War is a vile enough business without breaking its rules."

"Rules, priest? Do you dare to talk to me of rules? I make the law here. And you shall suffer its consequences if you do not tell me what he told you."

"Imprison me if you will. I have nothing to tell you other than of his ill treatment."

Furious, Marmont dismissed Doctor Curtis and sent for his Chief Clerk.

"Bring me that letter requesting Major Grant's exchange... Yes, as I thought. He offers a Colonel in exchange. He must think me a fool. Well, two can play that game. Draft Milor *sacré* Wellington a reply... 'I have the great honour to have received his request, etc, etc... I note his courteous offer to exchange any one of the Colonels who he holds prisoner for Major Grant...' The idiot. To think that I should fall for this nonsense... Say 'I note his kindness in offering that I should choose which Colonel I would like exchanged...' Tell him... 'It would give me inexpressible pleasure to grant his request. I am deeply honoured to have the opportunity of doing something - anything - that might be agreeable to such an illustrious character as Milor Wellington, of whom, of all others, I am the greatest admirer... Would he have the goodness to inform me the names of all the Colonels he holds so that I can decide which one I would wish to be exchanged, etc,

etc...'   Pad it out a bit... Damn fool. Does he really think me naïve enough to return his chief spy?

"Ah, General," - General de la Martinière had come in at that moment - "Pray have the goodness to send a despatch to the Ministry of War in Paris informing them that Major Grant is in all but name an accomplished spy and I do not want him back in Spain under any circumstances. It would no doubt be advantageous to us if he is never again in any position to threaten us in any way. Ever. Ever, you understand? Make sure your despatch gets to Paris before Grant reaches Bayonne. General Savary's police should be waiting for him when he gets there. You understand?"

"Perfectly, sir."

"Good. And that cursed priest. He's up to something, I'm sure of it. He's been twice to see Grant. He questions our treatment of him. I will not stand for his impertinence. Expel him from his damned Irish College. Confiscate his belongings. I'll not have a doddering old fool of a priest making an idiot of me."

General de la Martinière mulled for some time over his despatch to General Clarke, the Minister for War in Paris. He was pleased with the result:

Army of Portugal.   Salamanca.
28th April 1812.

Monseigneur.

His Excellency the Marshal Duke of Ragusa has ordered an officer of his army to accompany as far as Bayonne the English major, Colquhoun Grant, of the 11th Regiment of Infantry, taken prisoner by the French army in Portugal. This outstanding officer was found alone with one servant on the flank of our columns: found on him were papers and notes which indicate clearly the role of a man of importance to the English army, having the most accurate and the most detailed ideas on the marches, the composition, the strength and the movement of the French army. Nevertheless, as he was captured in the uniform and badges of an English officer, the Marshal has treated him with much consideration and has been willing to receive his parole of honour. Enclosed is a copy of the undertaking he has given. But His Excellency thinks that he should be watched and brought to the notice of the police.
With the greatest respect for your Excellency.

Your humble and obedient servant,
 Monseigneur
General Chief of Staff de la Martiniére

He read it through with savage satisfaction.

"And that, you damned spy, will be the last we shall see of you."

Somewhat to his own amusement Colquhoun felt improperly dressed as he discarded his worn out boots in favour of the Spanish shoes - sandals, really, rope soled with leather uppers. He would be marching with his legs bare from the knee down and with the addition of the bandana he felt more like a Spanish guerrilla than an officer of Lord Wellington's army. He was soon to discover that it was much cooler wearing the bandana and easier to march in the sandals which were surprisingly comfortable.

He was not alone. Like all units of both armies that had been months or even years in the field without proper resupply, seen close to the *4ᵉ Léger* looked more like itinerant vagabonds than soldiers.

To a man, their uniforms were faded, stained, torn, patched or replaced with clothes from some other formation. A fair proportion of the soldiers wore sandals similar to the ones Colquhoun was wearing. Many wore bandanas. Their equipment similarly was borrowed liberally from a multitude of sources, though Colquhoun noted with professional approval that muskets, bayonets and the short broad bladed sabres, where worn, were scrupulously maintained, clean, polished and well oiled.

Everything about them impressed Colquhoun. Morale was obviously sky high at the prospect of leaving the horrors of the Spanish war and returning home. Nothing could be as awful as Spain. But that apart, they were as close knit and well trained a body of men as Colquhoun had seen - certainly on a par with the fabled green jacketed 95th regiment of Lord Wellington's army.

Their march discipline was impeccable. They were well aware that Don Julian Sanchez, the local guerrilla leader, was active in the area, and they marched closed up and alert. Colquhoun counted that they were somewhat under three hundred light infantrymen, their number including about forty men from the *2˚ Léger*. A party of lightly wounded convalescents from a variety of units marched with them.

Colquhoun marched in the middle of his escorting platoon. In a rough sort of way the soldiers were friendly: they knew who he was and had a certain admiration for him. Under the watchful eye of the *sous officier* they kept close to him the whole time, however, awake or asleep, mounting their own platoon guard at night irrespective of the watch that the column mounted around itself at every halt.

Unlike the English army which began its day's march at two in the morning, and hoped to reach its objective before the midday and afternoon heat made the movement of tired men extremely difficult, the French column did not begin to march until it got light. Colquhoun supposed that it was the lesser of two evils to delay and march in the crippling heat of the middle of the day rather than risk a guerrilla attack in the pre-dawn twilight.

Progress inevitably got slower as the heat mounted, not helped by having to skirt round heavily escorted supply convoys coming the opposite way. Inevitably, too, men fell out of the column - a few of the walking wounded - but Major Magaud was obviously not prepared to abandon any of his command. Picking them up and helping them along further slowed progress.

To Colquhoun's surprise they passed no columns of troops marching towards them to reinforce Marmont's army of Portugal.

At their bivouac the second night out he learned why. His

escort were by now used to his presence. They had to discuss what was on all their minds. It could not be contained. They could not help talking openly as he sat with them at their campfires.

Their talk was all of the rumours that the Emperor was massing his armies in the East of Prussia. There could be only one reason. The Russians had become more and more uncooperative, helping the English and defying the Emperor. They had cocked a snook at the Emperor once too often.

The Emperor was going to teach them a lesson.

It must explain their recall to France. The Emperor would need his best veteran light troops to spearhead his advance. There could be no doubt that they would be in the forefront of the attack.

They had beaten the Russians before. There would be no problems about doing so again. A chance to see what the Russian women were like. Russian booty would be as good as the rest of Europe's. A new campaign of proper soldiering. Not like this *sacré* business in Spain. Thank God, they would be out of Spain in a week or two. Proper soldiering again. Anything rather than Spain.

Colquhoun did not see much of Major Magaud during the first few days of the march. Magaud was fully occupied supervising the column's progress.

With justification.

The first morning out the column spotted a group of horsemen on rising ground about half a mile away. It was too far to be certain, but Colquhoun was pretty sure they looked familiar - they certainly were wearing some sorts of uniforms. There was an occasional flash of sunlight from what he thought must have been lance heads. But they certainly were not French lancers. And had they been

French they would not have kept their distance. English scouts to the North East of Salamanca were out of the question. Colquhoun had little doubt that they were guerrillas of Don Julian Sanchez' band.

He offered up a brief and unaccustomed prayer that the message had got through not to attack the column. He watched the *sous officier*. His hand was on the butt of one of the pistols at his belt. He turned and looked at Colquhoun, verifying where he was. His eyes were merciless. Despite himself, Colquhoun felt the hairs prickle on the back of his neck. The horsemen came no closer, however, and soon vanished.

They reappeared again on the second morning. The column closed up even tighter. The men shook their fists at the distant horsemen and shouted every sort of obscenity, daring the guerrillas to attack, contemptuous of their cowardice if they did not.

The *sous officier's* hand again went to the pistol butt. Again, he turned and checked where Colquhoun was. But once again the horsemen kept their distance, and again soon disappeared.

They did not appear again. To be sure, this was not likely country for a guerrilla attack on a strong convoy. The empty, rolling plains were too open for easy ambush. There would be ample time for a well drilled infantry unit to form square before the horsemen could reach them. The lack of cover would be disastrous for the guerrillas should they choose to press an attack. The French muskets would take a heavy toll. Magaud's veteran unit would make short work of them.

By the third day, when they were approaching Tordesillas, Magaud must have felt that he had left Don Julian's territory. He had his march discipline and routine well established, and he seemed to relax.

That night he appeared at Colquhoun's fire.

"Tordesillas tomorrow. We're a bit behind my schedule, but if we can re-provision quickly enough we'll clear the town and be two or three leagues beyond it before nightfall. Every step nearer France raises my heart."

"I regret that I cannot share your pleasure. Every step nearer France depresses my heart unutterably."

Magaud gave a short bark of laughter.

"Cheer up, Major. I tell you what I'll do. I'll find us a bottle in Tordesillas tomorrow and we shall share it together tomorrow night and tell each other a few tales from our days in this God forsaken Peninsula."

"I'll look forward to it, Major."

Re-provisioning the column inevitably took longer than Magaud had hoped. They crossed the river, marched up into Tordesillas and halted in the main square while the NCOs went off to find the commissary to draw their supplies.

Around them, the Spanish went about their business. Colquhoun watched them covertly. It was more than possible that there were guerrillas in the square, counting their number, assessing their strength, perhaps even someone he knew.

He could not see any familiar faces, but there was a young man lounging against a wall who undoubtedly was watching him, catching his eye and holding his gaze. He was a horseman, with wide hat, short jacket and leather reinforced flared trousers over dusty boots with long spurs, carrying a long, coiled whip, and smoking a black cheroot.

Surrounded by the soldiers of his guardian platoon Colquhoun could see no possibility of approaching the horseman and eventually the man must have come to the same conclusion, as he threw away the butt of the cheroot and vanished.

Colquhoun had little doubt that if indeed the man was a guerrilla he had been there because he carried some message.

Speculating was a waste of time: it was impossible not to, though. The guerrillas were aware of his progress. Were they planning an attack? A rescue? Unless they combined groups and could take on the French with overwhelming numbers they stood no chance of success against Magaud's men.

And if they did, he was a dead man anyway.

Inwardly, he sighed.

It was late afternoon before they left the town. By that time the safest place to camp for the night was within shot of the walls. Fires were lit. The men ate well with wine, *soupe* made with fresh meat, and bread. Colquhoun was sitting staring into the fire wondering about the horseman in the town when Magaud appeared, bottle in hand. He sat down beside Colquhoun, produced the two battered mugs from his bag, pulled the cork with his teeth, spat it out, and filled the mugs. He handed one to Colquhoun.

"To our safe return to France."

"Your good health, Major."

They both drank. There was a long pause.

"So. Tell me how you came into this business."

Colquhoun deliberately misunderstood him. Undoubtedly he was referring to Colquhoun's intelligence activities.

"The army? Oh, I have a lot of older brothers, most of whom went into the army. So the army has always been part of my life. There isn't much else to do in the North of Scotland. That's where I come from."

"You are Scotch, then? Why don't you wear a skirt like the rest of them?"

"I had the chance to join an English regiment. I've always

been happy with them."

Another silence. Magaud refilled the mugs.

"Me, I am the son of an apothecary. My father wanted me to follow him in the business. I stuck it until I was twenty one, but I hated it. So I left and joined up. The *Régiment de Beauce*, the *68ᵉ Régiment d'Infanterie* it became. I did well enough; they made me a grenadier. I'd have stayed in the ranks if it weren't for the Revolution. I was all for it. It opened up such opportunities for men like me. I left the army, thinking to make my way as a revolutionary firebrand, but I soon found that life wasn't for me. All big mouths, double talk and treachery. Nothing straight forward and plain.

"So I joined up again with the Jura volunteers. They made me a Captain in three months. What times those were. We starved. We were in rags half the time. But the fire in our hearts kept us going. Terrible hardships. That's how I came to lose my hand. Christmas night 1795 it was, serving in the Alps. You can't imagine the cold for men without proper winter clothes. I had no glove for my left hand. We'd got hold of some wine. I drank a bit too much, and when I woke up my hand was frostbitten. Then gangrene. So it had to come off. But they still needed experienced soldiers like me, be it with one hand or two.

"Then Italy. I'll never forget the first time I saw the Emperor. From a distance he seemed a skinny little man with dirty long hair and a big hat. But when I saw him close to... *Mon Dieu*... He had such presence. His eyes, once you looked into his eyes you knew this was no ordinary man. He burned you up when he looked at you. Massena, Augureau - all the generals - they cowered before him like children. He was so full of fire. And energy. And ideas. He was bursting with greatness. You knew his head was full of great things. I said 'This is the man I'll follow. He's the one to take us to victory'. And I've followed him ever since. All across Europe.

"I was at the bridge of Arcole with him. Got this there" - he drew a finger across his face - "though I'd been hit about the head twice before. 'Brave man,' the Emperor said, and he gripped my hand. Of course he wasn't the Emperor then. Only General Bonaparte.

"I was with him at the battle of Austerlitz, you know, with the *18ᵉ Léger*. What an army we were then. The finest army the world has ever seen. When we left Boulogne that autumn we knew he would lead us to the greatest victories. We knew we were invincible. Our morale was - it was like nothing I've ever known before - or since, come to that. Ah, what days those were. What a victory that was.

"The Emperor has spoken to me seventeen times. He always knows me" - he indicated the scars on his face again - " 'Ah, Joseph Magaud,' he says. 'My old comrade in arms from the bridge of Arcole. My old warrior.' He always talks to me when he sees me.

"I was posted to the 4ᵉ in '09 though I didn't come to this *sacré* country till last year. I came at the same time as Marshal Marmont, when he took over command of the Army of Portugal from Marshal Massena. I've known Marshal Marmont for years. I served under him in Dalmatia. He ruled Dalmatia, you know, for five years. Got his title from there. He was a marvellous commander there. They're a heathen barbarian lot in Dalmatia, I can tell you. But he civilized them. He's a great man. It wasn't like here in Dalmatia. Nothing works here except violence. These awful, bloody, vicious Spanish. I can't wait to get out of it. I hate this mindless butchery. You can't blame our men for retaliating.

"What I can't understand is why the Emperor didn't come back himself to finish the business down here. I can't understand it. He drove you out with no trouble when he came in '08. It only would have needed a little push from him and he'd have annihilated your army. I don't know why he never came back."

Colquhoun laughed.

"No more does Lord Wellington. Nor any of us."

"We have five armies in Spain. If he had come and joined only two of them together, and led them himself he would have pushed you back into the sea. Pouf. No problem."

He threw his hands up as though tossing something away.

"I can't understand why he didn't come. Without you English here the Spanish would have given up long ago."

Colquhoun was silent. It was hardly worth contradicting Magaud, hardly worth telling him that the Spanish would never give up until the last Frenchman was dead or had left their soil.

More to the point, if Magaud only knew it, he had asked the question that was always in Lord Wellington's mind, that always influenced his decisions, the question to which, above all others, Lord Wellington had always sought an answer.

Because it was a plain truth obvious to all.

Had Napoleon come back to Spain instead of trying to run the war from Paris, had he come and united his quarrelling and fractious Marshals and confronted Lord Wellington with vastly superior numbers, with his genius for manoeuvre and lightning movement the English army would have been annihilated.

"Well," said Magaud, "You'll have heard the rumours from the men, no doubt . It must be why the Emperor has never been able to come back and lead us here. Too busy with those damned Russians. Well, if the rumours are right he'll teach them a sharp lesson now."

They lapsed into a companionable silence, each busy with his own thoughts. Magaud divided the last of the wine between them, drank his share, held out his hand for Colquhoun's mug, bade him a good night and took himself off to do a round of his sentries.

Colquhoun sat on beside the fire, staring into the flames.

Magaud's *cri de coeur* that Napoleon had not come to deliver the English army and Spain into their hands had set him thinking.

Say the rumours were right and Napoleon was taking an army to crush Russia. And say he succeeded. As no doubt he would.

Would he then come back to Spain?

Surely he must. Spain was a running sore that he had to attend to himself one day. Only by uniting his armies and taking command in person would he have any hope of pushing Lord Wellington's army out of Spain. And if this was so, then when would he come?

This would be information so vital to Lord Wellington that it would justify any means to achieve it.

And where would be the best and quickest place to discover it?

Paris, beyond a doubt.

If they sent him to Verdun, as was normal with paroled officers, and say they refused to exchange him, what use would he be to Lord Wellington then?

And what if they imprisoned him somewhere, as Don Patricio had thought they might? In that case, his parole was worthless and had been from the moment he signed it.

Once again, he fell to wondering.

A hard day's march across the interminable plains brought them into Valladolid's vast main square.

Colquhoun gathered that they would be billeted in the town. It was of little concern to him where he slept but while he waited to be taken wherever it might be he scanned the square for any sign of a friendly face.

And sure enough, on the corner of a narrow side street the young horseman from Tordesillas was leaning against a wall, cheroot in mouth. He seemed less at his ease, as well he might. He had blended into the surroundings in the much smaller country town. Vallodolid was a real city, infinitely smarter and grander.

He looked totally out of place. His dress almost shouted 'guerrilla.' Worse, the town obviously supported a large garrison as there were soldiers everywhere. He must have realised quickly both that he had no chance of getting close to Colquhoun and that he might have attracted attention and been arrested. He disappeared into the side street, once again leaving Colquhoun to wonder who was trying to contact him, and why.

The next evening, camped beside the road on the plains North East of Vallodolid, Magaud reappeared at Colquhoun's fire. He sat down, produced a bottle from his bag and filled his two mugs.

"To another day nearer France."

"Your health, Major."

"Now tell me, Major, how did you come into this business?"

Colquhoun laughed. Why not? The information was unlikely to be of any use now.

" Our retreat to the lines at Torres Vedras was before you came down to Spain, I think?" Magaud nodded. "You'll know that Lord Wellington stripped the country as he retreated and took all the Portuguese with him behind the lines. There were a lot of mouths to feed, and food was short, despite us being supplied by our navy. The Portuguese were dying of starvation, some of them. It was a big problem."

"Not, I think, so big a problem as it was to Marshal Massena."

"No. No, I don't know how the Marshal managed to hang on there in that wilderness. A tough man, your Marshal Massena. Anyway, I thought I could do something about it. I speak Portuguese: you probably know that. The Portuguese talked among themselves, and to me, when they realised I could understand them. They kept saying that if only they could get into the hills on the other side of the lines and away from your army there was plenty of food, cattle, sheep, grain, olives - everything.

"So I suggested to Lord Wellington that I should go and buy whatever I could and bring it in to the lines. I think he might have had me locked up for a madman if it hadn't been that he knew some of my brothers in the army, and respected them. I told him there was a long history of cattle raiding in my family, up in the highlands of Scotland. Lifting cattle is in my blood. He laughed at that. He gave me a bag of money and told me to try it.

"It was easy enough. The two armies were facing each other from the town of Torres Vedras eastwards to the Tagus, but from Torres Vedras west to the sea in the other direction, along the river Zizandre, there was nobody from your army. Of course you didn't have enough men to cover the whole line of our defences.

"Oh, a romantic story grew up that I had slipped out through your lines, dodging the pickets, bringing cattle in to our lines through your army under the noses of your pickets and that sort of thing, but I didn't. I just crossed the Zizandre and headed into the hills where neither army had been.

"And sure enough, when I jingled the coin, the Portuguese came tumbling out of the woodwork. As long as I had coin and could pay them I could buy anything. All I had to do was organise to get everything back across the river.

"We went well downstream, well away from any likely interruption. The Portuguese both sides of the lines were only too keen to help. They produced flat bottom boats and we loaded everything onto them. Crossing the river was no problem to them, even where our engineers had flooded it.

"We took everything straight into our lines. Of course, there was a tiny chance that we might run into a foraging party of your men, but we had strong cavalry patrols across the river, and there was a fair amount of guerrilla activity as well - which your men tried to keep well away from. I would have known soon enough if any of your men were around.

"Anyway, Lord Wellington was more than pleased with the result. So when Massena started to retreat and us to advance Lord Wellington sent me to watch the flank of your army and report what it was up to. Things just went on from there. I enjoyed the excitement of it. I was on my own, my own master. A sort of freedom that suited me well."

"How come you speak Portuguese?"

"I was stationed in Madeira for eighteen months before we were sent out here. It's another thing I enjoy, learning languages. Then Spanish came easily to me as it's not so far off either French or Portuguese."

Colquhoun wondered why he was telling Magaud these things. He was not given to talking about himself. Perhaps it was the isolation of his position in the French column. Perhaps it was because he liked Magaud and felt him to be a kindred spirit, a decent man and a good officer.

Magaud poked at the fire with a stick.

"We have always regarded you as a spy - a notorious spy. I have heard men curse you more times than I can remember. But… I don't know. Time to do my rounds, I think…"

As the column marched across the interminable plains of Northern Spain it became a nightly routine. Magaud would appear at Colquhoun's fire and they sat and talked, often not much, but their silence was the silence of comrades. When Magaud had a bottle he brought it and they shared it, drinking from the battered mugs.

The column made good progress. Magaud was greatly respected by his men. They reacted quickly and willingly to his command. His march discipline was exemplary. If there were guerrillas around they did not appear.

Colquhoun, unhampered by weapons and the weight of a laden pack, soon found he could keep pace with Magaud's light infantrymen with no difficulty.

They passed through Burgos, across the river Ebro - very heavily guarded, Colquhoun noted, - and on out of the plains into the hills as they approached Vitoria.

This was dangerous country for Magaud now. The scrub covered hills could hide any number of guerrillas. Attack could be swift and without warning. An ambush could be mounted from the surrounding rocks and they would hardly even see their enemy.

The French had the road strongly patrolled and picketed, though. A large proportion of their Northern army must have been tied down just keeping it open.

The column marched up through a narrow, steep pass as they climbed up to the high plateau surrounding the hill town of Vitoria. French soldiers could be seen in force all over the heights above them. Without their presence it would indeed have been the perfect place for an ambush. Colquhoun smiled to himself. It was the first time in his career that he had been relieved to see a strong force of the enemy.

They had been on the road for the best part of two weeks. They marched up the steep hill into Vitoria and halted in the main square.

Colquhoun had thought that whatever message someone was trying to get to him, they had given up the attempt. The young horseman had not reappeared, and there had been no sign of any friendly face in Burgos.

But in Vitoria he was not so sure.

A woman with a large basket over her arm approached them in the square. She was selling eggs. She moved among the soldiers, offering her wares. She did not look at Colquhoun, but she was working her way towards him, no doubt of it. She had almost succeeded in coming up to him when the *sous officier* shouted at her to get out of it. She shot a look at Colquhoun, turned away, swore at the soldier, sauntered off and out of sight.

If Major Magaud had relaxed his attitude towards Colquhoun the *sous officier* certainly had not. He was the sort of man who backbone all the best armies in the world. Leader and driver, intelligent, smart, alert, he had not for one second relaxed his vigilance. He assigned three of his soldiers every day as close escort to Colquhoun. Effectively, one or more of them never left his side. He changed the close escort every day, ensuring that there was no possibility of any of his men becoming too friendly. Even his marching order was changed every day, so that Colquhoun never marched beside the same man on any consecutive occasion. With a man like this to do his bidding, Magaud could afford the friendship of enemies that grew between them.

"We camp here tonight."

Magaud came over to Colquhoun, looking pleased.

"There's a home bound convoy here already waiting for support before taking on these mountains. Better still, General Souham is expected here tomorrow with a strong escort, on his way back home. We'll join up. With four or five hundred men we'll be safe enough from any terrorist attack."

Information that was as reassuring to Colquhoun as it was to Magaud.

That evening there was a sudden ripple of excitement in the camp that spread through the men like fire through dry grass and erupted into an enormous cheer. The news reached Colquhoun's camp fire within seconds.

"The Emperor has left Paris for Russia."

"It's war with Russia."

"The Russians are for it now."

"The Emperor has the greatest army the world has ever seen. Troops from every corner of his Empire. He'll crush the Russians like a beetle. It'll be another Austerlitz."

"This is going to be the Emperor's most glorious campaign. And we are going to lead it."

Colquhoun sat silent among the cheering men. Their excited babble of chatter washed over his isolated figure.

Could Napoleon really conquer Russia?

Why not?

He had humbled the Russians before.

How long would it take him?

He would surely have to bring the war to a conclusion before the winter. Of course, he had never experienced it, but Colquhoun had heard stories of the cold and the endless Russian plains without cover or fuel or anything to sustain life. It would have to be one of Napoleon's classic lightning campaigns.

One major battle, perhaps - a brilliant stroke that would crush the Russian army and bring them to terms. Indeed, a second Austerlitz.

Colquhoun had put the question of his parole rather to the back of his mind, an unresolved problem that might perhaps never have to be faced. Magaud had treated him as a gentleman. Perhaps he should forget de la Martinière's treatment. He was a long way from Marmont's sphere of influence. Surely in France he would be treated correctly.

Maybe, he had been thinking, he should go to Verdun where he would be held until his exchange came through, behave honourably even though his captors had not done so.

But should he?

That might be the easy way. The cowardly way, even. Because there was no getting away from it. They had not honoured his parole.

Father Curtis had exonerated him from it. He had pardoned him in advance for any breaches of it, - albeit Don Patricio was a Catholic and maybe a Catholic absolution did not count with Colquhoun's Scottish God - and if he could find some way of discovering Napoleon's intentions when he got back from Russia and of getting the information to Lord Wellington, it might make a vast difference to their fortunes in the Peninsular.

He wrapped himself in his cloak beside the fire. What a

dilemma.

As soon as they left Vitoria Colquhoun appreciated why Magaud had looked so pleased. They were marching through real mountain country now, endlessly up and down, clinging to the mountainsides, zigzagging round perilous drops, on tracks that ran through narrow valleys enclosed by towering heights with rushing streams below.

It was perfect ambush country, the fief of an infamously brutal and merciless guerrilla chief known as Mina, a man who had once been a farmer, whose family had been ill-treated or worse by the French and who, as a result, had abandoned his land and now waged the cruellest and most heartless war of any of the guerrilla bands.

Once a sharp eyed soldier yelled a warning as several enormous chunks of rock dislodged themselves from somewhere far above and came hurtling down on them. The column scattered and the rocks flew past, missing the track and crashing down into the valley below. There was no sign of life above them, nothing they could do except form up again and carry on. The incident left an uncomfortable feeling of being watched.

General Souham had joined them in Vitoria, surrounded by an escort of two hundred men or more. He was grey haired, a man in his fifties, Colquhoun thought, and sagging with fatigue. He was apparently on his way back to Paris on three months' leave. He and Colquhoun bowed frostily to each other. Colquhoun hardly saw him again as, although the various convoys had come together, they kept their separate identities and commands and scarcely intermingled.

"I suppose my luck must have been running out."

Colquhoun still did not know why he was confiding in Magaud. He seldom did in anyone else. Was it the loneliness of a single prisoner surrounded by the soldiers of his enemy? A desire for human warmth and friendship in hostile surroundings? He supposed it must have been these or similar reasons, faced with circumstances he had never had to cope with before. Whatever the reason, he was finding it hard not to speak openly to Magaud.

"You nearly caught me twice in the last month or so. Idanha a Nova was the third time. I think my luck just ran out - or maybe I was getting overconfident and a bit careless."

They were perhaps three or four days away from Bayonne, camping in a mountain village no better than a collection of hovels. The night was cold, the fire welcome. Magaud reached out a hand for Colquhoun's mug and refilled it.

"The first time was at Salamanca when you were concentrating for your foray into Portugal. I wanted in particular to find out if you were going to lay siege to Ciudad Rodrigo again, and what preparations you were making. I got rather too far in amongst your lines on the North bank of the Tormes when the river was too high to cross easily. It's difficult to remain unseen in that country, particularly at that time of year. And of course I was spotted a time or two.

"You remember General de la Martinière's briefing that 'the notorious spy' was in your cantonment, and the extra vigilance demanded to catch him? Well, I knew it was high time to go. I might, if you hadn't been on the lookout for me, have risked the bridge at Salamanca, but that was out of the question. The only chance I could think of was the ford upstream at Huerta. A big risk. I knew you had it guarded. But if I didn't take the risk I was trapped on the wrong side of the river and it must have only been a matter of time before you caught me.

"Anyway, I managed to get there unseen at night. There was an infantry unit camped outside the village and a unit of dragoons picketing the ford. But not very cleverly.

"It was a two man picket, patrolling apart about a hundred and fifty yards up and down stream. But they were timing it to come together at the ford, so at the far limit of their patrol there was a couple of minutes when the ford was open. Enough to give me a chance to get well out into the river before they could get back into carbine range. So I picked my moment and rode like the devil for the ford just when it was beginning to get light enough to see what I was doing."

He did not add that León had gone on ahead to contact the local Spanish, to arrange for him to steal into the village to be hidden close to the ford, nor that two of their womenfolk had bravely gone to the water's edge and had busied themselves shaking out some blankets, the signal, when they both shook one of the blankets together, that the sentries were at the far end of their beat.

"It took a second or two for the sentries to realise what was happening. Instead of firing and alerting the district they both turned and galloped back to the ford. It gave me a few seconds more. And I needed them. The water was deep and flowing hard and I could scarcely see where I was going. My horse stumbled and threshed about, damned nearly throwing me. It took me a while - it seemed like for ever - to get him under control and going on. I expected a bullet in my back every second.

"The sentries fired at last, and brought the place alive, but by the time the infantry arrived I was fairly well out of shot, even for a marksman in that bad light. The dragoons came across the river after me, but they didn't give chase once they got into the trees on the far side. They were too vulnerable by themselves over there. So I got away. But it was a near run thing."

"You were lucky. I remember it well. We all heard about it. We cursed you, I can tell you."

"Yes, well, I'm sure you did."

No need to tell Magaud that his escape then had been thanks to León and the Spanish villagers. They had judged it too dangerous to hide more than one of them and for both to cross by the ford at Huerta. León had bravely gone back into Salamanca and had simply walked out over the Roman bridge the next morning, right under the noses of a strong and alert guard.

"Well, it wasn't long after that you nearly got me again.

"When Marshal Marmont left Ciudad Rodrigo I was curious to know what you were up to. I knew you had scaling ladders with you, so it looked as though you might be going back into Portugal to lay siege to Almeida again. But I didn't think it likely as you had no siege train, and rations for two weeks only.

"I wondered if it was a blind and Marshal Marmont was heading off South to join up with Marshal Soult to chase us away from Badajoz. And then I wondered whether perhaps the Marshal had produced the ladders for my benefit hoping that I would send the wrong message to Lord Wellington. So I waited for you at Tamames, where the road branches west or south, Almeida or Badajoz.

"Do you remember that day? The rain was pelting down. I was lying up in the trees on the hillside. Your army came past me, heading West, soaked to the skin and looking downright miserable - but no scaling ladders. So it answered some of my questions.

"I waited till you'd passed, then I went back to the village to see what had happened to the ladders. There they were, sure enough, thrown down by the road, but what I didn't realise was that a group of your officers were still there, sheltering from the rain in one of the houses. I nearly rode right into them. Fortunately for me they were downing a bottle or two and not too interested in what was happening outside. I whisked round and made off at a gallop. It was a close shave."

Again, no need to tell Magaud that León had gone on ahead into the village, and that it was Leon who had saved him. Drunk or sober, had he ridden into the village the French officers would have shot him down, and made fine sport of it as they did so. Quick witted León had ridden past them, slowly, head down against the rain, a Spanish farmer going about his business. They had ignored him. Once past, he had doubled back behind the houses, only just in time to warn Colquhoun as he came into the village. He had been no more than fifty yards from them. A second later, and they would have seen him.

Magaud laughed.

"Well, we're both out of it now. I hope to God I never see Spain again - unless when the Emperor finishes this Russian business he comes back here himself. I'd be happy enough to come back then. I can see now that's why he has never come back. Watch out next year. He'll come and finish this damned Spanish war then and push you into the sea."

Magaud took a long pull at his mug, smiled, and sighed.

"Ah, well, two or three days now, all well, we'll be over the border and safe into Bayonne. Out of these cursed mountains. I don't know which is more dangerous, the plains or the mountains. Easier to lay an ambush here, of course, no doubt of it, but then, we have more patrols and more outposts up here. I think we'll get through all right."

'Amen to that,' Colquhoun said to himself. Never for one moment had the *sous officier* relaxed his vigilance.

The mountains were reluctant to concede their territory to the sea. But abruptly, two days later, the road crested a hilltop and the sea lay bright in front of them, maybe two or three miles down across a narrow coastal lowland. There was a cheer along the length of the column, and involuntarily the pace quickened.

For the first time in three weeks the *sous officier* smiled at Colquhoun. He tapped the pistols at his belt.

"We made it, then," he said.

They crossed the Bidassoa river and were into France.

The horrors of guerrilla attack behind them, the column took on a carnival atmosphere as they marched into Bayonne.

104

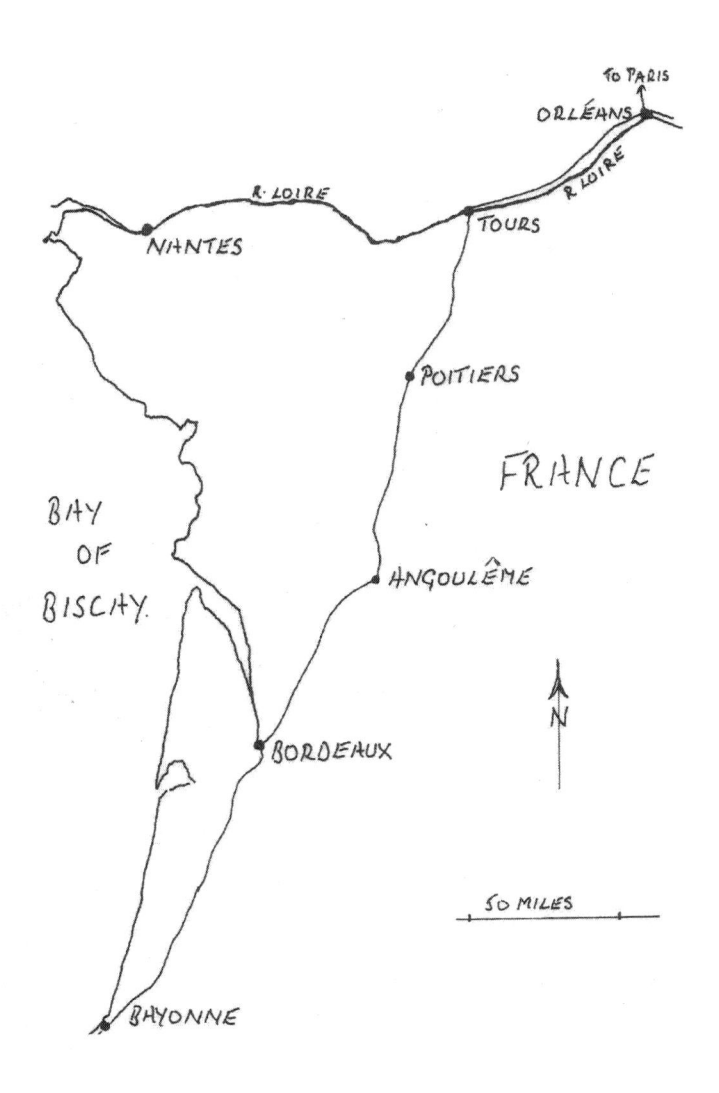

Chapter 5

ORLÉANS

"You are in great danger, Major Grant."

Bayonne was swarming with uniformed Frenchmen. Gold lace, silver lace, plumes, tassels, braiding, frogging - every colour of the rainbow, every unit of the army. Hardly surprising. Bayonne was the clearing station for four of the French armies in Spain.

Colquhoun imagined it would be similar to Belem, the Lisbon suburb which acted as the clearing station for the English army in the Peninsular, the haven for every shirker - blustering red faced field officers with stomachs stretched over their tunics; sharp, cunning eyed sergeants; malingering soldiers, - and for all the scum of the army. He imagined it would be the same here, and if it was so, and there were men here who would take great pleasure in proving themselves against an unarmed prisoner, it would probably be as dangerous as anywhere on the battlefield.

"My orders are to take you straight to the police and hand you over to them."

Magaud looked uncomfortable. He had not mentioned this before. He shrugged.

"I don't know why the police and not the military authorities, but no doubt they will give you your *feuille de route* to Verdun."

Magaud had halted his command short of the town. He had called the men round him and told them to be back at the same spot in twenty four hours exactly and to keep out of trouble in the meantime. Colquhoun was impressed. It would not be so in the English army. Let off the leash in a strange town after three weeks on the road they would have got blind drunk, set about demolishing the town and at least some would have taken the opportunity to desert. The drummers would have been busy with the lash for days.

"Will your men be back?" he asked.

"Of course. Some will get into trouble, no doubt, and I shall have to bail them out, but, yes, to a man they will be here."

Magaud sounded completely confident. If he really was right, it was a remarkable tribute to his leadership.

The men of *4ᵉ Léger* had looked like marauding itinerants when they had left Salamanca. Now, after three weeks of marching, they looked like the most desperate of cutthroats. Uniforms that had been threadbare then were rags now. Some were barefoot. All wore long unkempt beards. Their faces were blackened by the sun and framed by matted hair. They were covered with the sweat and dust of three weeks' marching. Hardly a man had washed any part of his body on the road. Probably the garrison at Bayonne would steer very clear of them.

Colquhoun felt a twinge of pity for the girls who would have to accommodate them in the wine shops and brothels.

Well, no doubt they were used to it.

Colquhoun and Magaud were directed to the police post. A bored police sergeant sitting at a high wooden desk looked at Colquhoun with massive disdain.

"He is dirty enough. He looks a great rogue. More like a terrorist than an English officer. No doubt he should be hanged. But has he done anything against the law?"

"No."

"Well, then." The sergeant spread his hands eloquently and hunched his shoulders.

"I don't want him. Why bring him here? He is a matter for the military, not for the civil police."

"But my orders were to bring him here."

The sergeant shrugged again.

"I know nothing of such orders. There is some mistake."

Magaud looked relieved.

"Quite so," he said.

And, as they left, "I am glad, my friend. I was not happy to do this. That policeman is right. General de la Martinière must have made some mistake. So, we are stuck with each other for a little longer. I feel much happier to take you to the garrison headquarters. They will treat you properly."

The street was crowded.

Either by accident or by deliberate design they were separated by several paces. Colquhoun felt himself jostled heavily on his left side, and then, a second later, jostled again on his right.

This was no accident.

He stopped. Two blue coated French officers had drawn level with him, one on each side. They stopped with him. One stamped down hard on Colquhoun's sandaled foot. It hurt, but mainly he felt flaring anger. The officers moved in front of him. Their eyes were malicious, bright with spiteful pleasure. They were expecting him to retaliate. He stood still.

One of them said:

"You trod on my foot. You owe me an apology."

Colquhoun said nothing.

"Perhaps you did not hear me? Apologise. You trod on my foot."

The other said:

"Apologise. Or give my friend satisfaction."

The first one raised his voice.

"You deliberately trod on my foot. I demand satisfaction."

One or two passers-by had stopped. They were not yet hostile, just curious.

Colquhoun held his gaze.

"He's afraid."

"Lost your tongue, arsehole?"

The officer turned to the passers-by. In a loud voice he said:

"Look at him. Look at this apology for an English officer. He's a coward. He refuses to give me satisfaction. What a specimen. He's filthy. A disgrace…"

The insults stopped abruptly as Magaud's hand seized the man's collar, twisting the coat violently, choking him, pulling him backwards off balance.

Colquhoun saw surprise, then fear in his eyes. The man's face was suddenly red, his eyes bulging.

"You are the disgrace, sir, a disgrace to the French army, you and your companion."

The second man turned aggressively. One look at Magaud's hideously scarred face was enough.

"Just a bit of fun. No harm intended."

"Get out of my sight."

With a harder twist of the collar Magaud thrust the first

man at the speaker. Both seemed mesmerized by Magaud's face. They backed off and were lost in the crowded street. The passers-by melted away.

"Thank you."

"Scum." Magaud's livid face was enough to frighten anyone. "I am ashamed, my friend, ashamed of the French army, ashamed that any officer in the Emperor's uniform could behave so. I cannot apologise enough. They are men without honour. They should be shot."

"Please, think nothing of it." Colquhoun took his arm. "It was nothing."

Thank God, he had kept his head. He could have knocked the first man down and turned on the second before they realised what was happening. But had he retaliated, had Magaud not come to his rescue, he might well have been spitted on the sword of one of the men, the other swearing that Colquhoun had insulted and attacked them.

That would have landed him back with the police, had he not been dead from the sword thrust or lynched by a whipped up mob first.

He smiled. "I am sure I do look a villain in these clothes."

He had given up shaving as just too difficult on the march. He had nearly three weeks' growth of beard. His hair was badly in need of a barber. His red coat was faded to a russet brown, his breeches, once white, were dirty dark grey. No doubt his face, although he had not seen it for weeks, was burnt as black as the soldiers'. All in all, he was sure he looked a lot more like a Spanish guerrilla than an English officer.

Magaud laughed, echoing his thoughts.

"So you do. Like a Spanish terrorist. We'll have to do something about you or you'll be in trouble again."

Their reception at military headquarters was a lot more

civil. The duty field officer, a smart young major of cuirassiers with one arm, shook Colquhoun's hand.

"I am honoured to meet you, major. I know something of the frustration of capture and exchange myself. I was wounded at Talavera and taken there. Your army showed me every courtesy and indeed saved my life with this." He indicated the missing arm.

"Not much good for active work now, I fear. Now, you'll need a *feuille de route* to get you to Verdun, and some money for subsistence en route. Not much, I'm afraid. Tell you what. I'll include for board and lodging on the *feuille de route*. Our honest hoteliers won't like it and no doubt will refuse to honour it. Sadly, they don't trust the government to repay them. They're right, of course, the rogues. The chances of them ever getting any payment are absolutely nil. Still, one or two of the more naïve ones may be taken in. You'll have to live very simply, but it'll get you there."

"Would it be an imposition to ask for some new clothes. These are quite worn out."

The cuirassier laughed.

"So they are. I would hardly take you for an English officer had Major Magaud not vouched for you. You will have to travel in uniform, of course, but, yes, I'm sure we can find you some overall trousers. Some boots, too, I see."

Magaud said: " I think that the sooner Major Grant can leave, the better. He was set upon in the street. It might have gone ill for him had I not been there."

"Ah. Sadly, that is not the first time I've heard that story. You have my deepest apologies, major. It is inexcusable. Everyone seems to have gone a little mad since we heard that the Emperor has left for Russia..." He rummaged on his desk and extracted a sheet of paper. " Hmm... Yes. The stage coach leaves for Paris tomorrow morning. I'll arrange a seat for you. It'll have to be outside. The coach will be full. I suggest you go to the *Hôtel de l'Empereur* - they say he dined there on his way to Spain four years ago - which it leaves from. I'll have you escorted there. I doubt whether the Emperor really dined there. Its kitchens leave a lot to be desired. Don't leave the hotel. Just get straight on the coach. I'll send word to Paris that you've left and are on your way to Verdun."

"Our ways part here, then, my friend," said Magaud. "I have enjoyed your company. I hope we may never meet again so long as these wars go on."

Colquhoun took his hand in both of his.

"I hope we may meet again in happier times, then, and that I can repay your kindness to me one day."

Magaud shrugged.

"Perhaps. Let's hope it is not in Spain when I return there with the Emperor to drive you *sacré* English out."

They both laughed, genuinely sorry to part.

"Wait a minute."

Magaud squewed the bag round from his left hip. He pulled out a small leather pouch and shook coins out onto a table.

"How much have I got?"

He counted and divided the coins into two lots. He pushed one lot towards Colquhoun.

"Here. Take this. It'll ease your journey. No, don't thank me. It's nothing."

He scooped the other pile deftly back into the pouch.

"*Adieu*, then, my friend."

And abruptly he turned and strode from the room.

Armed with his *feuille de route* and now wearing a pair of infantryman's overall trousers and boots which the cuirassier had produced for him, Colquhoun was escorted by two soldiers to the *Hôtel de l'Empereur*.

On the way he stopped and bought himself some soap.

There was, he sensed, an atmosphere in the town, excited or nervous, he was not sure which, with the news of Napoleon's incipient Russian invasion. Napoleon had indeed reportedly assembled over half a million men - a fantastic figure. Perhaps in actual fact it was the greatest army the world had ever seen. It could not fail. Cynically, Colquhoun wondered if the atmosphere was based at least in part on relief that the base camp soldiery were not included in it and would not have to face the inevitable hardships of such a campaign.

As predicted by the cuirassier officer, the hotel did not live up to its exalted title. Colquhoun asked for a room.

"A room, Monsieur? A room? How will I find you a room? A bath, Monsieur? Monsieur the English officer is a joker, no? Where will I find such a thing for the Monsieur? If you wish, there is the pump in the courtyard. I do not object if you wish to bath there. But a room... If you wish you may pass the night in the taproom. I do not object. Come here, boy," he shouted to an urchin squatting at the door of the hotel, "Show the Monsieur the pump in the courtyard and pump the water for him. There, Monsieur, that is the best I can do for you."

The boy took Colquhoun through into a square central courtyard. One side was stables. Comforting horse noises came from the stalls and the chatter of the ostlers who presumably were getting them bedded down for the night ready for the stage coach in the morning. From the opposite side of the yard came a clatter of cooking and women's voices from the kitchens.

The courtyard itself was empty. The pump stood in the middle of the yard, a stone trough beside it. The evening was warm. Colquhoun could bear his filthy clothes and body no longer. He stripped off and began to splash the cold water over his body as the boy pumped, then, armed with the soap, he climbed into the trough and immersed his head in the water rubbing vigorously at his hair.

"Do not look up at me, Major Grant. Carry on with your ablutions."

Momentarily Colquhoun froze. A man's voice. He did not look up.

"You are in great danger, Major Grant. Milor Wellington intercepted a dispatch to the police in Paris from General de la Martinière. The General informs them that you are a spy in all but name. He proposes that you be taken into police custody - the secret police, have no doubt. Milor considers that the French have no intention of exchanging you. If the secret police take you, you will never be seen again. Milor orders you to consider your parole void and act accordingly. Do not stop your ablutions, Major. If you can get back over the border the partisans - Mina's men - will be watching for you and will look after you. Be very careful."

The pumping continued for a moment, then stopped, then, after a pause, started again, and the boy's voice said:

"Haven't you had enough, monsieur?"

Colquhoun looked up and quickly round the courtyard. A man was disappearing under the archway to the street. He was dressed as a labourer. Then he was gone.

Resisting an intensely powerful temptation to run naked through the archway after the man, Colquhoun forced himself to finish washing. Deliberately, he shaved and used the razor to trim his hair to what he hoped was a reasonable length and shape.

So this was the message they had been trying to get through to him as he had crossed Spain.

This was why Magaud had been ordered to hand him over to the police. If de la Martinière's dispatch had got through and been acted on the secret police would have been waiting for him.

The cynicism of de la Martinière's conduct - and no doubt Marshal Marmont would have been party to it, if not the author - left him cold. They would not touch him as a paroled officer in Spain under their jurisdiction. Indeed, Marmont had given his word that no harm would come to him in Spain or Portugal. But once in France, out of their jurisdiction, no longer their responsibility, he could simply disappear: no blame, no dishonour, could attach to them.

Come what may, though, he realised now that the dilemma over his parole had been an enormous weight on his mind. Lord Wellington's command to consider it void had lifted his heart. It had cleared all the doubts and puzzling over what he honourably could or should do. Far more so than Father Curtis' easy absolution, much as he admired and respected him. It overruled everything. Despite all the dangers he faced he felt an overriding sense of relief.

Damn the French. If they played false with him, as they had, he would do his damnedest to confound them.

The fact that the dispatch had been intercepted did not of course necessarily mean that the police would fail to get the message. Usually dispatches were sent in triplicate, by separate messengers. If one fell foul of the guerrillas, even two, still maybe the third would get through.

He tried to calculate mentally how long a mounted dispatch rider would have taken to get to Paris and for the order for his arrest to have been relayed back down to

Bayonne. De la Martinière must have thought there was sufficient time or he would, presumably, either have sent his dispatch direct to the police in Bayonne or have ordered Major Magaud to escort him further into France rather than hand him over here. That might suggest that the message had not been delivered.

Or maybe Magaud had made better time to Bayonne than de la Martinière had expected.

Or, if a copy of the dispatch had reached Paris, maybe there had not been time for the message to be relayed back down to Bayonne.

Whatever the reason, by the grace of God, they had not been there waiting for him.

So what now?

Bayonne was probably not much more than fifteen miles from the border. An easy night's march. But once there he would have to get back across the river Bidassoa, heavily guarded and patrolled and with a strong French army presence on both sides. His chances of escape would not be high, even with a night's start. He did not know the country. He could expect every man's hand to be against him. He would have to travel on his feet. A cavalry patrol would probably pick him up within hours. As a parole breaker he could expect the harshest treatment, if not immediate execution. The direct road back to Spain was probably not the best option.

If he was to try to escape back to Spain he would have to go inland and cross the mountains.

But was it really what he wanted to do?

If - and it was a very big if - he succeeded in crossing the Pyrenees and the whole of Northern Spain and found his way back to Lord Wellington's army, would there not always be a nagging guilt that he had taken the easy option?

There was no doubt where he could now be of the greatest use.

Paris.

The fountain head of all information. The last place they would expect him to go. The first place to hear of Napoleon's plans when he returned victorious from Russia. Worth the risk. And what a challenge. It would put anything he had done in the Peninsular into the shade.

Yes, that was it. He should be taking the gamble that the message had failed to get through, take the gamble that he could get to Paris and survive there and somehow manage to warn Lord Wellington before the victorious Napoleon moved in person against him.

Given that both Lord Wellington and Father Curtis had exonerated him from his parole, clearly that was where his duty lay. Daunting: but what a challenge. His heart beat faster at the prospect. He felt again all the anticipation and excitement that he had known in Spain as he had sat his horse on some lonely hilltop and trained his spyglass on the French.

He was well over half way to Paris already. Maybe this had been his destiny from the moment of his capture.

So how to achieve it?

What better than the stage coach? Let the French take him openly at least part of the way at their expense.

What was more, no doubt someone would be watching the coach's departure and reporting back to the authorities. If he was not on it the alarm would almost certainly be raised.

And even if an order for his arrest were to arrive tomorrow he would still be going North and would probably be miles from Bayonne before the police realised that he had come and gone. At the very worst, the coach would probably have at least a day or two's start over any messenger sent after him.

So, get on the coach, go as far as Orléans, and make contact with Father Curtis' contact there at the cathedral of Sainte Croix. The next move after that would have to remain in the lap of the gods

It did raise an immense problem, though. How on earth would he survive without any money?

It was all very well living off the land in Spain with a saddle bag full of coin supplied by the army and a friendly populace to look after him. France would be an entirely different matter. Despite the ease with which his forebears had salved their consciences - if they had such things - and removed their neighbours' property - four legged, usually, but also sometimes two legged - the idea of stealing was anathema to him.

It would be supremely difficult for him to live by his wits in the capital of France. But damn the French. He would do it. His fingers tingled with excitement at the prospect.

Despite his thrill of anticipation of the challenge ahead, Colquhoun spent an anxious night in the taproom of the *Hôtel de L'Empereur*. He made himself as inconspicuous as he could, sitting quietly in a corner wrapped in his cloak, but it was impossible not to dread every opening of the door and feel a tremor of apprehension at every new arrival into the room. Beyond the odd incurious glance, however, no one paid the slightest attention to him and at last the room emptied and he was able to stretch himself out first on a bench which proved too short and then on the floor.

He slept fitfully, dreaming that a faceless secret policeman was beckoning to him, saying again and again that Fouché wanted to see him. It was absurd, he knew it was. The evil Fouché had been dismissed by Napoleon a year or two ago for plotting to overthrow him and presumably to restore the Bourbon dynasty.

The head of the secret police was now, Colquhoun was pretty sure, General Savary, a much less sinister and more human figure. Even so, he had no doubt that the French secret police were no less dangerous than they had been under Fouché's direction. The dream was not pleasant.

He rose as soon as the hotel began to stir, and ordered bread and coffee from the sleepy serving girl who appeared yawning and tousle haired from the kitchen.

The courtyard was already awake. The stage coach was wheeled into the yard. He watched as the horses were brought out of the stables and harnessed up. It might draw unwelcome attention to himself to appear in the yard too soon, so he waited until a small group of people - travellers, servants and no doubt the curious, had gathered round the coach, and for the first passengers to get aboard before he went out into the yard, presented his *feuille de route* to the guard and climbed aboard himself.

His fellow outboard passengers were civilians. They were probably used to seeing English officers leave Bayonne in this manner. Hundreds of paroled officers must have passed through the town over the years of fighting in the Peninsular. They nodded a greeting and made room for him on the wooden bench.

The inboard passengers appeared to be a family couple and a major of French engineers. Not as full a coach as the officer of cuirassiers had implied.

The coachman mounted his box. The guard heaved himself up next to him, carrying an enormous circular horn.

Colquhoun breathed a prayer of relief. Thus far, his gamble was paying off.

But was it?

The coach did not move. The horses fidgeted. The coachman and guard sat talking to each other on the front box. Ostlers held the impatient horses' heads. They waited. The other passengers began to complain. Still they waited.

Colquhoun tried not to show it, but he began to feel real fear. Could word have reached the police? Could the delay be while they got together an arrest squad? All he could do was sit tight, and hope.

There was a commotion at the door of the hotel. Officers. Surely they would send a squad of soldiers to arrest him, not officers. Heart in mouth, he waited.

To his surprise, out strode General Souham with the manner of a man who has just enjoyed a good breakfast, looking important and rather less exhausted than he had at their first meeting at Vitoria. He was surrounded by a small retinue, one of whom hurried forward to open the coach door. The General shook hands and embraced his followers.

He turned to the coach. As he did so he glanced up incuriously and started with surprise at the sight of Colquhoun. He must have seen an equal surprise in Colquhoun's face. He said nothing. Both inclined their heads to each other in the smallest, frostiest greeting. The door banged shut behind the General, the coachman picked up his reins, the ostlers stood back, and they were off.

The road was excellent. They passed frequent groups of ragged, blank faced Portuguese prisoners of war living out their captivity armed with shovels, picks, rammers and wheelbarrows keeping the road in condition. Colquhoun wondered why they did not use the implements as weapons, set on their guards, and escape. He supposed their life here was probably not so different to that in Portugal - endless hard physical labour and a bowl of stew at the end of the day if they were lucky. And at least they were no longer required to risk their lives fighting for their country.

At first there was a lot of military traffic. There were supply convoys heading South, hospital convoys heading north, occasional columns of marching infantry - all going North - and endless dispatch riders hurrying both ways on sweating horses. Every mile that they progressed Colquhoun felt marginally more at ease though whenever a messenger passed them on his unknown errand Colquhoun felt his throat constrict and his stomach churn.

Had he known it, one of the riders was indeed carrying a letter to the Ministry of War in Paris, signed by the Bayonne garrison commander and dated 26th May 1812, stating that Monsieur Colgahorn - the French never could pronounce or spell Colquhoun - Major of the 11th Regiment of English Infantry, captured by himself on the 16th April last by the troops of Monsieur the Marshal Duc de Raguse, left on the 25th May to report himself to Verdun, under parole of honour.

To Colquhoun's quiet amusement there was the usual coolness between the inboard and the outboard passengers, the former no doubt considering themselves a superior breed. General Souham had presumably reserved one whole side of the coach seating for himself as there were only four inboard passengers, though it was not long before the lady was seated beside him. Her husband's closed and sulky face suggested that he was not particularly amused by the

General's attention.

The four inboard passengers sat together to eat when the coach stopped for meals and to change horses. They appeared somewhat embarrassed by the presence of an English officer travelling outboard. Influenced no doubt by General Souham they got round the problem by ignoring him.

The outboard passengers ate together at a separate table. Their initial surprise that Colquhoun spoke fluent French quickly broke any ice that might have existed. To his surprise they appeared to have not the least resentment that he was an English officer, almost the reverse, in fact. He sensed there was more animosity in them towards their own officers and army. At first he was not sure whether this was directed at General Souham and was the natural dislike of people travelling uncomfortably towards those who were travelling comfortably, but sensing that it was something deeper he gently began to draw them out.

As long as they were out of earshot of any strangers or the officers in the coach, they had little hesitation in confiding in him. It was as though they all had a great burden on their minds and were glad to share it. They all had some family members or knew of families whose men were either in the army or disabled by the wars or indeed killed. They were all sick of the fighting, though none dared say so outright.

This latest adventure of the Emperor - what would it achieve?

More widows. More mothers with dead or missing sons. Less men-folk to work the fields. More misery. Of course the Emperor was right to teach those Russians a lesson. They raised their voices as they said this sort of thing, and glanced round, seeing who might be watching them. Then they lowered their voices. They wished an end to it all. France was being crucified by the endless fighting. Whatever the military might think of their Emperor's latest ambition, this tiny cross-section of the people of France wanted none of it. Colquhoun wondered whether they spoke for the people generally. It was information that would certainly be of interest to Lord Wellington.

Conceivably, just conceivably, the people of France might one day rise up against their tyrannical Corsican Emperor and demand an end to the wars.

Bordeaux, Angoulême, Poitiers, Tours, where the coach crossed the busy river Loire and turned right handed to follow its Northern bank, they rattled on through the lush green early summer of France. Once they had left the flat plains and marshland of Aquitaine the countryside was at its most beautiful. The journey was too long, though, to remember it well. The harsh rocky landscape, the scrub, the pine trees, the vast open spaces, the heat of Spain were in any case too fresh in Colquhoun's memory for him to appreciate this softer and kinder land.

The outboard passengers came and went as they passed from town to town. The post houses, like the countryside, merged into a blur.

As the cuirassier officer had predicted, the hotel owners, the women particularly, were vociferously scornful of his *feuille de route* and refused to comply with its order to provide Colquhoun with free board and lodging. So far as the lodging was concerned, Colquhoun was not in the least put out. He had slept rough every night for the last two years, usually wrapped in his cloak on the ground. If the innkeepers had given him lodging it would have been in some crowded attic where the apologies for beds would have been running with fleas and other assorted vermin.

As for the board, occasionally, - quite frequently - despite the initial fury at the demands of his *feuille de route*, he charmed an hotelier's wife and was rewarded with a bowl of *soupe* and some bread. It helped to eek out the small amount of money that was all that stood between him and starvation.

So he ate simply, slept under the stars when the weather was good, begged a space on the taproom floors when it was not, suffered the long hours of jolting on the back of the coach, and considered his next move.

He was pretty sure that no one from Bayonne would catch up with them now. There was always the risk that the police might be waiting for him at the next town, but with every passing stage he felt more and more confident that de la Martinière's dispatch could not have got through to Paris.

The married couple disappeared somewhere en route, to be replaced by some sort of officials. General Souham continued to ignore his existence. The major of engineers became embarrassed by Colquhoun's presence and his own boorishness and made to befriend him. He was sharply reprimanded by the General. He shrugged, raised his eyebrows apologetically, and abandoned the attempt.

At the end of a long, hot day the coach rolled into Orléans. Colquhoun climbed stiffly down. He took his leave of his fellow travellers.

"This is as far as I go on this coach. I go on to Verdun from here."

They all knew this already, but it did no harm to say it. The coachman directed him to the post hotel from which the Verdun coach would leave. He waved to his companions and walked away.

The first thing was to see whether he was followed. Although no one had said it outright, his fellow passengers had given a very definite impression that there were watching eyes and listening ears all about them. Several times he had thought that there had been men watching the arrival and departure of the coach and presumably reporting to some authority on the passengers. It was a fair guess that if the police ever bothered to correlate all the reports they would have a picture of his progress through France.

The streets were crowded, mostly with householders and their families sitting around their doorsteps to enjoy the cooler air of the evening. After some minutes - he could not be sure - he thought he had seen the same man several times in amongst the playing children and gossiping parents, but he might have been mistaken. He decided to play stupid. He stopped often and looked about him, went part way down a street and turned back, scratching his head, peering round corners, looking for street names.

The Sainte Croix cathedral was unmistakable. He had asked the coach passengers what sights he should see, should he have some time to kill in Orléans. The cathedral had been top of their list - second only to Notre Dame cathedral in Paris, known throughout the whole of France for its magnificence. It was indeed a vast building, and it was magnificent with immense twin towers, a spire and an extravagantly decorated façade - not to Colquhoun's Scottish taste, but impressive nonetheless.

Colquhoun did not go in. He wandered uncertain in the square in front of it and asked someone the way to his post house. It would be safer to go there, find out when the coach to Verdun would leave, and ask for board and lodging. Even if the coach went the next morning, he would still have time to vanish in the night.

The post house keeper was as unimpressed by Colquhoun's *feuille de route* as had been all the other hoteliers.

"Another bloody goddamn, here to cheat an honest Frenchman with his fancy paper. The coach does not leave for five days, Monsieur. Do they expect me to feed you for that amount of time? I suppose you want the best room in the hotel? Who is going to pay me? Not the military, with their swagger and their graces, you can be sure of that. I will be beggared. Why they send the likes of you to me, I don't know. You'll get nothing free here, paper or no paper."

He calmed down a little when Colquhoun apologised for his presence. He assured the man he would not have been there if he could have helped it, but he was under obligation to present himself to the authorities at Verdun. A bed would be quite unnecessary. He was not used to such luxury. Mine host must not trouble himself. With some huffing and puffing the landlord supposed that Monsieur could bed down in the taproom, though there was a charge for the privilege, of course. As for meals, Monsieur could forget it unless he could pay. Colquhoun assured him that he could and would. The hotelier immediately looked suspicious.

"And where does a goddamn find money to pay his way?"

It was Colquhoun's turn to shrug and spread his hands.

"Don't worry, Monsieur. If I eat, I pay."

"Well, I don't want you hanging round the hotel all the time. You'll give me a bad name. Bloody redcoats."

Colquhoun stayed at the hotel overnight. If anyone was reporting on him, it would be to say that he was quietly waiting there for the Verdun coach. He paid for his food and his night spent on the taproom floor - it was, after all the hectoring, only a few *sous*,- gathered his few belongings and left the hotel. He wandered around the town until he was sure that he was not being followed and eventually made his way back to the Sainte Croix cathedral. The interior architecture was breathtakingly beautiful, the trappings of its Catholic religion, to Colquhoun's prejudiced Scottish eye, less so. He sat down towards the front in one of the pews.

From time to time there were several priests in evidence, black robed, busy about whatever their Godly tasks might be. Impossible to tell which, if any, might be Father O'Shea.

He waited - half an hour - an hour - just sitting quietly - an hour and a half, hoping that his uniform and his continued presence there might attract Father O'Shea's attention.

He wondered whether to go away and try again later, or whether to risk asking one of the priests if Father O'Shea was there.

After two hours he decided that he would have to risk it. One of the priests seemed to be taking an interest in him, looking quizzically at him from time to time, busying himself quite close to Colquhoun.

"Excuse me, father, I am looking for Father O'Shea."

"Then you have found him. I am Father O'Shea."

"I am a friend of Father Patrick Curtis in Salamanca."

The priest nodded. They looked at each other. The priest's eyes were shrewd, inviting Colquhoun to say more.

"Father Patrick asked me to tell you that the wild geese have flown early this year."

"Did he, now? I thought maybe they had." He glanced round the cathedral.

"Is anyone following you?"

"I don't think so, but I cannot be sure."

"No, I don't think so either. I have been watching for some time. I don't think there are any strangers. Do you see up there," he flicked his eyes towards the altar area, "a door on your right. Wait a while, then go through it. I will be waiting for you there."

Colquhoun sat on for another ten minutes. The sense of relief that he might have found a friend was immense. He stood up. He sauntered to the door. It opened to his push. He slipped through and shut it behind him.

The room was full of robes, rich garments, huge silver candlesticks, solid gold and silver processional crosses, a life size figure of the Virgin Mary in a long, deep blue gown embroidered in gold with a great silver crown on her head, vivid colours, the smell of incense.

"How can I help you, my son?"

The priest was of medium height, dark eyed, dark haired, dark skinned, every inch a Frenchman. He said again:

"How can I help you?"

"I am Major Grant of the 11th Regiment of Foot. Colquhoun Grant."

The priest bowed slightly. Clearly the name meant nothing to him. He said nothing.

"Father, I have to disappear."

Father O'Shea contemplated this for some time. He looked doubtful.

"But you are on parole, no? You could not be here by yourself in your English uniform if you were not."

The eloquent raise of his eyebrows put the question that he was too tactful to ask.

"Yes, I am. I was captured in Portugal two months ago. I am on parole. I am supposed to be on my way to Verdun.

But I have learned that Lord Wellington intercepted a dispatch from General de la Martinière to the police in Paris. They regard me as a spy. I am to be handed over to the secret police."

"Ah. I see. That would be unfortunate. But why? If you are a uniformed officer? If you are on parole? Why should they consider you a spy?

"I am - I was - an intelligence officer. My task was to gather information about the strength and dispositions of the French army in Spain - that sort of thing. Indeed, I was fortunate not to be hanged for one when they caught me. But I am not and never have been a spy. We always wore our uniforms openly wherever we went."

"I see." Father O'Shea was silent again, perhaps contemplating the treatment of the clergy during the Revolution and more recently in Spain. Their cloth had been no protection for them.

"And you know Father Patrick in Salamanca?"

"I have worked with him for over a year."

Father O'Shea nodded, looking shrewdly at Colquhoun.

"A curious business, war, is it not? I am here because my great grandfather fled from Ireland with the Wild Geese to escape your army and your persecution."

"Ah. No. We were no part of the English army then. My clan fought for Prince Charles Edward at Culloden."

"Ah. You are a Scotsman. I thought so. A Jacobite?"

" Scottish, yes. Jacobite, no. That's all past now. My allegiance is to Lord Wellington."

Father O'Shea nodded again.

"Yes. It seems he is the best hope we have."

He had made up his mind.

"Well, now. For you to disappear is easy enough. You walked in to the cathedral a soldier. You will walk out a priest. We can get you down the Loire to Nantes. You will know that your navy blockade the mouth of the Loire? There is a regular intercourse between them and the local fishermen. The people of the Vendée are royalists still. They have no love for Napoleon Bonaparte. We can find a boat to take you out to an English ship."

"If I can - if I can make it possible - I must go to Paris, Father. If I go to Paris I can get first hand information on Napoleon's Russian campaign and can find out what he plans to do next. If I could get such information to Lord Wellington it would be of the greatest help to him in the Peninsular."

"That would be very dangerous. You may already have the secret police looking out for you, no? You will put your head into the lion's mouth if you go there. I do not advise it. The secret police are a force to be reckoned with, even now that Fouché is in disgrace and no longer directs them."

"My mind is made up. If I can find the means, I must go."

Father O'Shea nodded.

"God go with you, then. Very well. We have a contact there. He is very old, a Jacobite also, a fugitive from the very battle you mentioned, though he cannot have been more than a mere boy then. This will take some thought. First, we must for now make you a priest. Come."

They went further into the recesses of the cathedral, to a small robing room where Father O'Shea searched along a row of hooks carrying an array of vestments. He took down a long black cassock.

"This will fit you, I think."

He contemplated Colquhoun's uniform.

"Less the epaulettes and your badges of rank. They will show. Hardly appropriate under this."

They took the epaulettes and insignia off Colquhoun's coat. He put the cassock on. It came full length to his feet, hiding his uniform completely. Father O'Shea fastened a wide sash round his waist. He selected a black biretta from the hooks and set it on Colquhoun's head. He stood back.

"There now. And haven't I made a holy father of you."

They walked together to Father O'Shea's lodgings, two black robed priests going about their business. So far as they could tell, no one took any notice of them other than to greet Father O'Shea. He appeared well known, and, from the friendly smiles and greetings, well liked.

"You will have to stay here until we can think of the best way to get you to Paris. Papers will be the problem - apart from money, of course. I do not think that in all conscience I can rob the poor box for you."

He laughed at Colquhoun's rather shocked reaction.

"Don't worry. I am not serious. And for any hue and cry to die down if your failure to go on to Verdun is noticed. My lodging is, I fear, simple, but I have a good library of books to which you are most welcome. The coach to Verdun leaves in four days, you say? We will have to see whether you are missed at the hotel and more particularly when the coach leaves. If so, the police will undoubtedly be alerted. In the meantime I will see what I can do to find you a new identity."

Father O'Shea's lodgings were two first floor rooms at the front of a handsome house overlooking a small square. They had not been there many minutes before a middle-aged woman dressed in black appeared in the doorway. She looked at them without speaking.

"Ah, Madame Marie, there you are. This is a friend of

mine who needs succour and rest for a few days. Father Pierre, this is Madame Marie. Madame Marie, this is Father Pierre."

Colquhoun bowed. He gave Madame Marie his most charming smile.

"I am delighted to meet you, Madame, and I must apologise for intruding on your house."

"Hmm." She looked at him, eyeing him up and down, intelligent dark eyes in a face that was etched with sadness.

"He will need the small back room."

"Please, Madame, do not disturb yourself. I am very happy to sleep on the floor."

There was a quiet chuckle from Father O'Shea.

"Priests do not usually sleep on the floor, father. Unless you are undergoing some unusual penance, of course."

"Sleep on the floor! I'll have no such thing in my house. The very idea. Father Pierre shall have the small back room."

"Madame, you are too kind. I cannot inconvenience you. And indeed, I regret that I cannot pay for such a lodging."

"Who said anything about paying? Be off with you, father, back to your work, while I show Father Pierre to his room. He looks famished. Off you go, father. I'll look after him."

Father O'Shea winked at Colquhoun.

"She is my guardian angel. You may look forward to your *déjeuner*. She is a divine cook."

Madame Marie looked simultaneously complimented and disapproving, and, Colquhoun thought, rather pleased at the presence of her unexpected guest.

He also suspected that she had already realised that he was not a priest.

The small back room reinforced this suspicion. It was

little more than a cupboard with a very small window looking onto a blank wall, unconnected to Father O'Shea's rooms, very unobtrusive and completely private. He wondered how many times it might have been used for similar purposes.

As Father O'Shea had predicted, Madame Marie was an inspired cook. She left the house with a shopping basket on her arm, returned with it laden, and an hour later sat Colquhoun down to the best meal he had eaten for many months.

She asked him no questions, but, in the way of the lonely, was happy to talk about herself. He learned that the house belonged to her. She was the widow of a prosperous businessman who had been denounced and guillotined in the revolution. His only crime had been his success in business. Probably he had been denounced by someone who had a grudge against him. It had happened a lot.

She had only escaped a similar fate because she had been fever ridden in bed when they came for her husband. She had looked so ill that they had left her, fearing to catch the fever from her if they touched her. They had left the house laughing that she would be dead in a day or two in any case and why waste the executioner's time? They seemed to have forgotten about her, as they did not return. She had not left the house for eighteen months, until Robespierre had himself been arrested and guillotined. Her elder daughter had hidden her and looked after her all this time. It had been a time of terrible fear and danger. Her daughter had left Orléans after the Revolution and gone to Paris. She never wanted to see Orléans or its people again. It was a great sadness.

Madame Marie had at first welcomed the rise of the Emperor. Order was restored. The terror of the Revolution was past. She could breathe again.

But soon she had realised that the Emperor's order came at a terrible price. She had lost touch with her elder daughter. Two sons had been gobbled up by Napoleon's war machine and both had been killed on foreign battlefields. Her other daughter had married a soldier and was somewhere abroad following the army. She did not know exactly where. Germany, perhaps, or on the march to Russia.

In the following days Colquhoun listened quietly as Madame Marie unburdened herself of her tragic story. She was terribly alone. Yes, of course, she loved Father O'Shea, but he was always so busy, and a priest. She respected his cloth. She could not talk to him as she was talking now to Father Pierre.

She made it plain that she found him attractive. Her face lost some of its sadness. She smiled more often. Their midday meals stretched longer into the afternoons as they sat together, her talking, him listening.

It was unspoken, but she knew he was not a priest, knew he was a fugitive, had known it from the first moment she set eyes on him. She did not ask him why, nor what or who he was fleeing from. She must, Colquhoun thought, have had implicit faith in Father O'Shea and total trust that if the Father believed what he was doing was right, then right it must be. He was not, he was sure, the first to pass through her house in this way.

Father O'Shea left the house early each morning and did not return until late in the evenings. Then they ate together, Father O'Shea relating the happenings of his day with quiet and gentle humour. He spent a lot of his time working at an infirmary that was run by the Church, and much of it ministering to the poor. He was, Colquhoun quickly realised, a genuinely good man leading a genuinely Christian life. To put him and Madame Marie in jeopardy on his behalf was deeply uncomfortable, but the priest would have none of it.

"This house is safe. Madame Marie is, of course, perfectly well aware that you are not a priest, but you already know that you may trust her with your life. So long as you continue to appear to be a priest no one will ask questions. Madame Marie's maid is similarly trustworthy. No one knows you are here.

"Besides, you add a little excitement to my humdrum life, for which I am in your debt. And if your passing through here helps to shorten the war in Spain and the rule of Napoleon Bonaparte and restore our rightful monarchy, to be sure, won't I feel that I have been of some little use?"

On the first morning he had told Colquhoun to give him the *feuille de route* and anything else that could identify him. He had demanded that Colquhoun take off his uniform and to give it to him. Colquhoun had parted with it with mixed feelings. His red coat had saved his life in Sabugal. It was like parting with his passport. Though now, of course, it was more likely to be his death warrant. In any case, the weather was too hot to wear it under the cassock. Madame Marie had already suggested that she should wash his undergarments. It could not have been long before she or her maid would see his red coat.

On the third evening Father O'Shea said:

"I do not think they have given you a second thought at the hotel. I am very hopeful that no one there will ask any questions if you are not on the coach. The police, however, have, I think, noted that you arrived here on the coach from Bayonne. If they are alert, they may send someone to check whether you leave as you should. We will just have to wait and see what happens when you fail to do so."

Colquhoun did not ask him how he came by this information.

And two days later:

"The coach for Verdun left this morning. As I thought, the hotelier did not comment on your non appearance. He does not much like the police. I think we can forget him. Regrettably, I also think the police have noted that you were not on the coach. I do not think they will take any immediate action, - indeed, short of mounting a full scale search of the city there is not much they can do, - but it will be on their file. They will be on the lookout for you and they are not to be underestimated. It is all the more important you stay quietly here until they forget about the missing Major Grant."

Despite the pleasure of Madame Marie's company and her memorable *déjeuners,* and the quiet enjoyment of their evening meals together, the time hung heavily on Colquhoun. Confined to the house, he longed to get out and stretch his muscles. He longed for action, to be on his way to Paris, to face the challenge of survival there.

Father O'Shea might have a good library, but all the books seemed to be on religion, and Colquhoun was in no mood for the niceties of Catholic doctrine. He set himself an exercise routine and spent hours stripped of his cassock, sweating with exertion. It kept him fit, but did little for his frustration.

"Be patient, Father Pierre."

Father O'Shea said it over and over. In truth, there was little else Colquhoun could do. With no papers, no money, not even any civilian clothes, all he could do was rely on Father O'Shea and pray he would soon come up with a solution.

He began to query the wisdom of his decision to go to Paris. How could he hope to survive there? It was totally impractical. Mere bravado to have thought it possible. Stupid. The obvious thing to do was to take Father O'Shea's offer to go down the Loire and contact the fishermen there who could take him out to an English ship. He could be back with the army within a month, maybe, or two, instead of hiding here like a cornered rabbit. But he had given his parole. He had agreed on his honour not to fight again in Spain. And if only he could get to Paris and survive there… His thoughts seemed to go round and round in his head, never reaching any solution.

He put all his doubts to Father O'Shea. The priest was silent for some time. At last he said:

"Wait a little longer. I may have the answer. No, I cannot speak about it now. It may not work. But be patient a little longer. God works in a mysterious way."

And at last, one evening, it came.

Father O'Shea arrived home carrying a large holdall. He greeted Colquhoun with a beaming smile.

"God does indeed move in a mysterious way. I have a new identity for you and enough money to keep you in Paris for at least a month.

"God does mean you to go to Paris. Yesterday an American by the name of Jonathan Buck died in our infirmary. I hesitated to tell you about him in case he recovered and your hopes were dashed. Poor soul, I buried him today in your uniform. The authorities have been notified that a Major Grant, a paroled English officer on his way to Verdun, died of fever in the infirmary. Your *feuille de route* has been handed in to them. You are officially dead.

"Monsieur Buck was some sort of a merchant from

Boston. I do not know what he traded in. He was too ill or too guarded to tell us. There is talk of another war between America and England. - It is possible that war has indeed already been declared between them. - I suspect his business may have been connected with this, but I cannot be sure. He was trying to leave France. He had hoped to go down the Loire and find a blockade runner to take him back to America. Sadly for him, God rest his soul, he contracted the fever. He was just about your size. He has no further use for his passport or his identity papers. He was carrying a lot of money. He has no further use for that either. It seemed that as God had presented us with this opportunity it would have been a sin not to make use of it and pass everything of his on to you."

He opened the holdall. From it he extracted a handsome cut away swallow tailed brown coat and matching waistcoat, a full looking purse and a wallet.

"See here."

He opened the wallet and took out its contents. Colquhoun's heart was racing.

"Your identity papers - and look at this - Your passport to move freely about France, signed by the Ministry of Police in Paris. Whoever Jonathan Buck was and whatever his business, God could not have sent us a more perfect alias. Here, try these on. His breeches I felt I could not in conscience remove, poor soul, but we can soon find you a pair. Ah, and here is his hat. How does that fit?"

Jonathan Buck must have been almost exactly the same size as Colquhoun. The clothes and hat all fitted as though made for him.

Father O'Shea stood back and examined him critically.

"Perfect," he said. "Are you still absolutely sure you want to go to Paris? You could be at the mouth of the Loire in days, and back in England within weeks."

"With this identity, Father, I should be a coward and a deserter if I was to quit now. I am quite sure."

Father O'Shea nodded.

"In that case I must tell you that the Emperor officially declared war on Russia two days ago. His army will by now have crossed the river Niemen and violated Russian soil. France is again committed to untold bloodshed. It is too cruel. And all for one man's ambition."

"Then, Father O'Shea, it is all the more necessary that I go to Paris."

"Yes," he nodded, "as God has given us this opportunity he must mean for you to go there. The stage coach leaves for Paris the day after tomorrow. I think it would be safe for you to be on it."

"I could walk there in two days."

"No, not as Jonathan Buck, you could not. You are a merchant now, well dressed, well to do. You must do nothing that would draw attention to yourself.

"Now, listen. When you get to Paris you must go to the house of Angus Mcpherson in the Rue de Sèvres. You remember, I told you about him? He is very old, but a staunch Jacobite still, and a firm Royalist. He will help you in every way that he can. I expect he will be able to give you money as well. He can arrange for messages to be brought to me, and I can arrange for them to go on to Father Curtis in Salamanca. They must be brief and entirely to the point. Only send such messages as are completely factual and essential to your purpose. Not more than one or two sentences. No, don't ask me how I will send them on. It is better that you do not know."

Father O'Shea plunged a hand into a pocket somewhere inside his cassock and withdrew a tiny leather bag. He opened it and took out a ring.

"You must take this ring and give it to Angus Mcpherson."

Colquhoun took the ring from Father O'Shea. It was solid gold, delicately traced with the fluid lines of a Celtic design.

Father O'Shea laughed.

"Don't look so doubtful. This ring has made the journey between Orléans and Paris more than once. Angus Mcpherson made it and cut the design himself. He will recognise it instantly and know that you come from me and are to be trusted"

Madame Marie looked stricken at the news of Colquhoun's departure.

"Must you really go, Pierre?"

For the first time she dropped the charade of calling him 'Father.'

"Must I lose yet another man?"

She took his right hand in both of hers and squeezed it hard. He put his left hand on top of her hand and they sat silently together. At last she said:

"Of course you must. I will come with you to the coach tomorrow."

They walked together to the coach station, and when the time came for him to step aboard she flung her arms round him with all the passion of a woman who has lost her man, of a mother who has lost her sons. He put his arms round her and kissed her on the forehead and both cheeks.

"Come back one day, my Pierre," she said.

When he looked back as the coach moved off he saw that she was weeping.

The policeman watching the coach was sure that he had seen this man somewhere before. He could not think where. A well-to-do sort of a man. An American businessman, apparently. Not the sort of passenger you see every day. Where had it been?

No matter, it would come. He had certainly seen the woman before. She kept house for one of the priests at the Sainte Croix. He wondered what their relationship was. Aunt, perhaps? Sister? He had never heard she had any American connections. But then, why should he have heard. Could possibly be mother and son. She could have had a son who had gone to America to fight against the English in their war of independence. Quite a few Frenchmen had done so. Not very likely, but possible. He didn't look much like her, though. She would have had to have been very young when she had him. Lovers? Well, anything was possible.

And another funny thing. She had called him Pierre. The man's papers were in the name of Jonathan Buck.

Strange. It would come to him.

Chapter 6

PARIS

"Can we send word to Lord Wellington?"

Angus Mcpherson was a very old man. His elegantly brocaded long skirted coat, which would no doubt have been the height of fashion thirty years ago, hung loosely on his frail body. He rose slowly and stiffly from his wing chair as Colquhoun was shown into his salon. He was bent with age, though his bright blue eyes were alert. What little remained of his hair had probably once been red. He waited for Colquhoun to speak.

Colquhoun deliberately emphasised his Scottish brogue,

and spoke in English:

"Mr Mcpherson, it is kind of you to see me. Father O'Shea in Orléans recommended me to contact you."

"Father O'Shea?"

The old man's eyes were suddenly guarded.

"You are a Scotsman, Mr Buck? It is not often I am visited by my fellow countrymen. You are welcome. Come on in and sit you down. Monique, bring some refreshment and tell Madame Constance that we have a visitor."

The serving girl who had shown Colquhoun in bobbed a curtsey and left the room. Colquhoun took the ring from his finger and handed it to Mcpherson.

"Father O'Shea gave me this ring to give to you as a token of my good faith. He told me that you fashioned it yourself."

The old man took it carefully into his left hand and, with his right hand, took up the magnifying glass which hung on a ribbon round his neck.

He gazed at the ring for some moments, turning it slowly round in his fingers. He looked up at Colquhoun and smiled.

"Yes," he said, "this is my ring. I made it myself, you know, forty and more years ago. Father O'Shea has sent you to me for what purpose?"

"Can I speak plain, sir? He has sent me to you to ask for your help."

Mcpherson nodded.

"Speak plainly, sir. You are among friends here."

"Like yourself, sir, I am indeed a Scotsman. I am an intelligence officer in Lord Wellington's army in Spain. I am also an escaped prisoner and I am masquerading as an American."

Mcpherson held up a hand.

"Slowly, sir, slowly. Scotsman, English army, prisoner, American, this is too much for an old man to take in in one breath." He changed to French. "Ah, Constance, my dear, come in and listen. We have a most unusual visitor."

An elderly lady had come quietly into the room. She looked at Colquhoun with none too friendly a glance. She said nothing, and sat down.

The serving girl reappeared with a tray carrying a decanter and glasses. There was silence as she poured wine into the glasses, offered it round, bobbed another curtsey, and left, pulling the door to behind her.

"Now, sir, pray tell me - slowly - your story."

Speaking in French, Colquhoun explained who he was and how he came to be there, adding:

"I have come to Paris with the express purpose of trying to keep Lord Wellington informed of Napoleon's progress in Russia and of his intentions when he returns. It is of the utmost importance to Lord Wellington to know whether Napoleon intends to return in person to Spain when he has finished with the Russians. If it is humanly possible, I intend to get this information to him."

"I see...."

The woman spoke for the first time:

"You are too old, Angus. You are too old for this business. Your messengers are no longer reliable. I keep telling you to have nothing more to do with it. You must go, sir, and leave Monsieur Mcpherson in peace. He is too old. He is not well enough."

"No, no, Constance, my dear, I am well enough. Grant, you say? Your clan fought with us at Culloden. I was still a boy, you know. It was all the greatest adventure. I worshipped the Prince. He was so noble and so brave. We flocked to his standard, bursting to fight and to die for him...So many of us did... Brutal, the English army was, brutal... I was lucky to escape. How I ran. I ran till I thought my lungs would burst, and still I ran.... I was lucky. Friendly hands - at great risk to themselves - helped me to a French privateer....I have been in France ever since. I have never seen Scotland again, nor ever shall, more's the pity.

"France has been good to me, you know. I learned to make jewellery, beautiful things, and I made a good life for myself.... As you see. I made jewellery for the Court. The King himself was no stranger to me. Ah, it was a different world then, a different world. I pray I may live long enough to see his brother restored to his rightful throne."

"Do not distress yourself, Angus. Go away, Monsieur, go away. Can you not see he is an old man?"

"Hush, woman. Until the day I die I will fight to rid France of this tyrant. Sadly, sir, our Jacobite cause is lost. There remain no rightful claimants to the throne of England. But while I have breath left in me I will fight to restore the throne in France. Sadly, sir, I cannot do much myself these days, but I still have my ways and means. Lord Wellington shall have his information."

The woman glared at Colquhoun.

"Well, he cannot stay here. Don't be a fool, Angus. Please, for my sake, get rid of him. Go away Monsieur, and leave the old man in peace."

Colquhoun looked from one to the other. He had not bargained for this female intervention. He stood up.

"Then I must apologise for the intrusion, Madame, and will take my leave. I have no wish to distress either you or Monsieur Mcpherson."

"Sit down, sir, I pray you. Constance, you know that I must rely on your wit and your eyes now."

He turned to Colquhoun.

"There is nothing that goes on in Paris of which Madame Constance is unaware. Her circle of ladies have their finger on the pulse of everything that moves here. I can do nothing without her. Please, my dear, help us. I would rather be dead in this cause than alive and feel I am shirking my duty."

Madame Constance appeared somewhat mollified, either by Colquhoun's offer to go or Mcpherson's flattery and plea for her help. Colquhoun was not sure which.

She said "Well, he cannot stay here" again.

"Thank you, my dear. I am sure he would not wish to do so. We are far too old to be good company. Hmm… You have taken this American merchant's identity. Can you masquerade as an American?"

"I am not afraid to do so. My regiment was stationed in the West Indies for several years. There were often Americans there. Many of them were little different from Englishmen. My only concern is that I do not know what Mr Buck was doing here, nor who he met when he was in Paris, as I imagine he must have been."

"England and America are on the verge of war again. There is even a rumour that Napoleon agreed with the Americans that they would declare war on England before he crossed the Niemen. We will have to hope that Mr Buck's business here was not connected. He had nothing on him to give us any clue?"

"No."

"Then you must tread warily. But on the other hand if his business was military the chances must be very high that his contacts are now in Russia. All the Emperor's staff are there. As to how you will obtain the information that you are seeking here in Paris…" He shook his head. "The rumours of the Emperor's progress will of course fly round the city, be they true or false. But rumours will not be good enough.

You will need a good reliable military source for swift and accurate information. If we could find a contact in The Ministry of War, for instance, that would be ideal"

Colquhoun laughed.

"That might be difficult, I fancy. I am sure, though, that with your help we will separate the wheat from the chaff."

Madame Constance said: "Claudette d'Yves."

They both looked at her.

"Claudette d'Yves, of course. It is obvious. She is - friendly - with all the officers of the Ministry of War. Befriend her, and Monsieur will know everything as soon as it happens."

"Constance, my dear, Claudette d'Yves is almost of the *demi monde.*"

"Of course Claudette d'Yves is of the *demi monde*, Angus. And will Monsieur object to that?"

Colquhoun had no objection. The prospect sounded intriguing. He tried to look suitably neutral.

"Ha," she said scornfully. "Men."

There was a hint of amusement in her eyes.

He said carefully, "Who is Claudette d'Yves?"

"Claudette d'Yves is a girl who is no better than she should be who lives by her wits on the lust of the Emperor's officers, stupid creatures that men are."

There was no mistaking the amusement in her eyes now.

Colquhoun was not sure whether he was slightly shocked or just amused. He had no idea that old women could talk or even think in such a way. Come to think of it, the only other elderly woman he knew was his mother. The idea of her suggesting that her son cultivate a loose woman was quite unthinkable.

"Claudette d'Yves lives in the Rue du Bac, close to the Ministry of War. There must be lots of empty rooms round there with the whole army away in Russia. If we can find you some rooms there it will be up to you to make yourself known to the lady."

Mcpherson had been sitting silently looking embarrassed. He cleared his throat.

"Well, yes, my dear. Major Grant may not….."

"Fiddlesticks, Angus. Major Grant is no different to any other man, I assume? Well, then… I shall go myself this very afternoon to the Rue du Bac."

"Hmm…Well.. Such a contact would, of course be invaluable. But you, sir, you might not wish…"

"The prospect sounds intriguing, sir."

"Hmm…." Mcpherson changed the subject. "You are going to be conspicuous, sir, and excite comment, I fear, as a civilian on the streets of Paris at this time - hostile comment, in all probability. Napoleon has taken every able bodied man in France to Russia with him. You look like a soldier, too, if I may say so."

Madame Constance said:

"How do you know that this Jonathan Buck was not a soldier if he was here on some mysterious business that no one knows about?"

They all contemplated this in silence for a while.

"Well, I know nothing of commerce. I should certainly be happier to remain a soldier. Perhaps we should make Jonathan Buck a soldier instead of a merchant. With nothing to indicate what he was doing here - what he was buying or selling, that is, - he might have been a soldier, especially if there really is war looming between England and America."

They were silent. Mcpherson indicated the decanter and Colquhoun refilled their glasses. He sat down again.

"Why should Jonathan Buck not be a soldier?" he said. "Could we find a tailor who would make me up an

American uniform?"

"Do you know what the American uniform is?"

"I know it is a blue coat and white trousers. The tunic, as far as I remember, is similar to that of the *Léger* regiments. I expect there are a variety of uniforms and facings. I think it is simple and plain - not much gold leaf or ornament. There may not even be a standard uniform. If I don't know, I would doubt many people in Paris would have any better idea of it."

"This is a good idea," said Madame Constance. "You will be much more attractive to Claudette. She cannot resist a uniform, and a strange and plain one will be alluring to her. All the tailors in Paris are military tailors. Such a uniform will not pose any problems. You will say that you are visiting Paris and your baggage has been lost or stolen on your journey here. No one will question you. And if the uniform is not quite right you will say that you had to have it replaced here in Paris and the tailor did not make it correctly. It is simple."

Colquhoun understood now why Mcpherson had asked Madame Constance to join them. If he was too old for this game, she certainly was not.

Madame Constance returned triumphant from her visit to the Rue du Bac.

"It is all arranged. It was very simple. All I had to do was ask at the *Café Desmares*. They directed me to the next door shop - the *Au Petit-Saint-Thomas*- the shop where they sell the muslins and linens. They have empty rooms above the shop, the rooms of an officer who has gone to Russia. They will be only to pleased to let them to an American officer while he is away. You can move in tomorrow."

The uniform proved equally simple. Mcpherson directed Colquhoun to the nearest military tailor who saw no difficulty in making up the desired dark blue coat and white trousers. He professed to a familiarity with American uniforms, a familiarity which Colquhoun did not like either to accept or question.

On the basis that to show any hesitation would be dangerous he confidently ordered a single breasted cut away coat with plain silver buttons, silver epaulettes and a gold lace shoulder rosette. Top boots completed the outfit. As the tailor did not demur he assumed either that he had remembered correctly or the tailor knew no more than he did.

Colquhoun had no idea what sort of hat the American army was currently wearing. The tailor was similarly vague. Colquhoun reckoned that a forage cap could not go far wrong and while he was thinking about it decided that he would grow his side whiskers down and across his cheeks to merge with a moustache.

With the army away in Russia business was slack. The uniform would be ready for a first fitting within the day.

Mcpherson was direct on the question of finance.

"Away, man, I may be old and unable to move. But with money I can help. I cannot take it with me and it will give me pleasure if the money I have earned over my lifetime can be put to good use. I shall finance you, Grant, and your Lord Wellington can pay me back when he comes to Paris and sets our rightful King back on his throne. When you have the information you want bring it to me here, and I will make sure it goes on its way. I will die a happy man if I can achieve something positive in my last days."

The rooms over the linen shop could not have been better placed for Colquhoun's purposes. The Ministry of War, housed in the former *Couvent des Filles de Saint Joseph* in the Rue Saint Dominique was no more than a few minutes' walk from the Rue du Bac. There was a constant coming and going of uniforms in the area, some fairly similar to Colquhoun's. He thought that he would be able to blend in without attracting attention.

The absent officer's quarters consisted of two rooms on the second floor of the linen shop, one looking out over the street and the other looking out at the back over a small garden where a little donkey lived, apparently kept for the children of the shop's customers to ride while their mothers chose their materials inside. The rooms were as spartanly furnished as Colquhoun had expected, a table and several chairs in the front room and a simple bed, an empty chest of drawers and a large locked wardrobe in the back room.

The proprietor of the shop explained that the rooms were normally occupied by an officer of the *Grenadiers de Cheval de la Garde*, a Major Henri de Bacquencourt, who had left his spare clothes in the wardrobe. Major Buck would have to move out when Major de Bacquencourt returned. That would not be for two or three months, the proprietor supposed, with a knowing look at Colquhoun, and in the meantime, why, it was better for the rooms to be in use.

Business, the proprietor explained, was so difficult nowadays. The small extra income would be a great help in these hard times. The blockade of France by the English navy stifled his trade. He wished to God that the fighting would stop, that people - he was careful not to explain who 'people' might be- would have the sense to make peace, and now, - had the Major heard the news?- England and the

Major's country had declared war on each other.

It was madness, sheer madness. All it did was beggar honest tradesmen and make widows.

Perhaps the Major was in Paris because of this madness?

Colquhoun did not answer. He gazed out of the window at the donkey in the garden below. So the rumours were correct. England and America were at war again. Three thousand miles apart, how could they carry on a war? Presumably it was over trade and the blockade of Europe.

Well, let them fight it out at sea.

And when Napoleon returned triumphant from Russia, how would it alter the war in Spain?

The proprietor was speaking again. Did the Major have a manservant?. There was a room on the top floor which he could hire for such a person. No? A pity. But with the café next door there would be no problems with meals. There was a barber's shop just one side street away. And they could - indeed would - send up a maidservant to keep the rooms clean. Of course, there would be a small charge for the service.

And perhaps the Major would be kind enough to pay one month's rent in advance? Colquhoun handed over the money and shut the door on the man.

So far, so good. Almost too easy, in fact.

Claudette d'Yves lived twenty or thirty yards along the Rue du Bac.

Colquhoun saw her first that afternoon.

A light carriage pulled up outside her lodgings, driven by a splendidly uniformed officer of *Chasseurs à Cheval*. Colquhoun could not see her face under a wide brimmed hat as she swept out of the house and was gallantly handed abroad. She was elegantly dressed. Her figure, so far as he could tell, was very well proportioned.

The two seemed very familiar with each other. She tucked her hand under the officer's arm as the carriage set off down the street.

Whilst his moustache and whiskers were growing Colquhoun kept a low profile in the Rue du Bac. He used the time to familiarise himself with the streets of Paris in the same way that he had reconnoitred the country in Spain and Portugal to be sure that if need be and he had to flee he would know which way to go and what lay in front of him. The day might come when he would have to leave Paris in a hurry. Should that day come he would have to know exactly what he was doing.

He walked purposefully for miles each day, striding out confidently whether or not he had the slightest idea where he was or where he was going, lest any sign of indecision should draw attention to himself.

As he came to know the city and to begin to feel its pulse, he realised that France was war weary. The people longed for an end to the incessant fighting, the shortages of food and materials, the discomforts, the endless drain on their youth.

Paris was holding its breath, fearful perhaps, apprehensive certainly, denuded of all its able bodied young men, waiting, waiting, for news from Russia, the news that their Emperor had brought the Tsar's army to battle, that the Tsar had capitulated, that peace had been agreed and that the Grand Army would be returning.

The talk that he overheard in the cafés, though, spoken in hushed voices, seemed to hint at a different story.

Rumours were trickling back that despite the early success in capturing Vilna, the capital of Lithuania, within days and without a fight, the Grand Army was beginning to lose horses and men to exhaustion in the sweltering summer heat of Russia.

The dust clouds were so dense as they marched that they could not breathe.

Food was already short.

There was not enough water for such a vast army. Men were falling out from hunger and illness.

The Russians kept falling back in front of them. They were refusing to give battle as they should.

The Emperor had an insatiable need for more troops. Old men were being rounded up to garrison Germany to free the soldiers there for active duty in Russia. Even the sick and the maimed were not exempt. The 10th National Guard Cohort of the Paris garrison, for instance, was now composed of men with such physical disabilities that they could not march or fight.

The seeds of a tiny hope began to take root and grow in Colquhoun's heart.

After two weeks Colquhoun had learned the layout of the Paris streets well enough to be confident that if need arose he could get out of the city quickly. His whiskers, although not fully grown, were respectable enough for him to engineer a meeting with Claudette d'Yves.

The afternoon was wet. He had had enough of wandering the streets. Colquhoun decided to go back to his rooms. He would begin to establish the pattern of Claudette's daily movements.

To his surprise, the door to his rooms was ajar. He

pushed it open. The front room was empty. He stood and listened. Someone was in the back room. Its door was open. He crossed quietly and peered in. The big wardrobe stood open. A woman - a remarkably shapely woman - was standing in front of it. He could see uniforms hanging in it. She seemed to be going through them, stroking them, almost caressing them.

Colquhoun said: "Madame."

The woman turned. Colquhoun sucked in his breath. She was ravishingly beautiful, high cheekbones in a perfectly proportioned face, full lips, masses of black hair braided round her head, and, above all, stunning green eyes below arching black eyebrows.

She stared back at him boldly, without a trace of embarrassment.

"Ha," she said, "the American officer."

"Jonathan Buck, at your service, Madame. May I ask, Madame, who I have the honour of finding in my lodgings?"

He swept off his forage hat and bowed.

"Jeanazon Buck," she repeated.

Her eyes travelled audaciously over his body. She smiled slightly to herself.

"May I enquire your purpose here, Madame?"

"You may, Major Buck. I am Claudette d'Yves."

She turned back to the wardrobe and fingered the uniforms. They were well used tunics and waistcoats of the *Grenadiers à Cheval*. Worn boots stood on the wardrobe floor. There was a tall white plumed grenadier bearskin cap, somewhat battered, looped and tasselled in faded red and gold, worn gauntlet gloves, brass buckled white belts, white breeches, some pieces of horse harness thrown in a corner.

"How did you get in here, Madame?"

"I have the keys, of course."

"Ah... You have the keys? May I ask...?"

Her eyes flashed at him. A formidable woman.

"You do not know? Henri is my lover."

Colquhoun opened his mouth. He could think of no suitable reply. He said: "Henri, Madame? Henri de Bacquencourt? Major Henri de Bacquencourt?"

"Of course."

"I see."

"I miss Henri, Monsieur. I miss him dreadfully. Henri is a real man."

She turned back to the cupboard, closed the doors, locked it and dropped the key into a pocket. She sighed.

"You should not be in these rooms, Monsieur. These are Henri's rooms. They are waiting for his return."

"Of course. I am only here temporarily, Madame. Of course, when he comes back, I will leave."

She looked at him searchingly.

"Yes," she said bleakly.

Without another word she swept past him, turned, looked him up and down once again and was gone. Her enticing scent filled Colquhoun's nostrils as she passed him.

"Phew," he said.

He had not reckoned on such a dramatic first encounter.

The next morning there was a knock on his door. An urchin stood outside, a sealed letter in his hand.

"For you, Monsieur," he said. "The lady wants an answer."

Colquhoun broke the seal.

Dear Major Jonathan Buck,

> Will you forgive me, I beg you, for my intrusion yesterday? It was, I acknowledge it, unpardonable. Pray do me the kindness, to show there is no offence taken, to come to my lodgings at midday today to take coffee with me. Do come. Coffee, as you will know, is in very short supply, so this is an invitation you should not refuse.
>
> Claudette d'Yves.

Colquhoun looked at the urchin. The urchin looked back at him.

"Tell Madame that I will be there at midday."

He gave the boy a coin. The boy touched his forelock and retreated to the stairs. Two steps down he turned back with a leer and made a rude gesture.

"Gorrr.." he laughed and dashed off down the stairs.

The maid who answered Colquhoun's knock was as bold eyed as her mistress, though nothing like as beautiful or shapely. She took Colquhoun through a fair sized hall into a handsome salon. There was a welcoming smell of fresh coffee.

Claudette was seated at a small table in front of the fireplace. She looked heart stoppingly attractive. She smiled at him and held out her hand towards him.

"Ah, Jeanazon, you have forgiven me - I may call you Jeanazon, no? It was unpardonable of me to be in your rooms yesterday."

He crossed to her and took her hand in both of his. He bent over it to kiss it, and as he did so looked up into her face. Their eyes met. Her marvellous, calculating green eyes were at first speculative, then amused, then, he was sure, as eager as his own.

"There is nothing to forgive, Madame."

"But you must call me Claudette. Madame is so formal, so cold. Besides I am not Madame." She giggled delightfully. "Now, come and sit here beside me" - she patted the chair placed close to hers - "and let me give you a cup of this coffee. We are so lucky to have it. It is impossible to find now, unless from a friend. It is good, no?"

It was. The best Colquhoun had tasted since leaving Spain.

"Please, tell me all about yourself."

"I would rather hear about you. But, well, I am an American, as you know. I come from Boston, Massachusetts. I am a major in the 11th Massachusetts Infantry."

"Ah, does America have beautiful cities, like Paris?"

"Not quite like Paris. It's a new country. We're plain, straightforward folk compared to you Europeans. Our cities are much simpler."

"Tell me, then, what do you do in Paris?"

"I am here as an observer."

"An observer?" She looked amused. "What does an observer observe?"

"Well, we are at war with England again and allies of France, as you know. We need to keep in contact with each other. I am here informally, though. I have indefinite leave of absence from my regiment. I wanted to visit France and see all your cathedrals and buildings: your palaces and chateaux - we don't have anything like them in America. Then I had intended to accompany the Grand Army into Russia, but I arrived here too late."

"But how did you get here? The English have closed all

our ports with their blockade."

"Not quite all."

He indicated the coffee, and she smiled.

"There are blockade runners. I took the chance and we slipped into La Rochelle."

"How long will you stay in Paris?"

This was becoming more of an interrogation than a conversation. Was she asking these questions out of curiosity, or had someone instructed her to find out about him? It would explain her presence in his rooms. But then, she could not have known that he would arrive back when he did. He laughed:

"I cannot say. It depends on when the Emperor gets back and helps us to see off the English. Tell me about yourself."

"Ah, yes," her tone changed. "When the Emperor gets back. But when will that be, Jeanazon? Every day he sends demands to General Clarke. Find me more men. I must have more men. I must have more horses. More everything. All the time. At the Ministry of War they tear their hair out at his demands. You cannot make men, they say. Where can we find more men? We have scraped the bottom of the barrel with every man we can find. But the Emperor will not hear this. If he wants something, he thinks he shall have it. Are these the demands of an Emperor who conquers Russia? I think my Henri is in terrible danger there. All the time men are sick and dying and this is before we can make the Russians fight us. Henri is strong, but I am so frightened for him."

She laid her hand on the table, close to Colquhoun. The invitation was unmistakable. He put his hand on top of hers, then took it up in both of his. He squeezed her hand and kissed it.

"Your Henri must be an experienced soldier. He must

have faced hardship and danger many times already. Indeed, he could not have won a place in the *Garde* if he had not proved himself many times over a brave and gallant officer, and no doubt a resourceful one."

"Yes. Yes, all that is so. But I worry for him... And are you a brave and gallant soldier, Jeanazon also?"

Colquhoun laughed.

"I hope so. We have not had the chance to prove ourselves in battle in America as you have here in France. But I hope so."

"Perhaps you should be in America, fighting the English?"

"I don't think there will be much fighting on land. It will be a sea affair, I fancy. Besides, I plan that when your Emperor returns victorious and turns his attention back to Spain, I shall ask if I may accompany him. There will be plenty of action there."

To his surprise this idea had not occurred to Colquhoun before. It had just come out in answer to Claudette's question. What a way to get back to Spain - openly with the French army. It certainly would merit further thought, but all in good time.

She seemed to echo this thought.

"Ah, but there are many hills to climb before that day comes...There will be no help for Spain while the Emperor is in Russia. General Clarke will take more men from there... I think, Jeanazon, that you are a brave and gallant soldier. You are like my Henri. You have the ambiance of my Henri. I think you have seen more fighting than you are telling me. But you will tell me, of course, in time. In time, I think, Jeanazon, we will have no secrets from each other"

"Claudette..."

There was a cough from the door. The maid had

appeared. She bobbed the merest curtsy.

"Colonel Fournier has arrived, Madame."

"But he is too early."

She glanced at the ornate clock on the mantelpiece.

"He should not come for another hour."

The maid almost shrugged. She said nothing. Colonel Fournier brushed past her into the salon. Claudette withdrew her hand from Colquhoun's grasp.

"Colonel, you are early. The Colonel and I are to drive together in the Bois de Boulogne this afternoon, Jeanazon."

The Colonel, middle aged, overweight, bristling with whiskers and moustache, shot an unfriendly look at Colquhoun.

"Got away early, my dear. Thought I'd give you a little luncheon before the drive."

He looked at Colquhoun again, a look that said 'my turn now.'

Colquhoun rose. He took Claudette's hand again, kissed it, looked into her eyes, winked, bowed at the Colonel, and left.

He was surprised to find it raining outside. He had thought that the sun had been pouring in through the windows of Claudette's lodgings.

Colquhoun went straight to Angus Mcpherson. He was rather glad that Madame Constance did not appear to be at home. The amusement that he guessed he would have seen in her eyes would have been a trifle embarrassing. Perhaps she was with the ladies of Paris picking up the latest gossip.

Mcpherson welcomed him warmly, however, and showed no trace of levity when Colquhoun told him that he had made contact with Claudette D'Yves and that he thought she would be a mine of first hand information

"Can we send word to Lord Wellington?"

"Yes. It must be brief - on the smallest scrap of paper. It may take some time to reach him."

Colquhoun nodded. He had already decided on the wording:

> 'Am in Paris. N demanding all possible men for R. No decisive battle yet. No reinforcements likely for S this year. CG. 17 July 1812.'

"If that gets to Lord Wellington," he said, "it should help him to know what he can expect to be up against at least until the winter and probably well into next year.

His note to Claudette was more explicit, if hardly less brief:

Madame,
> 'Will you do me the honour to join me for *déjeuner* at the *Café Desmares* tomorrow, say at one o'clock?
> Jonathan Buck.'

He gave the note to Claudette's maid who somewhat maliciously told him that her Mistress was out.

He did not sleep well that night. After two years in the field where the only females were Spanish or Portuguese peasants Claudette was altogether too alluring.

When the knock came on his door the next morning

Colquhoun's heart quickened. He opened the door to find the same urchin who had delivered Claudette's first note. He was standing at the stair head poised for flight in the event of retaliation for past misdeeds. Colquhoun laughed as he took the note that the boy proffered at arm's length.

It read:

> Dear Jonathan,
> No. I cannot today. But you must come for *déjeuner* here with me tomorrow. The food will be much better.
>   A warm embrace.
>   Claudette.

"What's your name, boy?"

"Jacques."

"Well, Jacques, you run errands for Madame, no? Will you do the same for me if I ask you?"

Jacques looked suspicious.

"What's the game then?"

"No game, Jacques. Nothing at present, except this." He indicated the note. "But if I need you…?"

Jacques grinned back at him. "All right."

"Good lad. Take the message back to Madame now that I'll be there at one o'clock tomorrow."

Interested, and perhaps, were he to admit it, a little jealous, to see who Claudette's escort today might be, Colquhoun drew up a chair near the front window and sat down to watch the street below. Waiting was no particular hardship. Much of his life for the past two years had been spent waiting and watching. He was able to put part of his mind into neutral while part was alive to any movement that might concern him.

After a while he saw Jacques, squatting in a doorway smoking the butt end of a cigar that someone had thrown down in the gutter. This part of the street was presumably Jacques' fiefdom.

The boy might be useful if he needed a second pair of eyes.

As one o'clock approached the street grew less busy. The day was hot. People were going indoors to get out of the sun for their midday meal.

Colquhoun was beginning to wonder whether Claudette had some other reason for putting off their meeting when an infantry officer appeared rounding the corner into the Rue du Bac from the direction of the Ministry of War. He walked with a limp, with the aid of a stick. He passed under Colquhoun's window, a young man no longer fit for active service. He vanished into Claudette's lodgings, and they reappeared some minutes later.

For all the world it looked as though she was more than fond of him. She tucked her arm through his and turned a dazzling smile on him as they strolled together past Colquhoun's window and out of sight up the street in the direction of the Seine and the Tuileries.

"Damn," said Colquhoun. "Damn it."

It was quite illogical. He knew perfectly well how Claudette lived and what she was. He had every intention of using her to get information. Their acquaintance would necessarily be brief. He could never see her again once he left Paris. And yet…

Punctually at one o'clock the next day Colquhoun was at the door of Claudette's lodgings. The bold eyed maid let him in. Her eyes were bright with some unspoken excitement. She was almost smirking. She showed Colquhoun into the salon and shut the door behind him. The room was empty.

Colquhoun strolled over to the fireplace and checked his appearance in the mirror above it. As he looked he saw a second door open behind him. He turned.

Claudette was wearing a long dressing gown open from top to bottom to reveal a green, silken shift. Her hair hung loose, masses of thick, lustrous black hair framing her face, flowing over her shoulders to her bosom.

She was smiling, a little enigmatic smile as she glided across the room towards him.

Then they were in each other's arms, and he was kissing her passionately, hugging her close to him. He felt her hand slip down the front of his trousers. She gave a little squeak of excitement and pleasure. Her hand moved upwards. She was undoing the top buttons of his trousers. His hands, already inside the dressing gown, slid down her body to her buttocks. Her hand was inside his trousers now, on his stomach, stroking downwards. Involuntarily he clamped his hands tighter.

She squeaked again, laughing. "Ah, Jeanazon…Jeanazon, but you are as big as Henri….Ah, Jeanazon you are a real man…"

Chapter 7

MOSCOW

Claudette was a sparkling river of information.

Maybe it was a similar warm evening. Maybe it was the same driver. Maybe the coach drove into the yard and pulled up in the same way. Whatever the reason, the secret policeman whose job it was to watch the arrival and departure of the stage coaches in Orléans suddenly had a vision of a red coated English soldier climbing down off the Bayonne coach. It had been on his mind for weeks, like an itch that would not go away.

That was it!

The man he had seen bidding such a fond farewell to the woman who looked after the priest. Surely it was the same man. Could it have been? Surely not? They had looked very alike. He consulted his report book, thumbing back through the pages until he found the entries for the beginning of June.

Yes, there it was. A Major C - something unpronounceable - Grant, of the 11th Regiment of English Infantry, on parole, on his way to Verdun.

And the man getting onto the Paris coach? He thumbed on through his report book.

There it was. Jonathan Buck. American. He remembered it well.

The policeman voiced his suspicion to his superior

officer. The superior officer consulted his file headed 'English Prisoners of War.'.

"I thought that name rang a bell," he said. "He died. See here. Entry in June. Died in the infirmary, he did. Or so it says. They handed in his *feuille de route*...Hmm.. About the same time as the American left. It's possible. Have a word with the woman. Don't alarm her. Just a routine enquiry. It might lead somewhere. I don't trust those damned priests not one centimetre."

The policeman called on Madame Marie.

"Just a routine enquiry, Madame. Nothing to worry about. There was a man you saw onto the Paris stage coach - oh - four, five weeks ago. D'you remember? Bit over medium height, well built, well dressed. We're just not sure who he was. Nothing important, you know, just routine."

"But of course, Monsieur, how could I forget? It was my great friend Jonathan Buck."

"Jonathan Buck, eh? Did you not call him Pierre?"

"But of course. That is my pet name. Jonathan is such a mouthful. Pierre is so much easier. He is an American. I can tell you, he wanted to get back to America. It was at the time that the talk was of America and England wanting to go to war with each other. He had been to Nantes to find a ship, but with the war looming and the blockade there was no boat going to risk putting to sea. So he came back and decided to go back to Paris. He is a dear friend of mine."

"Came back? So how long have you known him? How did you come to know him?"

"Oh, I have known him for months. He came and asked me for lodgings on his way to Nantes. I sometimes take in lodgers, you know. I need the income. I am a widow. It is difficult to make ends meet as a widow, you know. He stayed then a week or two. And then on his way back he stayed much longer. We found we had much in common and grew very fond of each other. He was not sure what he should do. That was why he went on staying here with me. He was lonely and undecided."

"So when did he first come here, then?"

"Oh, it was in the winter, I remember. It was cold. February, I think, or maybe even January. Then he went away for some weeks, looking for a ship. It was a bad time to look for a ship, he said."

"So where did he go in Paris?"

"Ah, Monsieur, regretfully, there I cannot help you. Sadly, I have not heard from him. I do not know. Perhaps, after all, he has found a way to go back to America. I do not know."

"What was his business in France?"

"Ah, Monsieur. You must know that gentlemen do not discuss matters of business with women. Regretfully, he did not talk of his business. I cannot help you. I am sorry."

The policeman departed, frowning, feeling irritated. If the woman was speaking the truth, it could not be the same man. Major Grant had died. The woman had known the American long before the English officer had arrived in Orléans. It must have been coincidence. And yet.... And yet....

Perhaps they should take her in for some proper questioning. But she had seemed open and honest enough. His chief was probably right. Better to keep a sharp eye on her and those cursed priests at the Sainte Croix.

Maybe, who knows...? It might lead to something.

Madame Marie had always wondered what this moment would feel like. She had always known that one day it might come, ever since her life had fallen apart when they had arrested her husband. Strangely, because she had imagined she would be terrified, she was not particularly frightened or worried. She had not the slightest of regrets about the shelter and help she had given to fugitives from the State's oppression. She was in no doubt that they had all been men – and women – who had been persecuted and wronged. If Father O'Shea had taken up their cause they must all have been deserving of her succour. She was also rather surprised and proud of herself that she had lied so effortlessly to the policeman and had seen doubt and frustration in his features as she spoke. All she hoped was if they came back to arrest her they would shoot her quickly.

She wondered whether to tell Father O'Shea of the police visit, and eventually decided that he ought at least to be warned. He, too, took the news philosophically. His life was dedicated to his Saviour. The risks that he ran were taken in the name of God and for His purposes. If it was God's will, so be it.

All he said was:

"Let us pray that Father Pierre has done what he set out to do and has left France."

In Paris, the rumours were being substantiated. Every gaunt, exhausted, sweat stained, dust or mud covered grim faced dispatch rider who arrived at the Ministry of War confirmed the talk in the cafés.

The Emperor's Grand Army had crossed the river Niemen into Russia in an ominous silence. There was no sign of the Russian army.

The troops had been issued with four days rations that the men ate in a day. Hungry, they had started to break ranks foraging for food. The roads were nowhere adequate for the supply wagons to keep up with them.

The weather was awful - an oppressive humid heat by day

and bitter cold at nights, interspersed with cold hard rain or hail storms.

Hungry soldiers were straggling and deserting. Worse, the horses were eating green, unripe corn and were dying in huge numbers.

The Emperor had halted at Vilna to try to sort out the supply problems. He had issued a flood of orders. But orders by themselves do not solve crises. Without the means to carry them out they are so much hot air.

Already, by the end of July the Emperor had accepted that the supply system could not work and the army would have to live off the land. But how could it? This was not a fertile country. There was nothing to forage. Not only horses, but men were beginning to die in their hundreds, if not in their thousands.

And still the Russian armies would not stand and fight.

Every day Paris seemed to draw a little more into itself.

"I think," said Claudette, "that the *Garde* will have food. The Emperor will make sure, even if all else fails, that his *Garde* will be fed. I think Henri will not have to starve."

Claudette was a sparkling river of information. Her many admirers and lovers at the Ministry of War kept her fully up to date with all the latest news from Russia. Always in the context of how it might be affecting Henri, Claudette passed everything she heard on to Colquhoun.

Theirs was a curious relationship. There was no love in it - at least, Colquhoun thought there was not. He had been two years in the field, operating on his own in potentially enemy country all the time, totally reliant on the local population. If he had abused their trust by seducing their women he might well have ended up suffering the same dreadful fate as any captured French soldier. Claudette, exciting, beautiful, immensely attractive, good company, willing, accomplished - how could he resist her?

The dam wall of two years of abstinence had broken in spectacular fashion.

And Claudette?

Were it not for Henri de Bacquencourt, Colquhoun would have said that Claudette was probably incapable of loving anyone but herself or of any action that was not to her own benefit. Certainly she had no feelings for any of her *beaux* beyond amusement or exasperation. They were her living, to be courted and cultivated, flattered and satisfied - in bed, for the most part: sometimes merely by her company.

But her Henri was different. She loved Henri, there was no doubt of it, and by some curious quirk of her character, she had taken Colquhoun to her as a substitute. Maybe in her uncertain, calculating world she needed a protector, someone with a heart that beat for her, someone she could rely on and turn to in the moments when she looked into the cold void of her existence.

Colquhoun began to meet the officers from the Ministry of War. To a man, they were unfit for active service. Legs, arms, internal injuries, ears, eyes, all carried the aftermath of serious wounds. Many probably lived in permanent pain. All, Colquhoun was pretty sure, found their desk jobs at the Ministry deadly boring.

Claudette, laughing and bright in their company was like sunshine to their shadowed souls. In her company they could forget the gloom and pain in their lives. They did not appear to resent Colquhoun. Without apparent question they seemed to accept him as her lover in residence, someone even to be cultivated as in so doing they might gain more favour with her.

And, thank God, no one seemed to have heard of

Jonathan Buck or come across him - if indeed he had been in Paris. It was probably not surprising. The Ministry of War was concerned with administration, recruitment and the movement of troops. Had Jonathan Buck been in Paris on some military mission he would almost certainly have been in contact with Napoleon's Headquarters, the active staff planning the Russian campaign.

Morale at the Ministry of War was bad.

The Emperor's constant stream of ever shriller demands for men and horses, the constant reports that they heard first hand, which from their own campaign experience told them that all was not well in Russia, these things weighed on the officers working there.

To cheer them up, Claudette had decided that she would hold a *soirée* to which Colquhoun must of course come.

It was a hot evening at the beginning of August. Claudette was at her most charming and delightful best. Her lodgings were crowded with brightly uniformed officers -many of whom Colquhoun had never seen before - and a bevy of pretty *filles de joie*.

The champagne flowed. There was a noisy roulette wheel in the hall and a game of *vingt et un* in the salon run by a stiletto eyed girl with a very shapely figure and very low cut dress that emphasised her perfectly proportioned bosom. She was dealing the cards from a shoe, though it seemed to Colquhoun, whose Scottish soul rather disapproved of gambling and kept him as a spectator rather than a player, that the girl invariably won whenever the stakes got serious.

He stood watching for some time, sure she must be cheating, but for the life of him he could not see how, other than that she leant forward over the table at these tense moments, and the eyes of the players invariably left their cards and feasted on her breasts.

Quietly amused, Colquhoun stepped back from the table.

Directly behind him an officer in a general's heavily embroidered coat and sash was standing talking with his back to him. In the confined crowded space Colquhoun could not help bumping into him. To his horror, the back was familiar. He had seen it in front of him too many times on the coach from Bayonne, striding into the post houses, climbing into the coach, always in front of him.

He had a second to compose himself before the general turned impatiently towards him with a mildly irritated frown.

"Your pardon, sir," Colquhoun emphasised his American accent.

General Souham almost turned away, then he started and looked sharply at Colquhoun.

"I've seen you somewhere before."

Colquhoun looked perplexed.

"Have you, sir? I don't recollect our meeting before. Have you been in the States, sir? Could we have met there sometime?"

"Ha." General Souham looked scornful. "The States!"

To Colquhoun's enormous relief at that moment one of the officers struck up a marching tune on Claudette's piano. Several voices immediately took up the words. In a moment the whole room took up the refrain.

General Souham shook his head impatiently, turned away and resumed his conversation.

It was light outside before the last of her guests left. Claudette did not invite Colquhoun to her bed. She looked tired and needed to sleep. She would not appear before midday next day at the earliest. He knew from experience that it was unwise anyway to approach her before midday and that anyone who did was likely to have his head bitten off. He felt pretty tired himself.

As he kissed her hand she said:

"That General Souham says he has met you somewhere before. He asked me who you are and what you are doing in Paris. I think he will ask General Savary who you are. Jeanazon, you are a man of mystery, you know. But one day, you will tell me your secrets."

He was still bending over her hand. Tired or not she was quite acute enough to feel the sudden tension in his body

Without looking up he said:

"Who is this General Souham? I have never heard of him before tonight."

"Oh, he is not an important man. The Emperor would not use him for many years. Maybe he is a Royalist in his heart. He has been on leave from Spain. He is just passing through Paris. He leaves for there again tomorrow, I think. Have you been in Spain, my Jeanazon, that he should think to know you?"

Colquhoun laughed.

"Spain? Not yet. Maybe one day, if the Emperor goes back there to drive out the English."

"Ah, Jeanazon, my man of mystery."

She took his head in her hands and kissed him.

"But perhaps it is your mystery that makes you so attractive to me. One day, Jeanazon. One day... But for now, my bed is calling. For now I am too tired to prise your secrets from you. *Bonne nuit*, my Jeanazon."

There was no point in panicking. After all, General Savary's secret police might take it into their heads at any time to wonder who he was and what he was doing here. Unless they produced a genuine American to challenge him it would be impossible for them to disprove his story.

And again he wondered uneasily whether Claudette probed his identity out of her own curiosity or at someone else's behest.

Who would be better placed to keep General Savary's secret police in touch with the goings on at General Clarke's Ministry of War than Claudette? There was bitter rivalry between the Heads of the two Ministries. General Clarke and General Savary hated each other and spent a considerable amount of energy trying to discredit each other in Napoleon's eyes. It would suit General Savary very well to have an agent in the Ministry of War. On the other hand it was such an obvious idea that the officers at the Ministry of War must have considered it and discarded it.

Colquhoun sighed as he climbed the stairs to his lodgings. He had, in any case, learned a great deal about the march into Russia from the talk at Claudette's *soirée*.

He just must be very careful.

Jacques, the street urchin, might be useful. He found the boy warming himself in a sheltered corner of the street next morning. Jacques had a black eye and several scratches on his arms and face.

"What have you been up to?"

Jacques grinned, slightly painfully.

"Got to look after me own territory."

Colquhoun grinned back.

"Did you see them off, then?"

"Um. He won't come back no more, he won't."

"Well done you, then. I want you to do something for me. Yes? Good lad. Keep a good eye on my lodgings up there. Tell me if anyone shows any interest in them or tries to go in when I'm not there."

"Who's after you, then? What you done wrong?"

"Nothing."

"Them police bothering you? Them nosey bastards."

Colquhoun grinned again.

"Not everyone likes Americans. Just let me know, eh?"

He gave Jacques a franc. The boy whistled, bit the coin, and laughed.

"Heard the news, have you, patron?"

"What news?"

"Looks like there's been a big battle in Spain. Terrible beating we got." He said this with great relish. "That Marmont's lot. Killed them to the last man, them English did. Horrid slaughter it was. Them redcoats bayoneted them every last man, bloodthirsty bastards that they are. Screaming for mercy, they was, but it didn't make no difference. Them redcoats bayoneted them every last one. Horrid slaughter it was."

Jacques stabbed viciously at the ground with an imaginary bayonet.

"Where did you hear this?"

Jacques grinned.

"On the wind, patron. You wait. It'll be all over Paris this morning."

And it was.

By midday it was on everyone's lips.

There had been a battle at Salamanca some ten days or two weeks ago.

Milor Wellington had treacherously tricked Marshal Marmont and fallen on him, decimating the Army of Portugal. Thousands had been killed. The Army was in rout. Nobody seemed to know exactly where the news came from. And it had probably been wildly exaggerated. Everyone knew that the English general Wellington did not attack, that he was only good in defence and that he certainly was no match for the young and brilliant Marshal

Marmont.

There must be some truth in the rumour, though. There must have been some sort of engagement. And it was just possible that the English had tricked Marshal Marmont into some sort of reverse.

Colquhoun felt a pang of regret that he had not been there.

But mainly an enormous relief. Surely, surely, if General Souham really had intended to alert the secret police to his presence this news would have driven the thought out of his head. If Claudette was right, and the General was leaving Paris anyway, surely all his thoughts would be on the situation in Spain. True or false, he was sure the rumours would let him off this particular hook.

There remained Claudette herself. But until Henri de Bacquencourt came back it was highly unlikely, even if she was an informer, that she would voice any suspicions she might have that he was not what he claimed to be.

He needed someone to talk things over with, and decided to call on Angus Mcpherson.

The old man greeted him warmly. He seemed frailer, said he was suffering from the summer heat and could not get out much now. Colquhoun must be his eyes and ears and bring him all the news from the city. He called for wine and sent the maid to find Madame Constance. She greeted Colquhoun with a very merry sparkle in her eyes.

"How is Madame Claudette?" she asked. "I hear that you are much in each other's company."

Colquhoun bowed. She laughed out loud.

"Oh, la, la, you men. You are too serious, you *Écossais*. Angus, he is the same. But she is beautiful, no?"

"She is indeed, Madame Constance, though she may be dangerous. I think she may be reporting to General Savary's police. She is too curious about me."

"Do not be silly, Major Grant. You are an attractive man from a foreign country. You are a bit of a mystery. Any woman would want to know all about you. If I was thirty years younger, I would."

Mcpherson coughed. He looked embarrassed.

"Well, yes, my dear, but I am sure Major Grant is right to be cautious. Now tell me, what is the latest news from Russia, Grant?"

"Madame Constance will no doubt be aware that Claudette gave a *soirée* last night, which a good number of officers attended. No? Ah, Madame, so there is something of which you and your ladies are unaware."

They both laughed.

"They talk carelessly. They are worried - very worried. They talk of massive losses of men through illness and desertion. They say discipline is collapsing. Insubordination is rife. There are huge differences between the day and night temperatures and violent hailstorms. They are playing havoc on starving men and horses. The horses are dying by the thousand as well. The figures are almost unbelievable. They say five to six thousand men a day are being lost and nearly twenty thousand horses have died."

Mcpherson said: "That is unbelievable. The Emperor boasted that the campaign would be over in twelve or twenty days at the most. It seems he gravely miscalculated."

"That is what the officers say too. They say that he has taken far too big an army into Russia. Nothing can cope with the numbers. The roads, where they exist at all, are no better than unpaved tracks. They are either ankle deep in dust which chokes the men or knee deep in mud which nothing can cope with. The supply wagons are tens of leagues behind the men with no hope of ever catching up. Hospitals are non existent, or completely inadequate for the numbers of sick. The whole army is just too big and too clumsy. It is impossible to feed or control it.

"And anyway, they say, why should the Russians give battle? Their armies are far smaller than Napoleon's. If they fight they will lose. So they go on retreating. And he goes on following. Getting deeper and deeper into trouble every day that he does so."

They were all silent, digesting the implications.

"Do you need to contact Lord Wellington again with this news?"

"I do not think so, not at the moment. Not until we have something hard and fast to report. A battle. Or Napoleon deciding to call a halt to his advance."

"I doubt he will do that. He is a gambler for high stakes. Such men will double their stakes rather than quit. What would he do if he did call a halt? It would be tantamount to admitting he was wrong to invade Russia. Tantamount to admitting defeat. No, I do not think that could be in his nature. He has always had to go on. Always before his gambles have worked. But now, I wonder. Russia is so vast. He must be in danger of being cut off. What a dilemma for him. He must be desperate for the decisive battle that he craves. But I think you are right. Until we know something for certain we should wait. It is dangerous to use my channels more than necessary."

"Well, if he cannot force a battle he will have to retreat. He could not risk being stranded in Russia when the winter comes on. Something must happen soon. That will be the time to contact Lord Wellington again. And have you heard the rumour from Spain? Paris is abuzz with rumours of a battle at Salamanca and a French defeat. I'll come back and tell you all about it when we get proper confirmation."

Confirmation was not long in coming.

Messengers were arriving in Paris now with definite news of the battle. It seemed that Marshal Marmont had been deceived by a dust cloud into thinking that Lord Wellington's army was retreating. He had thought that the two divisions of the English army that he could see were Wellington's rearguard and had given chase, hoping to cut them off.

What he could not see was that the dust cloud was being kicked up by Wellington's baggage train and that the whole English army was facing him, but out of sight. Marmont's leading divisions had advanced too quickly across the English front and had become separated from the rest of the army. The English had fallen on them, taking them in flank with cavalry and infantry. It had indeed been a serious reverse for the army of Portugal.

But Paris seemed to take the news in its stride.

The war in Spain had already been going on so long and so murderously that the Parisians seemed inured to what might be happening there. They could shrug off a minor Spanish setback.

All eyes were on Russia.

Colquhoun did not see Claudette again until the next day. The weather was very hot. Her mind was in Russia with Henri.

"It is so hot here, Jeanazon. What must it be like for Henri? They say it is far hotter in Russia, and humid all the time. And then it is so cold at night. Do you think he still has his horse, Jeanazon? And food? Do you think the *Garde* will be losing men? I think not. The Emperor will care for his *Garde*, I know it. But how can we know? Oh, I long for news of him. They say, what is the Emperor doing? He no longer makes up his mind. He no longer strikes hard and fast as he used to. Oh, Jeanazon, I fear for this Russian war. I fear for Henri."

Colquhoun took her hands in his and drew her to him. There was nothing he could say that could give her the comfort she needed. He kissed her lightly on her forehead and held her to him. After some moments she said:

"Let down my hair, Jeanazon."

He undid the pins that held it, and her shining black tresses fell down around her face.

She pressed her body hard against his.

"Kiss me properly, Jeanazon."

Afterwards she lay quietly in his arms for a while. Then she sighed.

"What will we do when Henri comes back, my Jeanazon? Will you be friends? Or will you kill each other for me? You must be friends. You will be friends. I will make you be friends...

"Now, Jeanazon, I cannot see you again until next week. Tomorrow, Captain Girard takes me to the Luxembourg gardens. The next day is Colonel Lefèvre. That is very important to me. - Why? - Jeanazon, you are so straightforward. Why do you think? A girl has to live and he is very rich. Then it is Major Dupont's time of the month. Ah, poor Major Dupont. Always I see him at the same time of the month. Poor man, some fragments of a shell took off his balls at Eylau. He lives all the time in horror of that battle. He dreams of his blood on the snow and the awful cold and he wakes screaming. I have to comfort him like a mother with her child. Always I tell him that regretfully it is the time of the month and always he says he understands and next time will be different for us. But of course it never can be. But it keeps him a little happy, I think."

August dragged on into September - at least, it dragged for Colquhoun.

Claudette was as enticing as the first moment he had met her. But her apart, he was bored. He was not a town man. He longed for a view devoid of houses. He longed for open country. Paris was stifling and airless. Its streets stank. He longed for fresh unsullied air. The constant presence of people all round him oppressed him. He longed to be back in Spain, on his own with only León for company and his horse under him.

He began to wonder what he was doing in Paris. He had not envisaged it like this.

He had imagined that Napoleon's invasion of Russia would be a swift and decisive affair. He had imagined that he might have been of importance to Lord Wellington if he could have relayed vital information to him days, weeks, maybe, before it could reach him by any other route.

He had thought the whole campaign would be a matter of weeks, that the triumphant Napoleon would have been back in Paris by the autumn, flushed with victory, planning another lightning campaign that would finish the Spanish war once and for all.

But now there was no end in sight.

He could do nothing that was of any value to anyone. And surely, at some point, the secret police or someone at the Ministry of War would begin to wonder what this unemployed American officer was doing in Paris. Should he go, get out while the going was good, try to get back to Spain or perhaps to England? What was he achieving here?

Claudette could sense his frustration.

"Jeanazon, my man of secrets. Why do you not tell me your secrets? I think they weigh on your mind. Do you have a guilty secret, Jeanazon, that you will not confide in me? You are so like Henri, you know. I think you have been in more campaigns that you tell me. I know you are a real soldier. I do not think you came to France to look at its cathedrals. You are a soldier of fortune, perhaps?" She giggled. "Tell me, where did General Souham see you before? Was it really in Spain?"

"General Souham must have mistaken me for someone else. I like to be out in the open. Paris walls me in."

"Ah, yes, Henri also. He is happy when he has his horse under him and an open sky around him. But I do not think General Souham was mistaken."

"Then Henri and I will be friends. I don't know, Claudette, whether I should try to get back to America. I am not sure what I am doing here."

"I am not sure also. But you are making me happy, Jeanazon. Is that not enough for you."

Colquhoun laughed. In a way, yes. In a way, no.

Angus Mcpherson was a help. They talked often, sometimes with Madame Constance present, sometimes alone. When they were alone they talked of Scotland, of the mountains and glens of the Highlands, of the heather, purple at this time of the year, of the rivers, the mists, the emptiness, the beauty.

Sometimes the old man spoke wistfully of the Jacobite

rebellion of 1745. Isolated events were still clear in his memory. In Colquhoun he found a sympathetic listener. One day he said:

"Do you know, one of our French marshals today is the son of a Jacobite follower - friend, indeed, - of Prince Charles Edward."

"I did not know. Which one?"

"Marshal Macdonald. His father was with the Prince when he fled the English army across the Highlands. His name was Neil MacEachen; he was a cousin of Flora Macdonald. He was with the Prince the whole time, often his only companion. He escaped with the Prince to France. Later he changed his name to Macdonald. I don't know why. Probably because the French could not pronounce his name, I shouldn't wonder. He died in poverty, poor man, I believe. He deserved better."

"Good God."

"Why do you say that, Grant?"

"Because my mother saved the lives of the Prince and Neil MacEachen. She loves to tell the story of how when she was a little girl she danced for some English soldiers who were searching for them. She danced so beautifully that the English were completely beguiled and forgot to search the house where the Prince and MacEachen were hiding. How extraordinary."

The old man was silent, looking back into the past. At last he said:

"Aye, well, 'tis likely enough. They had some narrow escapes. Ah, well..."

Mcpherson would never see the Highlands again. He was very frail and hardly stirred from his chair. But he helped Colquhoun. He encouraged him to hang on, sure that when it came the information he would pass to Lord Wellington could and would be vital to him. It could not be long in coming.

But still it did not come.

Instead, impossible Russian town names were becoming familiar to them.

Vilna, Vitebsk, Smolensk, Moscow.

At Vitebsk Napoleon had nearly brought the Russians to battle, but they had slipped away. Napoleon had stayed there for days, trying to organise his army, undecided whether to go on. There had been furious arguments with his Marshals. All of them wanted to call a halt to the advance. Napoleon had overridden them. He had decided to go on, even though his army was reduced already - before they had even engaged the main Russian armies - by over two hundred thousand men - two hundred thousand, an unimaginable number. The bloodiest battles might see ten thousand men lost, but two hundred thousand! How many sons, fathers, brothers would never come back?

Morale in Paris sank deeper as the days went by.

Smolensk.

The Emperor said the Russians would stand and fight when the army reached Smolensk. It was a holy city. The Russians would never give it up without a fight.

There would be a decisive battle when they reached Smolensk.

Paris held its breath.

There had been fighting there, certainly. But after a day of fighting to take the city - which had cost another ten thousand men - the Russians had set fire to the place and gone.

All Napoleon's Marshals except Davout had urged him to go into winter quarters there. But Moscow was under three hundred miles away.

On the twenty fifth of August Napoleon had ordered the army forward again. In the appalling late August heat, in rain, in sandstorms, without adequate water, the horses starving, a hundred and sixty thousand men - out of the four hundred and fifty thousand who had crossed the Niemen with their Emperor - marched on towards the Russian capital city.

Once there, Napoleon assured them, the Russians would surrender.

There was a dreadful foreboding of impending catastrophe. Everyone's thoughts were on the dwindling army of suffering soldiers so far away and in such terrible danger.

For now to add to all the other disasters, stories were told that the Russian peasants were retaliating with appalling atrocities. Any soldier who fell out of the column, who straggled or fell sick or strayed too far from his comrades was likely to suffer a death too ghastly to relate at the hands of the peasants. There were even nightmare stories that prisoners were being sold to the peasants by the Cossacks.

And then, at last, at long last, at the end of September came the news that Paris had been waiting for. At a place called Borodino the Russian army had dug in and had given battle. The Emperor claimed a great victory, of course.

But Paris wondered.

They were suspicious of the Emperor's rhetoric.

And quite rightly. What they did not know was that forty thousand more soldiers of the Grand Army had died or been wounded there, and that the Russians had vanished from the battlefield in the night, surviving to fight another day.

Colquhoun knew, though. He knew because the Ministry of War knew the truth, more or less, of what had happened that day, and the officers working there could fill in the gaps for themselves from their own experience of past battles.

Worse, the battle could have been won. The Russian army could have been annihilated. And if it had, the Tsar would have had to sue for peace.

There had come a time when the Russians had been forced back. It could have been turned into a rout. The Marshals had implored the Emperor to send in the *Garde*. The Russians would have broken if the *Garde* had advanced. The exhausted soldiers of the line leaned on their muskets, gasping for breath. They had done all they could, and more.

They waited, to feel the ground shake under the tread of the *Garde*, to see the massed ranks advancing through their lines in perfect order. But they did not come. The Emperor had refused to commit them. The Russians had reformed. The army was too drained to go forward again.

Had it really been a victory?

True, it had left the road open to Moscow. But Moscow was another week's march into Russia. Another week further from home and safety.

There was little rejoicing in Paris. Already the summer heat was a memory. The weather had broken. The days were drawing in. The nights were cool. Autumn was touching the trees. Winter was round the corner. It had taken over three weeks for the news of the battle to reach Paris. Where was the Emperor now? In Moscow? Had the Russians surrendered to him when he had reached the city? What was happening in far off Russia?

Claudette told Colquhoun everything she heard.

"The Emperor would not commit the *Garde*. Marshal Bessières kept whispering to him that they were his last reserve and he is eighteen hundred miles from Paris. The Emperor was not himself that day. He was ill. He listened to Bessières. He let victory slip through his fingers. But, Jeanazon, that whisper may have saved Henri's life. I can picture him, sitting on his horse at the head of his men, furious to go, to charge the Russians, fuming with anger that the Emperor will not order the charge. But I am glad. It is selfish of me, I know, but I am glad. They will not publish the casualty figures - indeed they do not know the full list - but it was a day of terrible slaughter. They attacked the Russians time and time again until at last they so nearly broke them. But for Henri I am glad."

"Can we send a message to Lord Wellington?" Colquhoun asked Mcpherson.

"This battle will be reported as a great victory in Napoleon's newspapers. Without a message from us it might be all the report of the battle that Lord Wellington hears. It could make a difference to his plans."

Mcpherson agreed, though, Colquhoun could see, with some trepidation. As Madame Constance repeatedly said, he was too old for this game. He remained unwilling to talk about his channels of communication with Spain, but he had probably lost his grip on whatever they were and whoever ran the messages for him. He probably knew that he could no longer trust either his own judgement or the loyalty of his messengers. He knew that he ought to close his operation down, that the dangers increased as his faculties decreased.

He looked miserable, but he nodded his agreement.

"Yes," he said. "Whatever we can, we must go on and

do."

Colquhoun kept the message as short as he could.

> R gave battle 7 Sep. Indecisive. N lost 40000. N advancing to Moscow. Now has 100000 effectives only. CG. 1 Oct 1812.

"We must be near the moment of truth," said Colquhoun. "If Napoleon has reached Moscow, and if the Tsar has surrendered to him, we will have to inform Lord Wellington as a matter of the greatest urgency. I think we will have to contact him again shortly anyway, because it will be just as important - perhaps more so - if the Tsar holds out. What on earth will Napoleon do then?"

Mcpherson shook his head: "I can see no reason why the Tsar should surrender now. The scales have tipped so heavily in his favour. The Emperor commands less men now than the Russians must have in the field. He can cut the Emperor off, surely, then starve him out and let winter do the rest. It is unbelievable that the Emperor should have allowed things to come to this pass. As to our operations, we must be prepared to send information to Lord Wellington as and whenever necessary."

Mcpherson looked so old and so tired. Should he use the old man's operation, Colquhoun wondered? Perhaps it had already broken down or even been broken into by the secret police. But what was the alternative? Unless he went himself. But that would achieve nothing. Assuming he managed to leave France and get back to Spain his news would be months out of date and common knowledge anyway. And then he would not be in Paris when at last any important news should arrive, as one day soon it must. No, there was no help for it. He must rely on Angus Mcpherson.

Claudette was doing her best to keep up the morale of the officers of the Ministry of War.

For all their fine uniforms, their whiskers, their swagger, their bravado, these were lonely and sad men. For them death in the heat of battle, in front of their comrades, leading their men, this would have been glorious. There was no glory in a desk job in Paris with a broken body and an empty future. Claudette gave them laughter and lightness and a moment's escape from themselves.

Colquhoun watched her with a mixture of admiration and exasperation: admiration at her ability to lift their spirits and appear as though she had not a care in the world. Exasperation because she was so occupied with them that he hardly saw her and when he did she discarded the mask and snapped at him.

"Do you have to spend so much time with them?"

"Yes."

"But why?"

"Oh, Jeanazon, don't be so stupid. Because they pay me, that's why. And the worse it all gets, the more they need me and the more they pay me. The day will come when I am no longer attractive to men. How will I live then if I have not made enough money now?"

"You will always be attractive to men. And you will have Henri."

She laughed bitterly.

"And will Henri come back from Russia? I am not a fool, Jeanazon. They will be cut off in Russia. The best I can hope is for him to be taken prisoner by an officer who will treat him honourably. But you know as well as I do what the Russians are doing to their prisoners. I may never see him again, and if he does come back do you think that he will not be changed?"

At the thought her body sagged. The anger was gone and she pressed her body hard against his, her arms round him, clinging to him.

"Oh, Jeanazon, I am so sorry to tear at you. I am so frightened for Henri. What will they do to him? Those Russians are savages. They are so cruel. And I fear that one day you will go too. Forgive me." She was weeping now. "It is all so... so stupid, so senseless. I am so lost. Forgive me, Jeanazon. I need you so ..."

On a cold, wet October day the news reached Paris that Napoleon had occupied Moscow.

It was not a cause for rejoicing.

There had been no reception party waiting to hand him the keys to the city.

Moscow had been a ghost town, empty of all but the meanest of its inhabitants. Fires had been started, either by the Russians or by the soldiers, nobody seemed to know who, and they had taken hold and roared through the wooden buildings lighting up the night so brightly that you could read by the firelight. Most of the city had burned down. The army had run amok. They had looted everything they could lay hands on. The place was a squalid shambles.

Paris heard the news in sombre silence. Everyone - everyone except the Emperor, it seemed - knew now beyond any doubt that the invasion of Russia had been a disaster.

The news from Russia was getting sparser now.

Very few messengers were coming in with first hand reports from Moscow. It was well nigh impossible for dispatch riders to run the gauntlet of the Russian partisans who swarmed like infuriated bees over every inch of the route, let alone the Cossack cavalry and the Russian army.

It seemed that the Emperor was hanging on in Moscow, dreaming - it could only be dreaming, - that tomorrow the Tsar would sue for peace. All the world could see that it was not going to happen. Why could not the Emperor? Had he lost touch with reality?

Whenever his orders did arrive at the Ministry of War, it was to demand reinforcements. He wanted surgeons, troops from all parts of his Empire, sailors, men who had served their time and been discharged, the sick, the lame, the disabled - anyone he could conceivably think of.

Every demand confirmed that the Emperor seemed to have taken leave of his senses.

As if all this was not bad enough Paris awoke on the morning of the twenty third of October to find the National Guard out in force on the streets. There had been a *coup* in the night. General Malet, who was mad and should have been in a lunatic asylum, had managed to arrest General Savary in his bed, as well as the head of Savary's Security Division. Malet had almost succeeded in taking over the police and the entire Paris military garrison before someone had recognised him and seized him. By mid-morning the coup was over. The ringleaders had been arrested. The National Guard went back to barracks.

But the *coup* did nothing for morale. The head of the secret police had been arrested in his bed by a certified lunatic and a handful of unfit National Guardsmen. What were things coming to! The mad General Malet had claimed that the Emperor was dead. Apparently he had had no possible grounds for this claim. Apparently letters had been received from the Emperor written after the date General

Malet claimed he had died.

It shook the already demoralised city. The authority, the absolute authority of the Emperor had been challenged.

Even if the army managed to fight its way back to France, could things ever be the same again?

It was, Colquhoun thought, all part of the malaise that gripped Paris. Nobody seemed capable of doing anything. Life went on, but until the fate of the Emperor and his army was known, nobody could take any initiative, think any positive thoughts, take any positive action.

So far as he was concerned, of course, it was all to the good. It probably explained why nobody had questioned his purpose or presence in Paris. Fervently he hoped that it would remain that way, and that the failed *coup* would not spur the secret police into action that might start them looking in his direction.

But he yearned for an end to his days in Paris.

He had been there too long. He felt stifled. He was neglecting his duty as an officer of Lord Wellington's army. He should have made good his escape and bent all his efforts on getting back to Spain. He could have been of use to Lord Wellington there all this time that he had wasted in France.

What good had he done in Paris? Two messages that might or might not have reached their destination. It was not much to show for six months of inactivity. But if he left now he would have achieved nothing. He had to stay, to sit it out until he knew the end of Napoleon's gamble. Only then would he have the cast-iron information he craved.

October dragged into November. Dark days, cold winds, cold rain, cold nights.

What must it be like in Russia now?

It was not until well into the month that Paris learned for

sure that the Emperor had at last given up his dream of Russian surrender.

Napoleon had ordered his army to abandon Moscow and march back five, six, maybe seven hundred miles to the relative safety of Poland just as the Russian winter was about to begin. A hundred thousand men had left Moscow with him, all that remained of the Grand Army. Apparently they had left the city loaded with booty, looking more like a vast troop of travelling mountebanks than an army.

Claudette's officers shook their heads.

Such a retreat would need the strictest military discipline if it was to stand any chance of success. Every man should be carrying every scrap of ammunition and food that he could. To waste energy and space on booty was asking for disaster.

Almost unnoticed, Colquhoun's relationship with Claudette had changed. Her efforts to raise the morale of her officers left her exhausted and tearful. She no longer took it out on Colquhoun, just needing him near her to comfort her when her door closed behind her suitors, and the ready laugh and lightness were turned off. He found himself reacting to her need for him. Their lovemaking was more tender, even perhaps touched with a genuine love, all the more extraordinary in that it was Henri de Bacquencourt for whom she grieved.

"Henri will never come back, Jeanazon. They all say that there is no hope for the army now. The Russians have two or even three times the soldiers that we still have in the field. They are on their own ground. Everyone says that they will surround the army and cut it off. The stories of the cruelties are so awful. What hope will there be for Henri? He will die fighting, I know it. He will not be taken prisoner to be tortured to death by Russian peasants. Oh Jeanazon, my poor Henri."

And Colquhoun would take her in his arms and hold her and try to comfort her.

He could not reassure her. There could be no escape for Napoleon and his Grand Army. By now, surely, the Russians must have closed in on the frozen and starving remnants of the French army and annihilated it.

But they hadn't. At any rate, not yet.

At the end of the month they heard that the remnants of the army - now no more than half the number that had left Moscow - had reached Smolensk. It should have been a haven. It had good stores of food and clothing. But the starving, freezing soldiers had broken into the stores and ransacked them. Within twenty four hours everything had disappeared in a chaos of looting and indiscipline.

Numbers were dropping by the thousands every day. The snow was falling in heavy blizzards. The temperature was thirty degrees below freezing. The daylight lasted, if they were lucky, for eight hours. Less than forty thousand men had struggled on from Smolensk. The Russians had armies behind and on both sides of them.

Two weeks later there were reports that the army had somehow managed to fight off the Russians at a place called Boritsov where they had had to cross the river Beresina. General Elbe and four hundred pontooners had waded waist or shoulder deep in freezing water with vast chunks of ice swirling past them to build bridges over the river. Most of the soldiers still capable of fighting had crossed to safety.

Thousands had died in the river.

Thousands more, all the stragglers and all the remnants of the camp followers, had been cut off on the far bank and slaughtered by the Cossacks.

It was thought that not one of the brave four hundred pontooners who had built and kept open the fragile bridges had lived to tell the tale. Truly those gallant men were the heroes of their Emperor's invasion.

On December the sixteenth a bulletin from the Emperor arrived in Paris. It was printed immediately. The people of Paris rushed to read it, as starved for news as the army had been for food. At last, from the Emperor's pen they read something of the disaster that had been the invasion of Russia. Colquhoun read it and then reread it in disbelief.

According to Napoleon the catastrophe had not begun until the snow had started.

He read:

'To the 6th of November the weather was fine, and the movement of the army executed with the greatest success. The cold weather began on the 7th; from that moment every night we lost several hundred horses...

'In a few days, more than 30,000 horses perished...

'It was necessary to abandon and destroy a good part of our cannon, ammunition, and provisions...

'This army, so fine on the 6th, was very different on the 14th, almost without cavalry, without artillery, and without transports...This difficulty, joined to a cold that suddenly came on, rendered our situation miserable.

'Those men, whom nature had not sufficiently steeled to be above all the chances of fate and fortune, appeared shook, lost their gaiety - their good humour, and dreamed but of misfortunes and catastrophes; those whom she had created superior to everything, preserved their gaiety, and their ordinary manners, and saw fresh glory in the different difficulties to be surmounted.'

"Good God."

Napoleon's cynicism was beyond belief. Colquhoun read on:-

'The Cossacks…this contemptible cavalry, that make only noise, and are not capable of penetrating through a company of *Voltigeurs*…

'The enemy had to repent of all the serious attempts which he wished to undertake… they… lost many men…the Russian army being fatigued, and having lost a great number of men, ceased from its attempts…Marshal Oudinot… took 2000 prisoners, six pieces of cannon, 500 baggage wagons…'

There was an account of the crossing of the Beresina river.

'During the whole of the 26th and 27th, the army passed…All the army having passed…the enemy was defeated and put to the rout, together with his cavalry, that came to the assistance of his infantry. Six thousand prisoners, two standards, and six pieces of cannon fell into our hands…Marshal Victor vigorously charged the enemy, defeated him, took six hundred prisoners…'

"Good God," Colquhoun shook his head, "This is nonsense."

Then came Napoleon's reason for retreating towards Vilna - the route that he had taken into Russia - rather than to Minsk where there should have been food and shelter. There was no mention of the fact that Minsk had been taken by the Russians, but a breathtaking claim that the devastated road to Vilna was 'through a very fine country'.

And then an extraordinary claim that:-

'*Matériel* and the horses are coming in; General Boureier has already more than 20,000 remount horses…

'The artillery has already repaired its losses…'

And an admission that 'The Cossacks have taken numbers of isolated persons…..of wounded officers who were marching without precaution, preferring running the risk, to marching slowly, and going with the convoy'.

And, as if to rub salt into the wounds of the grieving families of the men who would not return, the bulletin ended:-

'The health of his Majesty was never better.'

There was one crumb of hope for Claudette in the bulletin.

'His Majesty has been well pleased with the fine spirit shown by his guards. They have always been ready to show themselves wherever their presence was needful: but circumstances have always been such that their appearance alone was sufficient and that they never were in a situation which required them to charge.'

It was impossible to know whether this was any more truthful or any more fanciful than the rest of the bulletin. But perhaps it could mean that Henri de Bacquencourt was still alive. Claudette wept tears of frustration and fury.

"How can I know if what the Emperor says is true? How can I believe anything he says when I know what has happened in Russia. It is no more than a fairy tale, this bulletin. Oh, how true it is when they say 'to lie like a bulletin.' Oh, Jeanazon, what will become of us?"

Two days later, in the middle of the night, a coach arrived at the Tuileries. It carried two passengers, General Armand de Caulaincourt, and Napoleon Bonaparte.

The Emperor had abandoned what remained of his army to its fate and had returned to Paris.

Chapter 8

RETREAT

Colquhoun's blood quickened at the prospect of action.

At first, no one could believe that the Emperor was back in Paris.

He was a thousand miles away, leading the remnants of his battered army home out of Russia.

It was a very poor sort of a joke.

But it wasn't a joke.

He really was in Paris. The very next morning he summoned all his Ministers, meeting them first in Council and then in private interviews.

Presumably nobody dared ask him what he had done with his army and why he was there.

He said, apparently, that it had been the Malet conspiracy that necessitated his precipitate return. General Savary, Chief of the Secret Police, was said to have been closeted with him for two hours. He had emerged smiling, despite having been arrested by the Malet conspirators in his bed. General Clarke of the Ministry of War, on the other hand, had been sharply reprimanded, both for failing to materialize more men out of thin air and for making out that the conspiracy had been much more serious than in fact it was.

Bad, probably, Colquhoun reflected, for the Ministry of War, which could expect to come under their Emperor's scrutiny, and bad for himself as the secret police would be cock-a-hoop and would probably wake up and become much more aggressive.

What was really extraordinary, though, was that Napoleon could appear back in Paris as though it was a puppet theatre, pick up the strings and continue his show with all the puppets dancing to his order again as though nothing had happened.

He was responsible for the destruction of his Grand Army, for at least half a million violent deaths, let alone the enemy dead, for God's sake.

What would have happened if Lord Wellington had engineered a similar catastrophe, abandoned his army and gone back to London?

It beggared belief. But it also showed the iron grip that Napoleon had on France. England should not imagine that this débâcle would topple him from his throne, nor, probably, that he would sue for peace.

But if Napoleon acted as though nothing had happened, General de Caulaincourt made no secret of what he had seen in his last days in Russia, and messengers from Poland and Germany were beginning to appear in Paris with first hand reports from the Russian frontier.

They all spoke of a frozen hell more ghastly than words can describe. Every inch of the road was covered with corpses of men and horses. The soldiers who could take no more just sank down in the snow and froze to death - if they were lucky, that is, and died before the Cossacks got to them.

It was so cold that water froze three feet away from a fire. Men who could get to a fire were so frozen that they could not feel the heat, so that they burned without knowing it. If they lived long enough thereafter the burns turned to gangrene. But often they refused to move again. Mornings would find a thick ring of corpses round the ashes of every fire.

Wherever they could find anything to burn, they burnt it, so that the air was dark with smoke and red with flame. Abandoned wagons and guns added to the chaos. If the starving, frozen men could find spirits to drink they literally drank themselves to death. There was talk of cannibalism, of men eating their own fingers.

Soldiers joining the retreat who had been garrisoned along the way and had not been hardened to the cold perished immediately. Two hundred Neapolitan cavalrymen who formed King Murat's bodyguard froze to death to a man the first night they spent in the snow. Twelve thousand conscripts going from warm barracks to a bivouac in the snow in thirty degrees of frost soon suffered a similar fate

On December the tenth some ten thousand soldiers had shambled out of Vilna. Double that number were left behind in the town to the mercy of the Cossacks. It was all that was left of the Grand Army. When they reached Kovno and the river Niemen they were down - no one could say for sure - to between seven and nine thousand men.

There were some stories of heroism. Marshal Ney had formed and reformed the rear guard of the army and had held off the Cossacks all the way back. At Vilna he had held them off with four men. He had been the last man to leave

Russia. The Emperor called him the bravest of the brave.

And apparently a thousand men of the *Garde* had kept their discipline, alone of the whole army, and had marched shoulder to shoulder out of Russia. There had been forty seven thousand of them six months before so it was scant comfort, but better than nothing.

It gave Claudette a grain of hope.

"Perhaps Henri is with them. He would have lost his horse of course. Everyone lost their horses. But perhaps he marched with them. Perhaps in a few days I will get word from him. Do you think I will, Jeanazon? Do you? Do you?"

There was nothing Colquhoun could honestly say. The story of the *Garde* keeping its ranks was probably apocryphal anyway. From his own experience two years before, when the English army had retreated to the lines of Torres Vedras pursued by Marshal Massena he knew the nightmare of a starving army when discipline breaks down. The weather then had been nothing compared to the Russian winter. The retreat had been a matter of days, the distance miniscule compared to this. The army had managed to stagger back to the safety of the prepared lines and restore discipline. There had been no such haven for Napoleon's army.

"Perhaps," was all he could say. "Perhaps. It is more likely, I think, that an officer of Henri's rank will have survived, especially an officer of the *Garde*. The Emperor will have made sure that if anyone fed it would be them. They are France's best troops, Claudette. We can only hope."

Colquhoun had gone straight to Angus Mcpherson when he knew for certain that Napoleon was back in Paris. Lord Wellington would of course get the news - it was widely known that *Le Moniteur*, the Paris newspaper, was regularly smuggled across the channel and immediately sent on down to Spain, just as the English newspapers were regularly smuggled into France and avidly read by Napoleon. But the story in *Le Moniteur* would probably bear little relation to the truth.

Mcpherson was even more unhappy about his communication channel than he had been the last time they had sent a message.

"Of course we must try it, Grant," he said, "but my organisation is not good now. I fear it is breaking down. My reliable men have gone. Madame Constance is right. I am too old for his game. I hardly trust anyone, either to make the journey or not to betray us. But, yes, we must try it."

"Can we try the French way and send two copies of the message? Or three?"

"Two is possible. Three, no. I do not have the men."

Colquhoun nodded. This information was worth any risk.

"You must keep the message very brief, just a scrap of paper that can be swallowed quickly if necessary.

"Of course. This covers it, I think:-

> "GA completely destroyed in R. Has ceased to exist. N abandoned remnants, is back in P. Eastern border wide open to R. CG. 20 Dec 1812."

Colquhoun was unsure whether to include the final sentence. Had he said it to Lord Wellington in person he could imagine the blisteringly sarcastic reply it would probably have received - 'That is obvious. I am perfectly capable of drawing my own strategic conclusions, Major Grant,' or some such belittling dismissal. He smiled to himself. He would not be there when Lord Wellington read the message, and, anyway, it reinforced the unbelievable truth that Napoleon had sacrificed the largest army the modern world had ever seen and was now himself open to an advance by the Russian army into his own Empire.

The question was, what would Napoleon do now?

Once this became clear, it would be time to go. There would be nothing more Colquhoun could do in Paris. He was anyway hating the confinement of the city and longing to leave. He never wanted to see a city again, let alone have to live in one. He longed for the great empty open plains of Spain, for fresh air, to be on his own again with a good horse under him. Every day he was feeling more frustrated, more strongly that his duty lay back there with Lord Wellington's army.

Napoleon's first reaction was not long in coming. It was to order a round of dinners, of galas and of lavish balls. He really did intend to act as though nothing had happened. By all accounts the balls were ghastly affairs - like dancing on graves, someone had described them. But coupled with Napoleon's refusal to acknowledge the catastrophe Colquhoun soon learned from Claudette that he had set the Ministry of War feverishly to work to find him the men for another army.

Almost certainly, Colquhoun had the answer to his question. Napoleon was going to fight on. All that remained to find out was whether it would be in Spain or on his Eastern boundary. Almost certainly the latter. He could not possibly leave it undefended.

Would he, in this case, withdraw his armies from Spain and seek to put an end to the war there? Almost certainly not. That would be to acknowledge defeat - defeat on two fronts. He would plan to hold his enemies at bay there while he dealt with the problems on his Eastern borders.

Early in January Paris learnt of yet another blow.

While the main body of Napoleon's army had been invading Russia Marshal Macdonald had been besieging the town of Riga in Latvia. In his army corps were twenty thousand Prussians under a General Yorck. When he had heard of Napoleon's débâcle this general had contacted a Colonel Clausewitz, a Prussian who was serving with the Russian army, and had negotiated for the whole Prussian contingent to change sides.

For Napoleon this was devastating news.

It must surely mean that Prussia would join with Russia and now fight against him, and there must be a strong possibility that Austria, pushed no doubt by the perfidious and treacherous English, would follow suit. Once again the three countries would combine against him. He had beaten them before, frequently and comprehensively, but never from such a weak position as now. And the talk was that the Prussians had secretly been building up their army, that it was far stronger than Napoleon had realised.

There could be no doubt of it. Napoleon would have to face East to defend his Empire.

"Can we send one last message? And then I must leave Paris."

Mcpherson nodded. He appeared terribly tired and hardly stirred in his chair.

"One more message," he almost whispered, "and then goodnight."

"Angus, you have been more than a friend to me. I am wrong. No more messages. Let us leave it. I will go myself. Once I get to Orléans Father O'Shea may be able to send a message on ahead of me. In any case I will make my best time back to Spain. Who knows, I may get there before your message. Lord Wellington will anyway have realised for himself that Napoleon has got to protect his Eastern boundary. He will be planning accordingly already."

"No, Grant. We must send him word. One final word. Pour me another glass of that wine... Ah, that's better. Now, what will you say?

" 'Prussia has changed sides. N desperate to muster all resources. Must face East. R advancing. CG. 10 January 1813.'

But, Angus, the danger to you is not worth the risk if your network is breaking down and you cannot trust it. Let us leave it."

"No. We must risk it. We will send two copies. Write it down for me. I feel better for seeing you and the thought of some action."

As he wrote out the message Colquhoun said:

"Tell me about Marshal Macdonald."

"They say he is solid rather than brilliant. I believe him to be a decent and honourable man. Perhaps because he is half Scottish, for a long time the Emperor did not trust him or indeed employ him. He might also have been mixed up in a Royalist plot. But he led the great column at Wagram in '09 that broke the Austrian centre and won the battle. After the battle the Emperor embraced him. He said 'Come, let us be friends from now on,' and awarded him his Marshal's bâton then and there. But he says, maybe half in jest, that he will not let the Marshal fight the English. He would not trust him if he could hear the sound of the bagpipes."

Madame Constance snorted.

"He is a vain man. He has lost all his hair, and must wear a wig. It greatly concerns him."

They all laughed.

"He has a chateau at Beaulieu sur Loire. A beautiful place, they say, which he greatly loves. It is called Courcelles le Roi. He has spent much time there and made many improvements."

"Courcelles le Roi. Where on the Loire is that?"

"Upstream from Orleans, perhaps thirty miles. I do not know exactly."

"I would have liked to have met this Marshal. I feel we would have had something in common."

Colquhoun walked slowly back to his lodgings, deep in thought.

Which would be quickest?

To leave Mcpherson's couriers to go South and himself head North to the channel and hope to find some smuggler who would take him across? It might work. If he could once get across the Channel the Navy could whisk him down to Spain in a fortnight. There must be a lot of illicit traffic across the channel. There must also be a lot of police and National Guard trying to stop them. Although they were probably in league with the smugglers an escaping officer would be too large a package to pass unnoticed. Risky. And probably the roundabout journey with inevitable delays would actually take nearer two or even three months than one.

No, it would make more sense to head South, to get back to Spain. Once over the border and in contact with the partisans a relay of horsemen would be able to take a long detailed message to Lord Wellington setting out everything that Colquhoun knew about the state of Napoleon's armies and his need to defend his borders. Lord Wellington could have the information within three weeks, if all went well. It was the obvious answer.

Colquhoun's blood quickened at the prospect of action and lifted at the thought of leaving Paris.

It would be a long way through hostile country. And how to travel?

It would have to be as Jonathan Buck, as he had no other papers and would surely be stopped by the police somewhere on the way. Jonathan Buck the merchant would be best. Buying wine from Bordeaux, perhaps. It would give a reason to be travelling through France. He would need a horse - a scarce commodity just now as Napoleon had lost countless thousands of horses in Russia and was scouring the country for every animal he could lay hands on, so Claudette had told him.

And what of Claudette?

He had come to feel protective towards her. For all her confidence and worldly wisdom there was a lonely and lost soul somewhere inside her. He had, he realised, become very fond of her. He must not hurt her, particularly as there was still no word of Henri de Bacquencourt, alive or dead.

It was all very well to say he must not hurt her. Inevitably, his sudden disappearance would hurt her. Perhaps Henri was still alive and would come back. In any case, they both had always known that the moment would come when he would leave.

If Henri did not reappear she would just have to find another 'real man.' It should not be too difficult for a courtesan as beautiful and accomplished as Claudette.

The police picked up a young man leaving Paris that evening.

It was only a routine road block, but the man was nervous. It was enough for them to be suspicious. They searched him. He was carrying a scrap of paper which he tried unsuccessfully to put in his mouth. Within hours all police in Paris had been alerted that someone signing himself 'CG' was sending sensitive information to the English in Spain.

It did not take the police long to beat everything he knew out of the man

That night they came knocking at Angus Mcpherson's door. They pulled the old man out of bed, but they had underestimated his age and frailty. As they pushed him downstairs his heart failed him. He crashed to the bottom. He was dead when they tried to haul him to his feet.

General Savary was furious. He was also shrewd. The contents of the message were almost common knowledge in Paris, though it would of course be of great interest to the English army who would not at the moment know what the Emperor was planning, nor perhaps indeed that the Emperor was in Paris or that the Prussians had changed sides. The old man would not have been 'CG.' It appeared that he had simply been running a courier network, a messenger service. Bad enough in itself, though it would not take long to smash now.

Clearly the old man's network had been feeding information to the English from this 'CG' and perhaps others. No, 'CG' would have to be someone with military connections, someone in a position to be told or to hear of the latest developments as they occurred. The message was written in English. The old man had been English - or Scotch: same thing as far as the General was concerned. So

'CG' was quite possibly - almost certainly - an English spy operating right here in the heart of Paris. The Emperor would not be in the least amused.

Much as General Savary hated General Clarke he decided to alert the Ministry of War, at the same time sending a general alert to all police between the capital and the Spanish border.

The alert ran like wildfire round the officers at the Ministry of War. It was passed on to Claudette that afternoon by the Major who was escorting her to the opera that evening. She was very pensive during the whole performance, ate her supper and was bedded by the slightly baffled officer without consciously noticing what she was doing. She startled her maid by appearing at eight o'clock the next morning and demanding the presence of the street urchin Jacques

"Go to Major Buck, Jacques. Tell him I must see him. If he is not there, find him, or wait until he comes back. Do not fail me."

Jacques, who would have died rather than fail the beautiful Madame d'Yves, swore that he would not blink an eyelid until he had found the Major, but he was not at his lodgings. Jacques had seen him go out quite early.

"How was he?"

Jacques was surprised.

"Same as always, Madame. He said good day. He asked me how everything was. Same as always."

"What do you mean -'how everything was?'"

"I watch his place for him." Jacques said it with a touch of pride. "See nobody goes in, that sort of thing."

"Do you." That in itself was interesting. "I see. And has anyone gone in? No? Very well... Go... Wait for him until he gets back. Give him the message. Do not fail me."

For the past few days Colquhoun had been seeking a horse suitable for a merchant travelling the country visiting the wine producers. He had decided to remain in his American uniform while he searched. A uniform carried more authority in Paris and it would be better that he gave no hint of his proposed change of occupation.

He had been round most of the stables of Paris. The owners were all reluctant to sell, if not somewhat suspicious of his motives. Every horse in France was going to be needed by the army, that was common knowledge, and a foreign officer looking to buy a mount would no doubt be planning to sell it on at a profit - either that or some equally underhand foreign motive.

Colquhoun was running short of cash; it was an uphill battle to find any suitable mount at a price he could afford. He was reluctant to ask Angus Mcpherson for more money but this would be the last time and within months - weeks, perhaps, - he would be in a position to arrange somehow for repayment.

He arrived back at his lodgings fairly pleased with his morning's work. He had found a cobby animal that was sound and looked as though it would go all day, if not fast, at least reliably. With saddle and bridle thrown in he had had to pay a lot more than he would have wished for the animal. He would collect it from the stable next morning and be off. He had bought saddle bags as well, and some spare clothes and hard tack for the journey ahead.

The transaction and his purchases had left him dangerously short of money. He would have to ask Angus Mcpherson to fund him one more time though he was sure the old man would not mind doing so.

He found Jacques waiting for him.

"Where you been, patron? I've been looking for you all morning. Madame wants to see you immediate. What you been up to upsetting her? She's all of a dither."

"Is she now?"

He felt that sudden contraction of his stomach and jump of his heart that warned of danger.

"What's up?"

"Search me, patron. You've upset her. What you been up to? Been dallying with another girl, have you? Found you out, has she?"

He laughed crudely.

"None of your business, young man. I'll go and soothe her down."

Claudette did not greet him. She just looked at him. She said nothing.

He smiled.

She backed away from him.

"What is it, Claudette? What's the matter? Have you had news of Henri?"

She shook her head slowly, staring at him.

"You have never told me your secrets, Jeanazon, but I have always known that you have them. I have always known that you are a real soldier. I have always known that you have been in Spain since General Souham recognized you. Oh, yes, don't deny it. He was in no doubt that he had seen you in Spain. He told me so. So tell me now. What do the initials 'CG' mean to you? Are you 'CG'? I think you are. I think you are not an American at all. I think you are an English spy."

They looked at each other. What was in her eyes? Anger, certainly. But also a sort of pleading, he thought; a sort of desperation, even the look of someone who loves you and fears for you.

"Why do you say this, Claudette?

"General Savary's men have arrested a man carrying a message to the English. It is signed 'CG.'"

"And would you tell them if you thought it was me?"

For long moments she stared at him. Slowly, she shook her head.

"No, Jeanazon, I do not think that I would."

He stared back at her. His last message must have been intercepted. That would need thinking about. But later. Right now, could he trust her? Dare he trust her? If he did, how much would it be safe to tell her - both in his and in her interests. Life would be difficult for her if the secret police found out that she knew his real identity.

Her eyes were searching his desperately. It was not the look of someone who is planning to betray you.

"Yes," he said. "I am CG. But I do not call myself a spy. I am an officer of the English army, I admit it. I was taken prisoner. I gave my parole and it was accepted. I was on my way to Verdun when I found out that your secret police were after me and that despite my parole they had every intention of killing me. I was in the middle of France when I found this out. I had no option but to disappear. I had to come here and pretend to be an American.

"Claudette, I will do anything I can to end the war in Spain. That is why I have stayed here. Europe has been torn by war for too long. Your Emperor is too careless with the lives of all the young men of Europe - not just the young men of France. I want an end to it."

Her eyes were still searching him.

"I am not sure that I entirely believe you, Jeanazon. I do not think you are as innocent as you pretend. I have known this, I think, always since you came into my life. Oh,

Jeanazon, I should run and tell the police. I should turn you in to them and hate you. But I cannot do those things. I think I have come to love you a little - I who love no man except my Henri. Oh, Jeanazon, must I lose you as well as Henri? I think my heart will break."

This time she did not back away from him. He went to her, took her in his arms and held her to him. She clenched her fists and hit him, a flurry of blows on his chest and back. He pulled her closer to him, tried to soothe her with gentle words, stroking her hair like a child's.

"When we met, Claudette, we had no thoughts of loving each other, not really loving each other. But I think we do. I think we have come to love each other, and I am sorry. I would not want to hurt you for the world. I am sorry, my Claudette, I am sorry."

The blows subsided. She sighed.

"Yes, I think we do love each other a little. How silly. How stupid. What would I have done when Henri comes back? I cannot have two men who I love. Oh, Jeanazon, you must go. They do not suspect you yet. But they do not know you like I do. And it will not be long before they find it is you. You must leave Paris quickly. General Savary's men are clever. They will not rest until they find you. You will be shot, for sure. They are hard men. You must go today, now…"

They were standing close to each other. Her pelvis pressed hard against him. She turned her face up and kissed him. He pulled her closer to his body.

When Colquhoun left her apartment a good two hours later his heart was heavy with the grief of their final lovemaking and their parting. Both knew that they would not see each other again, not, at least, while the Emperor Napoleon sat on his throne.

He did not have long to indulge this sentiment. Jacques was waiting for him.

"What you been up to this time? You're in trouble, you are, patron. While you been in there there's been two men at your lodgings. I can smell a policeman three hundred paces off and I'm telling you they was police."

"Are they still there?"

"No. They wasn't long. They went off when they saw you wasn't there. But they'll be back. You watch out for yourself, patron. They'll be watching out for you. They're bastards, they are."

The short January day was already dying. It was bitterly cold. His long stay in lodgings had softened him. The thought of living rough again was not attractive. Instinctively he pulled his greatcoat tighter round him.

"Good lad," he said. "Here."

He gave Jacques a five franc piece. Jacques bit it and grinned.

"You're a gentleman, patron."

It had probably been a routine visit. After all, he had lived in expectation of a police check. It did not sound too serious if the two men had simply knocked on his door, received no answer and decided to come back another time. Nevertheless...

The urgent need was to see Angus Mcpherson, both to warn him that his man had been picked up and to ask him for enough money to get across France. He should not have given Jacques five francs. It was needless extravagance at this time, but the boy had faithfully kept an eye on his lodgings and was always full of spark and gutter wit. He supposed Jacques would soon be swept into the army. He would no doubt make a resourceful soldier.

He must be careful approaching Mcpherson's house. If the courier had talked he might have named the old man, though Colquhoun imagined that Mcpherson would have passed the message to him via an intermediary.

The street lamps had been lit and the street was empty as he pressed into a doorway and peered towards Mcpherson's house. The windows were all dark. That was curious. The old man's living room looked out onto the street. He should have been there and certainly should not have been sitting in the dark.

He waited.

There was movement in the darkness at Mcpherson's door. The streetlight reflected dimly for a moment on something metal as someone shifted position. Then the sound of someone stamping his feet, no doubt numb with cold in the freezing evening air. It could only be a sentry posted there. The police must have broken into Mcpherson's network. The dark house ominously must mean that he had been arrested. Good, resolute old friend. He was hardly able to walk. What would they do to him? It did not bear thinking about. And yet he had bravely insisted on carrying on. Perhaps he would be happy to die in his cause. A true Scotsman, straight and determined to the last.

What about Madame Constance? Had she been arrested too? And the maid? And the other house staff? What would the secret police do to them? He felt real fear for them as he stood undecided in the doorway. There was nothing he could do to help them. Madame Constance would be a match for anyone. But if they started beating her? He cursed under his breath.

And, from his own point of view, without money it was going to be alarmingly difficult to cross France. How much did he have? He cursed his stupidity in giving Jacques the five franc coin. It would have fed him for many miles of his journey.

He watched the house a while longer. Apart from the freezing sentry nothing stirred. He slipped away into the night.

Would it be safe to go back to his own lodgings?

He would freeze to death on the streets. There was not enough money left in his purse to warrant taking a room in some hotel. He decided to risk it. He watched the road and the doorway beside the draper's shop below his rooms. All was quiet. He crept up the stairs. Empty. Nothing in the rooms had been touched, he was sure of it. He opened the window at the back. He could hear the little donkey munching and moving quietly in its stall somewhere below him. It was a hell of a long drop. He took the sheets off the bed, knotted them together and tied them to a bed leg. It would still be too far to fall. He added a blanket to his improvised rope, and then a second one. Better to be cold and have his emergency retreat prepared than warm and without one. He closed the window gently.

Colquhoun hardly slept. At five o'clock he took his saddle bags, stuffed with all his possessions, and cautiously took to the street. It was snowing. The snow flakes were falling gently through the circles of light around the street lamps. It had not been snowing long. The street was hardly covered He was still wearing his uniform. It might give him a small advantage if some early riser happened to see him and report him. The authorities would think they were looking for a uniformed officer. Jonathan Buck's clothes were in the saddle bags.

The stable was busy, grooming and preparing the horses for their day's work. They were mildly surprised to see him so early, but shrugged their shoulders and saddled up the horse. He fixed the saddle bags behind the saddle, led the animal out and rode away into the snow.

The watch on the road out of Paris was three parts frozen and half asleep in the dark of the January morning. He left his greatcoat unbuttoned so that they could not miss his uniform tunic. They glanced incuriously at his papers, and waved him on, an officer going about his business.

It was still dark as the houses thinned and he left the city. He turned into woodland, took off his uniform tunic and redressed in Jonathan Buck's coat, waistcoat and hat. The breeches and boots would be alright for the time. They would not draw comment. To his annoyance the clothes that had fitted so perfectly six months ago were now a little tight round the middle. Unless he could lay hands on some money that would soon alter. He smiled grimly to himself.

So far, so good. He stuffed the blue tunic and forage cap into the roots of a tree and emerged from the wood a merchant on his way to Bordeaux to buy wine.

Chapter 9

COURCELLES LE ROI

"Now clear off, and don't come back or I'll set the police on you!"

The officer commanding the secret police in Orléans read General Savary's alert with great interest. He called for the man who had noted Colquhoun's arrival from Bayonne.

"Remind me," he said, "what you reported about that English officer back in June. The one you thought you saw getting onto the Paris stage coach dressed as a civilian. The one they reported as having died in the infirmary... Ah, yes. Just as I thought. Major Col- something Grant. 'CG.' Could be a coincidence, but I think we'll have a look into this. Could be our man. Start with the infirmary where they said he died."

The infirmary orderly who had dealt with the body was quickly located.

The mere mention of the secret police was enough to terrify him into total recall. He pleaded ignorance. He pleaded that he only did what he was told. What he thought had happened - he couldn't be sure, the policeman must understand - it was only what he thought might have happened - he really didn't know, but it had struck him - well, not struck him, but he had noticed - the man they put into the red soldier's coat, he hadn't been a soldier when he was admitted to the infirmary, he had been wearing well-to-do civilian clothes because he happened to have been there when the man was brought in. He had noticed him because he was a richer looking sort of person than the people who usually were taken in. He hadn't wanted to touch him then because the man had been so sweating with the fever and he might have caught it, but of course once he was dead that didn't matter so much. Father Auchay had taken his papers. He had said the man wouldn't need them any more and he would hand them in to the Authorities. No, he couldn't remember the man's name. He was a foreigner with a passport though. He hadn't heard the man speak, but they had said he was foreign. No, not English, he didn't think. American, they had said.

For some unexplained reason there were no infirmary records for that June.

The police absorbed this information with great interest.

"I don't think this Colga - something Grant died at all. They switched identities in the infirmary. That *sacré* bastard cunning priest. You were right all along. That woman you spoke to who looks after him was lying. She knew all about it. Jonathan Buck, she called him. Her and the priest are both in this. This is our man, no doubt of it. Find Jonathan Buck and we'll find Major Colga- something Grant. Pull the damned priest in, and the woman. We'll get to the bottom of this."

Colquhoun took the main road South towards Orléans. The horse was excited by the snow and pleased to be trotting on an open road. For a while it snorted and shied in sheer high spirits, then settled down to a steady pace. As Colquhoun had thought, the animal would not get him anywhere in a hurry but it felt strong under him and he was sure it would go all day.

He stopped when it was light and bought some bread in one of the villages he passed through. To his irritation dismounting was uncomfortable and he walked stiffly into the bakery. He had not taken this into consideration. Six months on his feet, living comfortably, and he was unfit for a long day in the saddle. His buttocks were feeling sore already. The inside of his knees and thighs felt tender. He had hoped to do the seventy or eighty miles to Orléans in the day. He would be lucky if he managed half that distance.

He tipped the contents of his purse into his hand. Just enough for one night. Even if he tried to sleep rough the horse would have to have stabling and food. There was nothing for it to eat in the bleak January landscape which was slowly covering over with snow.

He had been unsure whether to contact Father O'Shea and Madame Marie, unwilling to put them into any danger by his presence. There was no question now, though. The horse would have to be stabled in Orléans and he would have to seek shelter with them. In his unfit state he would probably freeze to death anyway if he did not find a roof. He cursed as he remounted. This journey through France was going to be more trying than he had reckoned.

Snow fell steadily through the day. He rode in a silent, almost twilit world. There were few travellers out that day. That at least was an advantage. Heads down, muffled into cloak or greatcoat the few that he passed were far too preoccupied with their own discomfort to pay any attention to him.

He managed to reach Étampes before the light had gone. It was, so far as he remembered, the only fair sized settlement between Paris and Orléans. He had had enough for one day anyway. He was frozen and a great deal stiffer than he cared to think - though whether from cold or the day in the saddle, or both, he was not sure.

He booked in to the post hotel in the town centre. The hotelier seemed surprised to see a traveller on a day like this. As a matter of course he asked for Colquhoun's passport, made a note of his name and handed it back disinterestedly.

Colquhoun saw that the horse was properly bedded down and fed and went and thawed out at the fire in the hotel dining room. It would be better in a day or two. The stiffness would disappear and he would harden to the weather. He rubbed his bottom. He could not remember when, if ever, a day in the saddle had left him aching like this.

The hotel bill ate up nearly all his remaining cash. He paid the sleepy hotelier before breakfast, ate everything put in front of him, called for more bread and surreptitiously pocketed it. Then he went back to his room and shaved off all his whiskers.

He set out before it was light. The snow had stopped. The hotelier had said Orléans was about forty miles on. Had he been fit he would not have thought twice about such a distance.

The first few miles were uncomfortable. Then as his muscles warmed to the familiar rhythm he forgot about the stiffness. The sun came out. The snow lay thinner on the ground. The horse trotted merrily along. His spirits rose.

Colquhoun reached Orléans as the day was beginning to die. For much of the time he had been deliberating with himself whether to go to Father O'Shea's house or to the church of Sainte Croix to make contact. He had eventually decided on the church. It was unlikely, he thought, that the authorities would be on the look out for him in Orléans, but the church was more anonymous.

He found a stable on the outskirts of the city and lodged the horse there for the night. He saw it fed and watered, shouldered his saddle bags, and walked on into the centre. He was glad of the change of exercise. He was stiff and very cold, but nothing like as bad as yesterday. In a day or two his body would be back to its old self. He was mightily glad to be out of Paris and doing something positive again. He felt more cheerful than he had for weeks, if not months.

It was dark by the time he found the church of Sainte Croix, and even darker inside, the darkness relieved here and there by candles and wall lamps. He walked into one of the side aisles and sat down near the back.

As he expected there were figures scattered around, mostly women in black kneeling praying, a couple at the table where the votive candles lit a circle of the gloom, a cassocked verger doing something that he clearly considered important.

It was very cold in the church, a damp freezing chill that emanated from the stonework all around him. He knelt down and put his hands to his face as if in prayer, watching the high altar and the comings and goings around him.

At last a black robed priest appeared. He came out of the side door where Colquhoun had first seen Father O'Shea, genuflected deeply, and went up to the high altar. Colquhoun went forward.

As the priest left the altar Colquhoun said:
"Father."
The priest looked surprised and not particularly pleased.
"Forgive me, Father, I am seeking Father Auchay."
"Father Auchay? You... What do you want with him?"
There was no mistaking the reaction. The priest took a

step backwards. His head swivelled left and right to see whether anyone was watching or listening. Even in the dim light Colquhoun could see fear in his eyes, then calculation.

"He is a friend of mine."

"A friend? Yes, of course. Of course." His voice was ingratiating now. "Who shall I say wants to see him?"

What on earth had happened? It was almost impossible that they could have traced him so fast. But the priest's whole demeanour shouted that this must be so.

"Buck. Jonathan Buck."

"Ah! Yes. Jonathan Buck. He is not here at present, my son."

The voice was wheedling now, trying to soothe him.

"I'll find him for you. Wait here. Don't go away. I'll be back directly. Wait here. Don't go away."

The priest turned away and almost ran from Colquhoun, vanishing through the side door.

Colquhoun turned as well.

He strode quickly back down the aisle. Almost, he hurried out into the square, but he checked himself in the darkness of the doorway. A moment later a cloaked figure appeared from the side of the church, half running, one hand holding down a biretta on his head.

Colquhoun waited until the figure disappeared down one of the streets leading out of the square. He stepped out of the doorway, down the steps, across the square, found the dark recessed doorway of a closed shop, pulled his hat down and his coat collar well up, and waited.

His fears were soon confirmed.

He saw the priest come hurrying back into the square towards the church. Close behind him came a uniformed squad - soldiers, police, National Guardsmen, Colquhoun was not sure which. Their officer was calling orders. The squad broke up as they ran, some, no doubt going to cover whatever other doors there were to the church.

Colquhoun waited until they had disappeared into the church, then slipped from his doorway down a side street.

Somehow, he had been discovered. The police must have worked fast. Alarming as this was, he could not help feeling a certain admiration for them.

To go to Father O'Shea's house now would be madness.

In the space of less than a week his cover in France had completely collapsed

He thought of Claudette and his stomach lurched. He hoped to God that they would not have implicated her.

What had he done?

Angus Mcpherson, probably Madame Constance, probably their household, Claudette, now Father O'Shea, perhaps Madame Marie - what had he done to put all these lives at risk, perhaps worse, to have them all put to death? Probably there were others too, Mcpherson's network of couriers, men whom he had never set eyes on but who nevertheless could be in deadly danger if not already under arrest.

If Napoleon could dismiss the deaths of half a million of his soldiers as easily as he had, what hope could there be for anyone accused of spying?

Let alone his own predicament. Apart from a few *sous* he had no money. He had nowhere to go. Effectively he had lost the horse as the stable would undoubtedly refuse to give it up to him if he could not pay for its keep and stabling. He had nothing to eat and he was hungry.

He had automatically walked back to the stable. Its doors were locked. The place was in darkness. There was no hope of spiriting the horse away or bluffing the ostlers to let him have it. Not, anyway, until early the next morning.

But come the light the danger of capture would increase dramatically. All the roads out of town would be blocked. Police would be on the alert for him everywhere. Maybe already they would be setting up the road blocks. There was no help for it. He must abandon the horse, get out of Orléans, and fast.

Almost, he retraced his steps into the centre, thinking to cross the Loire by one of the bridges and head South. He checked himself. The first places that they would watch would be the bridges. He was at the North of the city. With luck they would not be expecting him to go North. Probably checking the roads out of this side of the city would be their lowest priority.

He headed on back up the Paris road. Orléans had bedded down for the night. The road was empty and he was soon into more or less open country.

It hardly lessened his predicament. For a start, if he stopped walking he might freeze to death. To make matters worse there was no moon, just a faint light reflecting off the snow and marking the darkness of the road surface.

He came to a junction, a wide well surfaced road branching off to the right. Presumably it would follow the course of the Loire upstream.

He stopped.

What had Madame Constance said?

'Upstream from Orléans, perhaps thirty miles.' If he branched to the right, then somewhere ahead of him was Marshal Macdonald's chateau.

It was a mad idea. An escaping prisoner seeking out a Marshal of France.

But what had he to lose?

Either he would starve and freeze to death or sooner or later he would be arrested.

He did not even know whether the Marshal was at his chateau. He knew he had returned from Riga and Claudette had told him that Napoleon had cut him dead when the news of the Prussian defection reached Paris. It was at least possible that he would be on leave at Courcelles le Roi.

Anyway, what alternative was there?

Colquhoun walked all night. He just had to hope that the road was following the line of the Loire. Of all the directions the police would look for him this - going inland and eastwards - was surely the most unlikely.

In the dead of night he passed through a small town. He dared not deviate from the main road to search for the river even though it was probably close at hand.

Dawn found him dead tired and very hungry but a signboard pointing onwards to Sully Sur Loire encouraged him that he must be going in the right direction. He thought he had covered about twenty miles in the night. It looked as though Madame Constance's thirty miles was an underestimate.

He had to take risks. He walked on, slow with fatigue, following the sign to Sully sur Loire.

The sun was well up on another cold and beautiful morning when the road came to the river. It was busy. Flat bottomed boats were plying both ways along it, loaded with sacks or barrels or indeterminate bundles. One had a superstructure that presumably sheltered passengers. There was a solid bridge across the Loire and on the far side were the massive stone walls of a turreted chateau.

As he crossed the bridge he could see that the chateau was moated, and then that it appeared to be uninhabited and perhaps falling into disrepair. Most likely, he thought, the last occupants had been forcibly ejected - or worse - in the Revolution. Beyond the chateau he could see the houses of a village or small town.

A horse and cart were coming towards him on the bridge. He hailed the driver.

"That's not Courcelles le Roi, is it?" He pointed to the chateau.

The driver turned and looked at the chateau for a long time as though he had never seen it before. He puffed silently on a pipe. He turned back and looked at Colquhoun speculatively. He removed the pipe and spat towards the river.

"It is not." He spat again. "Blockhead. How would it be Courcelles le Roi when it's Sully sur Loire? You're over six leagues from there."

This was bad news

"I am a stranger to these parts."

The man looked him up and down, taking in his dishevelled unshaven appearance.

He smiled as though at some private joke.

"I can see that. Going to see the Marshal, are we, blockhead?"

"Something of the sort."

The carter considered this for a while.

"Deserted, have we?"

"Deserted?" Colquhoun was genuinely surprised.

"Don't try to fool me, boy. I can tell you're a soldier. See it a mile off."

"And if I was a deserter would I be going to Courcelles le Roi, blockhead?"

The man laughed. A good natured chuckle.

"Well, you be careful. There's lots of your sort around and they're hot on picking you up. Was a soldier myself, once. In the Revolution. Didn't like it over much. Don't blame you, I don't. Courcelles le Roi, eh? Follow on, on this side of the river to Châtillon. Its not so far after that. In the middle of the woods it is. Careful does it, though. Don't get yourself picked up." He jerked his head towards Sully. "Don't tarry overlong in the town. They're hot on the likes of you there. Nor in Gien."

"Gien?"

"Three leagues downstream. Most of the town's on the North bank. Go straight on for Châtillon."

He clucked to his horse and moved on, chuckling to himself.

Colquhoun walked on, skirting round the chateau and through the village. He had intended to get out into open country again as quickly as possible but the smell of new baked bread coming from a bakery that he passed was so overpoweringly seductive that he glanced up and down, saw no one in uniform, and stepped inside.

The solid hard faced woman behind the counter looked at him contemptuously. He held out the few *sous* that remained. She snorted and gestured for him to hand them over. She counted them derisively, looked him up and down rather as the carter had, and shook her head.

"We don't want the likes of you here. Be off with you. Deserter, I suppose. I suppose you're on the run, eh? Here, take this."

She handed him a small loaf, little more than a bun.

"Now clear off, and don't come back or I'll set the police on you!"

"Thank you, Madame."

Gratefully Colquhoun took the loaf, tore off an end and crammed it into his mouth.

The woman snorted again. "Get out."

The bread was delicious, the best, he thought, that he had ever tasted, but all too quickly gone. 'I should have saved some of it,' he thought. It showed both how hungry he was and how soft his time in Paris had made him. It was not the first time that he had not eaten for a day, sometimes for two, even on occasion three, nor that he had marched all night, and in weather more inhospitable than this.

He hurried on through Sully Sur Loire.

Best now to lie up for the day and push on, hoping to find the right road, after dark. He left the road and went into some woodland. It did not look as though anyone had been there for some time. The snow was melting, almost gone, but there were no human footmarks and his presence sent some deer bounding away through the trees. Trying not to disturb anything he made his way into the thickest undergrowth that he could see and made himself as comfortable as he could in the shelter of the roots of a wind blown tree.

He managed to doze a little through the day, curled into a ball, knees drawn up to his chin, arms wrapped round his legs, but hunger and cold kept him mostly awake. No one came near. He wondered whether to jettison his saddle bags. Apart from his razor there was nothing in them. He had put on all the spare clothes as an extra layer. His Scottish blood was loathe to abandon the bags. As the light began to fade he picked them up, went back to the road and resumed his search for the chateau of Courcelles le Roi.

Sometime in the night he passed what must have been Gien, then two small villages. At least, he thought it was two, but he was so tired that as soon as he passed them they became jumbled in his mind.

An hour or so later he passed another settlement on the far bank.

Another hour, or more, he was moving so slowly now, and at last, he walked into the sleeping village of Châtillon Sur Loire. He was exhausted, frozen all through, light headed from lack of sleep and hunger. He longed to stop, to beat on one of the doors and plead for a bed and something to eat. Or to curl up in a doorway and throw himself on the charity of whoever lived there in the morning. He cursed himself for a fool.

The village was bigger than he had expected, with several streets. He got confused, wasting precious energy on finding the Courcelles road. But he had developed a sort of instinct for placing the river on his left and eventually he found his way out on what he thought must be the right road.

Another slow painful hour's walk.

It was getting light when he came to a crossroads. Somewhere to the left, although he could not see it, was the Loire. To his right the road dropped down a slope with woodland on its left. He hesitated. Straight on seemed to be open country.

There was a different feel to the land here. It was well ordered, well maintained, the woodland beautifully thinned with fine tall trees. The carter had said the chateau was in woodland. Or was it Madame Constance who had told him? He could not remember. He was completely numb with fatigue.

He turned down to the right. Some few hundred yards brought him to another little crossroads. Looking to his left along the line of the trees he could see imposing gates several hundred yards ahead. His heart jumped. This must be Marshal Macdonald's chateau of Courcelles le Roi.

There was no one in sight. He turned left, walking slowly on until he came to the gates. He peered through their iron bars. He could see the chateau a hundred yards or so away beyond the woodland on his left.

It was not enormous like the grey stone castle at Sully Sur Loire. It looked quite compact, more like a manor house, two handsome storeys high with a row of dormer windows above in steeply pitched roofs, a tall square tower and, at a lower level, conical steep tiled towers setting off a single storey extension. Its walls were partly rendered and partly a warm terracotta brick.

There was a cluster of neat looking buildings to the right of the drive that led on beyond the gates. The chateau seemed to be set in a great clearing in the woodland. There were lawns all round the chateau and the buildings, level ground with cut and tended grass, powdered still here and there with the last of the recent snow. It looked enchanting.

For a long time he clung to the bars of the gate, trying to think what to do now, half asleep, struggling to shake off the lethargy. Maybe he slept, head and chest resting on the gate, frozen hands holding himself upright.

A voice behind him said:

"Who are you? What are you doing?"

It was a woman's voice, speaking in French, of course, but - could it be? - with a Scottish accent.

Three parts asleep, without thinking he said in English:

"Are you Scottish?"

Stupidly, immediately, he realised that he had given himself away.

It jerked him awake. He let go of the bars and turned round. The woman was well into middle age, comfortably built with a homely face. She must have walked up the road behind him.

"Lord 'a mercy," she answered in English. "Look at you. Aye, I'm Scottish. And what in the name of the Lord are you?"

"A Scotsman, Madame, and in need of help."

"Lord 'a mercy, a Scotsman. Well. Well, well. What will the Lord send us next? You look all done in."

She sounded as though she had not spoken English for a long time. Her voice was heavily accented, the accent a mixture of French and Scottish.

"If you're a Scotsman you'd best come with me."

She moved past him, producing a large key from a pocket in her topcoat. She unlocked the gates, opened them, took his arm and together they walked up the drive towards the house.

"We can't turn a fellow countryman away now, can we. You'll be hungry I doubt?"

"Very."

She nodded. "You poor mannie. Come on with me. I'll find you a nice hot drink of tea and a fine big breakfast."

She was as good as her word. She took him into the chateau's kitchen. It was blissfully warm. She pushed him down into a chair and called to two startled serving girls to boil the water and bring food and stop gawping and get on with it.

She must be the housekeeper, Colquhoun thought, or perhaps the cook. She was clearly in authority. She demanded his greatcoat and handed it to a manservant who was hovering open-mouthed in the doorway.

"What are you gawping at, Gaston? Take this coat and give it a good brush. I want to see it as good as new."

She let Colquhoun eat and drink without further questions.

"Now, then, Scotsman," she said at last. "What is your name and your business at Courcelles le Roi?" She spoke in English again.

"Madame," he answered in English, " I cannot thank you

enough for your kindness in taking me in. I am a highlander, like yourself, I think. I am of the Grant clan. Marshal Macdonald owes a debt to my family, and I have come to ask him to redeem it."

"Lord 'a mercy. A Grant. Well, that's a good Jacobite name. Whatever next. They fought with the Macdonalds at Drummossie Moor."

"Are you a Macdonald, Madame?"

"Aye, and proud of it. Flora Macdonald is my name, kinswoman to the gallant Flora who rowed the Prince to safety in '46. My grandfather fought and bled at Drummossie Moor. He was lucky to escape after the battle."

"How come you are in France and speaking your mother tongue?"

"Well, that's a long story. My grandfather left his wife and bairns - my father amongst them - when he answered the Prince's call. He had to flee the country, of course, when the cause was lost. So his bairns were brought up in the highlands without a father. My grandmother always spoke proudly of him. So I had a mind to know my grandfather, I'd heard so much tell of him. So I came to France to find him when I was old enough. I liked it well enough and have been here ever since. But enough of me. What of you?"

"My father was in the linen trade in Forres. He had twelve children - I'm the eighth son. He died when I was a boy. My mother had to bring us up alone. Like your family."

With the food and the warmth his head was beginning to swim. He had to fight to keep his eyes open.

"Will the Marshal see me? Is he here?"

"Aye, he's here the past ten days. A clansman he owes a debt to! Well, I never heard such a thing. Lord 'a Mercy. I'll make him see you, though you come in a curious manner for such a request. What is this debt?"

"Madame, it is a matter of personal honour. You will forgive me that I must ask the Marshal myself."

He knew he was slurring the words, as though he was drunk. He folded his arms on the table. His head sank down onto them and he was asleep.

When he woke up it was dark. He was on a bed somewhere, with blankets covering him. He was too sodden with sleep to care. He went straight back to sleep. It was just light outside when he woke up again. He supposed he must have slept for twenty four hours. Maybe even forty eight. He sat up. His coat and waistcoat, cleaned and ironed, were on a chair beside him. From the steeply pitched ceilings and dormer window he reckoned he was in an attic room, perhaps in one of the towers of the chateau.

He got off the bed and went to the window. It looked Northwards back towards the gates. Below him, a long way down, he saw that the chateau was surrounded by a dry moat. He had been so done in when the woman had brought him in that he had not even noticed. It was early morning on a grey sunless day. The snow had gone.

He went over to the door. Inevitably, it was locked. He picked up the coat and searched through its pockets for his passport and papers. Inevitably, they were not there. He looked round the room for his saddle bags. Inevitably, they were not there. He sighed. He sank back down on the bed. He felt sleepy still, and very hungry, but vastly rested. He clasped his hands behind his head and waited.

Heavy, slow footsteps coming up a stairway brought him upright. There was a fumbling outside the door, a key turning, and the door opened to reveal a very large heavily moustached grey haired man who had certainly spent most of his life in the heavy cavalry. The man bent down and retrieved a tray that he had put on the floor while he opened the door. On it were a jug, soap, a razor, a towel and a comb.

They looked at each other

"Good day," said Colquhoun.

"Good day, sir."

The man crossed the room to a washstand, poured the water into the bowl, set the towel down beside it, and said:

"Marshal Macdonald will receive you in twenty minutes."

The water was comfortingly hot. Colquhoun tore off his cravat and set to. Shaving always woke him up and made him ready for the day. This morning was no exception. There was a mirror hanging above the washstand. Colquhoun retied his cravat carefully and inspected himself as he put on his waistcoat and coat. He did not look too bad for a man who had walked on an empty stomach from Orléans.

Marshal Macdonald was waiting for him in one of the high windowed ground floor rooms. He was somewhat over middle aged, probably around fifty, very strongly built, broad shouldered, holding himself ramrod straight, his head thrown back a little, very conscious of his physical appearance, a man accustomed to command. He probably was wearing a wig, Colquhoun thought.

He looked as dour and suspicious as a Kirk elder on a Sunday morning.

Colquhoun bowed.

The Marshal acknowledged the bow with the slightest inclination of his head. The old cavalryman, who had brought Colquhoun downstairs, took post beside the door.

"Thank you, sir, for granting me this chance to speak to you."

"You may thank Flora for that. She tells me you are a highlander come to claim a personal debt of honour. I know of no such debt to you, sir. You are a Grant, she says. Your passport says you are an American by the name of Jonathan Buck, a merchant from Boston. One way or the other you are an impostor. If you are a Scotsman I would remind you that your country is at war with France. As you are in civilian clothes and under a false name I must assume you to be a spy. Is there any reason why I should not have you shot?"

"I do not consider myself a spy, sir. It was necessary to borrow that identity in order to travel through your country."

"Then state your business, sir, before I have you shot."

"Sir, I believe your father to have been Neil MacEachen."

A frown and slight nod from the Marshal.

"He was a true friend to Prince Charles Edward. He accompanied him throughout his flight from the English after the battle at Drummossie Moor."

The Marshal's rather haughty face marginally relaxed. He looked guardedly interested.

He said "Yes, that was so."

"Did your father ever tell you the story of how Jean Grant saved both their lives?"

There was a long silence.

"He did." Another long silence. "Frequently."

"Of how she danced the sword dance to the English soldiers when your father and the Prince were in the house behind her? Of how she distracted them so they failed to search the house, dancing and offering them a cool drink so that they went on their way and your father and the Prince escaped capture?"

Another long silence. Marshal Macdonald appeared to be a man of few words.

"How do you know all this?"

"Jean Grant is my mother."

"Your mother? How do I know this is true?"

"You have my word as a gentleman of honour. How else could I possibly know this story?"

"Hmm...Then why is your name Grant? Your mother would have changed her name on marriage."

"My father was Duncan Grant of Mullochard in Strathspey, of the house of Grant of Freuchie. My mother is Jean Grant, daughter of Thomas Grant of Kylvemore of the Grants of Arndilly."

The genealogy clearly meant nothing to the Marshal but the strange Scottish names appeared to impress him.

He said "Hmm.." again.

"She brought us up with the words of the Prince repeated so often that I know them by heart. 'Jean, child,' the Prince said, 'I can never thank you for this. See, I have nothing now, but when I come back and claim my kingdom you shall have your reward. You shall sit at my side when I am crowned. Hear me Neil -if ever - ever- I say you or your kin are in peril, Jean, if ever you are in need - you or your kin - come to me and I will not disappoint you. D'you hear me, Neil? She's saved our lives. We owe this girl the greatest debt that any man can owe.'"

Still the Marshal was silent. He turned away and looked out of the window.

Colquhoun said: "Sir, I ask you to honour your father's debt to my mother, and further, that if you are unwilling to do so, you will do me the honour to shoot me here and now, for you are my only hope in France."

Without moving the Marshal said:

"Thank you, Gaston. You may leave us."

The old cavalryman bowed and left the room.

There was a long, long silence.

Then Marshal Macdonald turned from the window.

He held out his hand to Colquhoun.

"Shoot you, sir? My father would have died there that afternoon. He would have fought the English soldiers to the death rather than face the dishonour of capture for either of them. It was the closest they ever came to capture. If it were not for your mother I should never have been born. I acknowledge your debt. It is a debt of honour that no man could refute. You are welcome under my roof. Come, I expect you are hungry. Breakfast is on the table."

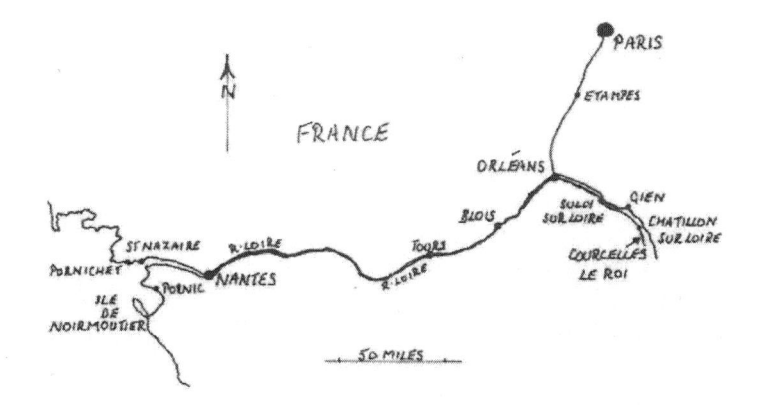

Chapter 10

THE LOIRE

The men of the river were a law unto themselves.

To the famished Colquhoun the Marshal's breakfast was a vision of heaven. The table was spread with cold fowl, cold ham, boiled eggs, fresh bread, made up dishes, butter, jams, what looked like oatcakes, the whole overlaid by the ravishing smell of hot coffee. Colquhoun felt faint with hunger.

The Marshal was not disposed to talk. He ate solidly in silence, indicating to the hovering butler with his knife which dish or meat he next wished to sample. From time to time he gazed speculatively at Colquhoun, then returned his gaze to his plate.

Colquhoun ate ravenously everything that he was offered, the butler cutting him slice after slice of ham and fowl until he felt his stomach would burst. At last he could eat no more. He sat back.

The Marshal had already finished eating and was sitting staring at him. He said:

"I'll not ask you what you are doing in France nor why nor how you came to this place. That you are on the run is obvious. I take you for a soldier, from your bearing, and as one soldier to another I admire your courage in coming here. I assure you, though, that were it not for the striking parallel between my father's situation and what I take to be your situation I should have had you arrested on the spot. And shot. A debt of honour is a debt of honour, however, and it cannot be denied.

"The less I know about you the better. You cannot stay here. It would be too dangerous both for you and for me if your presence here is known. I take it you want money? Of course. And that you need to leave the country as quickly and quietly as you can? Quite so. I thought as much. Have another cup of coffee. I will be back shortly."

He indicated to the butler to pour the coffee for Colquhoun, pushed back his chair and left the room.

He was gone a long time. Colquhoun forced the coffee down. It might well be his last good cup in France and it tasted excellent. He got up and went over to the window.

Within its dry moat the chateau was L shaped occupying the North and West sides of a square. He was looking onto a small courtyard open to the South with a square tower in the South Eastern corner connected to the main buildings via a main gateway and curtain wall on the East of the courtyard. Across the moat the even lawn stretched to the edge of the woodland, dotted with young cedar trees. Even in mid-winter Courcelles le Roi was the sort of place you would not wish to leave.

He sat down again, and waited.

When the Marshal at last returned he was carrying a small leather bag and a flat, polished wooden box.

He still had the look of a disgruntled Kirk elder.

"As regards this debt, I cannot physically aid or abet your escape from France. To do so would make me a traitor to my country. There is only one way I can help you. I shall lend you one hundred *Napoleons d'or*, a sum more than sufficient to enable you to do as I shall advise."

He pushed the bag across the table to Colquhoun.

"The debt will then be cleared in full. If we meet again I regret that we will almost certainly be on opposing sides. If this is so I will have no hesitation in ordering you to be shot. As a man of honour and a gentleman I demand that you never mention this meeting or the payment of this debt so long as France and your country are at war. Do I have your word on this."

"You have my word of honour, Marshal."

Macdonald nodded. "Very well. There are one hundred *Napoleons d'or* in the purse. And, with some misgiving, I will also loan you this."

He pushed the wooden box towards Colquhoun. Inside was a small pistol with powder flask, wads, ramrod, spare flint and ten balls.

"I will lend you this on condition that I have your word that you will not turn it on any soldier of France, that you will accept capture and even death rather than fire it at any French uniform. I have your word? Thank you. Take it. Nantes is a rough place. It would be as well to be prepared.

"You must leave now. If you are asked, you will deny that you have ever been to Courcelles le Roi or spoken to me.

Equally, I shall deny that I have ever set eyes on you.

"Flora will take you to Beaulieu Sur Loire. She has a house there and a son who runs a boat on the Loire. My advice - no, my command - to you is to go with him down river to Nantes. Under no circumstances should you break your journey or go ashore unless her son tells you to. Place yourself entirely in his hands and do exactly as he says. You may trust him. He knows every centimetre of the river.

"If you are lucky you will not be stopped on the river by the police, who I fancy may be on the lookout for you. Also if you are lucky you will find a boat on the coast there that will take you out of France. How you do this and how you cope with the blockade will be up to you, but I take you for a man of courage and resource in that you have had the temerity to come to the house of a Marshal of France to claim your debt."

"Marshal, you have fully repaid our parents' debt. I can only say thank you and hope that we will meet again one day as friends."

For the first time Marshal Macdonald gave a flicker of a smile.

"These wars go on too long, Monsieur Grant. One day, God willing, they will be over and I shall visit Scotland. I have an urge to see the land of my fathers. I am told it is both bleak and beautiful. Perhaps we shall meet again there in happier circumstances."

"Marshal, if this war ever finishes it will be my pleasure and my honour to show you the beauty of the highlands. You will not be disappointed. If ever this hope materialises send a letter to Mistress Jean Grant of Forres and it will eventually find me. In the meantime, I cannot thank you enough for your honesty in acknowledging our parents' debt."

Marshal Macdonald held out his hand.

"*Au revoir*, then Monsieur Grant. Let us hope for such a meeting."

Flora was waiting for him when he left the Marshal's dining room. She was holding his saddle bags, comfortably heavy with bread, cheese, and cold meat.

Flora walked with him to the village of Beaulieu. They talked of Scotland and the highlands. She loved France, loved the Marshal for whom she had worked for thirty years, loved her French husband and family, but still felt the pull of the empty lands of the North. Philosophically, she knew she would never see Scotland again. To talk and remember with Colquhoun gave her great pleasure.

As they came to the village Flora became businesslike.

"Lord 'a mercy but we are lucky," she said. "My son Jean has a full load. He would have left for Nantes yesterday, but I persuaded him to wait so he can take you. You must do as he says for he does not much like to carry a cargo such as you. He will put you ashore before you get to Nantes. He will probably travel mostly at night. He will anyway pass the main cities of the river at night. He does not think there is much risk that the boat will be checked at this time of the year. The police prefer their warm beds and do not like to be wet. He knows what he is doing. He will get you there, have no fear."

Jean was waiting for them at her house in Beaulieu.

He was an immensely powerful man with an enormous breadth of shoulders and hugely muscled arms. His surly taciturn unfriendly acknowledgement of them both confirmed his anger at his mother's persuasiveness and his misgivings about taking Colquhoun onto his boat. He looked Colquhoun up and down in an insolent manner that in other circumstances would have sparked an instant reaction. Their eyes met for a moment. Jean's look was contemptuously arrogant.

A dangerous man to cross, - perhaps more so than Colquhoun's erstwhile travelling companion, Major Magaud. Magaud had been the scarred leader of the wolf pack, but a creature similar to himself. This man was like a great bear, solitary, going his own way, probably striking down anything or anyone who stood in his path.

There would be no comradely reminiscing beside a warm fire over a mug of wine with this one.

But Colquhoun could well understand Jean's reluctance to abet what was obviously an escaping fugitive. He must have agreed to do this trip - which plainly was illegal - to please his mother and she must have decided on it and persuaded him to do it before Colquhoun had even seen the Marshal. Colquhoun wondered what sort of a hold she could have had on a Marshal of France, let alone on her sullen son. Whatever it was, - Scottish kinship, perhaps - she was a determined highland lass with a steely will and a romantic heart.

Not for nothing, like her fabled forerunner, was she called Flora Macdonald. Thank God, she had grown up with romantic tales of highland fugitives and dramatic escapes. Thank God, she had taken a liking to her fellow Scot.

Above all, thank God, she had seized the chance of carrying on her family tradition of spiriting a fugitive away by water. Colquhoun had no doubt that it was entirely her influence that had persuaded Marshal Macdonald to honour his father's debt and to help him as he had.

They set off down to the river immediately, Jean carrying a great basket of provisions which his mother had handed him.

The boat was larger than Colquhoun had imagined it would be. It was flat bottomed, about fourteen paces long and some two paces wide, somewhat like an enormous punt. It had a mast, though what Colquhoun took to be the sail was unattached and furled round a spar lying on top of the cargo together with two long punting poles and a great triangular shaped oar or steering pole. There was no superstructure on the boat, which was loaded with dusty, dirty looking sacks of what he soon discovered were charcoal, together with half a dozen barrels of wine and some nondescript boxes and bundles.

A bitter wind was blowing upstream. The river looked bleak and inhospitable. With satisfaction, though, Colquhoun realised that he was toughening up again.

The cold and wet were not going to bother him unduly.

Jean indicated to Colquhoun to get aboard. He untied the boat, picked up one of the poles and pushed the boat out into the river until the current took hold. Then he put the pole down and picked up the great triangular oar which he skilfully used to steer them into midstream. Colquhoun sat down on one of the barrels.

The boat moved at a walking pace, Colquhoun reckoned. Sometimes the current spurred it faster, sometimes slower. Jean was active the whole time, watching the water, steering with the oar, using it like a fish uses its tail, sometimes exchanging it for the pole and pushing the boat this way or that.

Colquhoun watched for some time, then, the next time Jean exchanged the oar for the pole Colquhoun offered to help, picked up the other pole, and, under Jean's surly and taciturn direction, managed clumsily to help push the boat in the direction Jean wanted.

As the day went on he became cleverer with the pole and in the afternoon he took a brief turn with the oar, steering the boat as Jean directed. It was plain that Jean knew the river like a landsman knows the twists and turns of a long familiar lane. He handled the boat with an expertise that immensely impressed Colquhoun even though he did not understand what Jean was doing or why, as he changed course or steered from one part of the current to another.

In the afternoon they glided past the great stone turrets and walls of the chateau at Sully sur Loire, just one of several boats plying up and down the river, cargo laden, crewed, to the casual observer, by two men.

As the light was fading they poled the boat out of the current and pulled it onto a sandy river bank in what appeared in the fast approaching gloom to be a desolate uninhabited stretch of scrub and trees.

There was no talk between the two men. Jean opened his food basket, ate and drank from it enthusiastically, evidently seeing no necessity to share food or drink with his passenger whom he ignored, produced a voluminous oil skin cloak from somewhere on the boat, wrapped himself in it and settled himself down in the cramped space of the stern. He was soon snoring.

Colquhoun's shoulders and arms were aching from his efforts with the pole and oar. He could well understand Jean's massive build and strength now. He ate some of the provisions that Flora had given him, drank water from the river, found himself a space in the bow and tried to sleep.

Not very successfully.

The sides of the boat gave some protection from the incessant biting wind but the space was too small to stretch out and his back and arms got scant respite from the wooden planks underneath him. He wondered how long the journey was likely to last and whether the bear like Jean would tell him if he asked.

On a whim he scratched a mark in the plank nearest his head, and finally he drifted off into some sort of sleep.

Heavy movement at the other end of the boat and a shout of "Come here, you. She's settled" pulled Colquhoun out of a half sleep.

It was still dark, though the stars glittered in their thousands overhead. He got up stiffly. Rather than clamber over the cargo he took off his greatcoat and dropped overboard into the river. He was wet anyhow and likely to remain so until they got to Nantes. He splashed to the back of the boat and joined Jean in heaving it back into the stream. At least he was not being treated as a despised supercargo.

They both climbed back on board as the boat started to slip out into the river. He picked up one of the poles and together they pushed the boat into the current. He had no idea what time it was nor why Jean thought it necessary to start in the middle of the night.

The reason came clear an hour or so later as they glided past a sleeping town. It was, Colquhoun imagined, the first town he had passed through on his way to Courcelles le Roi. No one was astir. No one challenged them. The dark houses and the small pools of light from the streetlamps vanished astern.

They stopped and tied up to a little deserted wharf in the afternoon.

Colquhoun was enjoying himself. As he had become

more familiar with the working of the boat Jean had seemed quite willing to let him pole where needed and take his turn with the steering oar. The physical exercise was good after the months of city life. The clean, cold river air felt like champagne after the months of breathing heavy, stale city air. He felt he was getting quite adept at it, and presumably Jean was reasonably happy with what Colquhoun was managing to do. He still scarcely spoke, but the atmosphere between them was less tense.

Who knows: perhaps Jean never spoke much anyway. His boat could not have been a more solitary way of life.

They did not start again until after dark. The moon was strong enough to light the water, silvering the ripples of the current. Colquhoun imagined Jean was timing it to pass Orléans in the small hours of the morning, and so it proved. The sky had clouded over when they glided silently past the sleeping city on the black water which seemed all the darker in contrast to the lights on the wharves and streets ashore. They had left the city well astern and the day had long dawned when Jean steered the boat to the shore and they tied up again.

It was a pattern that soon became familiar. Jean was judging exactly where he would be at any given time. He planned their stages to pass the major settlements at night. Blois, and then, the next night, Tours, he called them, not that the names meant anything to Colquhoun. He scratched another mark on the planking each night. All the time the river was widening. There was more traffic on it now, by day and night.

Downstream, all the boats travelled as they did, with the current, steered and propelled by pole and the massive triangular oars.

When going back upstream, they all hoisted a great square sail and travelled roped one behind the other in convoy, a big multi-sailed strong looking boat in the lead, avoiding the strongest currents, helping to pull a flotilla of smaller and smaller boats behind against the flow but with the incessant westerly wind filling their sails. The convoys hardly seemed to move. Colquhoun reckoned they probably would have covered a mile, perhaps two at best, in an hour.

The two men did not talk much, but Jean seemed now to have accepted Colquhoun, almost to be quite pleased to have a companion.

The third day, when they had finished all the food they had brought with them Jean motioned to Colquhoun to go ashore with him when they tied up at a small landing stage. There were three other boats tied up there, apparently deserted. They followed a track a short distance in shore to a ramshackle house with a peeling sign at its door proclaiming it to be *Le Coq d'Or*.

Jean pushed open the door and strode in as if he owned it. A cloud of tobacco smoke fogged the steamy air inside and vied with the river smell of damp clothes and sweaty bodies. The room was crowded with rough looking boatmen. Several arrogant pairs of eyes looked up at them from a long table.

Jean must have been well known. There were greetings or nods and the men seated at the table went back to their previous occupation, eating, drinking, smoking, just talking.

An old crone was tending a large cooking pot hanging over the fire in a vast open chimney place. She wiped her hands on a filthy apron and came across to them, eyeing Colquhoun suspiciously.

Jean said "He's with me."

The old woman nodded. She indicated empty places on the benches. They sat down. She put mugs in front of them and poured red wine. It was good, light and smooth. Colquhoun's face must have shown his surprise. The crone cackled with amusement.

"Loire wine," she said. "None to beat it."

She hobbled back to the fire and pulled a long white loaf of bread from the oven built into the side of the fireplace. She cut it into thick slices and heaped them into a bowl which she put on the table, together with the wine bottle. She ladled two platefuls from the cooking pot and set them down in front of them. It was some sort of stew or very thick soup. Best not to ask what was in it.

Like the wine, it was delicious.

Colquhoun did not attempt to join in the conversation. All the men knew each other. They were all boatmen. The talk was all of the river, of people and places that Colquhoun had never heard of, of boats and cargoes, of the currents and the wind, of women and the places they could be got, of charges and taxes, of shipwrecks and accidents, all in the grossest language the coarseness of which would have outclassed the lowest of the English soldiery.

Most interestingly, the whereabouts and activities of the Customs officers and the police figured large in the conversation, invariably in the context of avoiding their attentions or bribing their officers. Plainly, they were the hated enemy, to be outwitted, outmanoeuvred and outfought wherever possible. Colquhoun was fascinated. It was an insight into a world that he never knew existed.

The men of the river were a law unto themselves, with little regard for anyone or anything beyond their horizons.

Taking him on board, Colquhoun realised, had nothing to do with breaking the law. It had been the reluctance of a river man to take a stranger onto the river, one, moreover, who was a foreigner and had probably never done a day's physical work in his life.

There was a long stretch of river, three days' travelling, before the next major town.

They stopped twice a day now, tying up at little wharves and going ashore to eat. The hostelries were invariably squalid, earth floored, smoke filled, wooden benched dens which catered exclusively for the boatmen. Strangers were not welcome. Colquhoun's presence was only accepted when Jean growled "He's with me."

A fair proportion of the hostelries doubled up as brothels, though the women - Colquhoun could not bring himself to call them girls - were harridans as strongly boned as the boatmen, as dirty, and equally as foul mouthed and uncouth.

One of them took a fancy to Colquhoun. To the amusement of the company she started to strut and flaunt herself in front of him.

Colquhoun ignored her.

She lifted her skirt to her knees and with shouted encouragement from the company she danced in front of him until Jean rose from the table with a wordless roar. The woman looked startled, swore at him, turned away and retreated to an inner door. When she reached it she bent forward and threw her skirt over her head, exposing formidable white buttocks which she waggled at them open-cheeked before disappearing through the doorway.

There was a roar of laughter. One of the company got up and hurried after her.

Colquhoun was not in the least amused. Overt lewdness was not in his nature. More to the point, it often only needed a spark and places like this could erupt into violence. As a stranger and outsider the boatmen might well have turned on him.

Not a dissimilar incident to the jostling in Bayonne where Major Magaud had come to his rescue. Inwardly furious, he caught Jean's eye and was somewhat mollified to see respect in the look that Jean gave him.

The next town, Jean told him, was Angers, two days journey from Nantes. From here the river was navigable to ocean going ships. It was broadening and deepening all the time with ever increasing traffic.

Jean did not bother to pass Angers at night. The day had been fine with the promise of clear skies overnight. The moon was nearly full. The boat would have been clearly visible to any watcher on the silver water. Besides, it would only have been one of many, and the chances of their being stopped by the police on the wide, busy river must by now have been almost nil.

Colquhoun was by this time indistinguishable from the men they mixed with in the boatmens' inns that they frequented for their meals. Face and hands were filthy from the charcoal dust. His greatcoat was stained and torn, fraying all round. Underneath it, Jonathan Buck's fine cutaway coat and waistcoat had become equally shabby, sweat stained, fraying, buttons beginning to drop off, the brown dye fading to a muddy tan.

He had discarded his boots - useless in the river - and was bare-legged from the knees downwards. Bare feet were far nimbler on the boat and gave a far better purchase on the planking when he worked the pole and the steering oar. He had neither shaved nor brushed his hair for a week, and, apart from the constant spraying of the river water, he had not attempted to wash. In common with all the boatmen, he stank of sweat and the river.

But the wet and cold were no more than a minor inconvenience. He felt fitter and more alive than he had ever since that day last year when he and León had fled from the French at Idanha a Nova.

There were nine scratches on the planking when Jean put ashore some miles short of Nantes. There was a mutual respect between them now, the camaraderie of men who have lived and worked together. They shook hands with something like genuine warmth.

Jean refused to accept any money. It had, he said, all been taken care of at Courcelles. Whether by the Marshal or Jean's mother Colquhoun never knew. Jean just shrugged and dismissed the subject with a wave of his huge hands.

Colquhoun watched him cast off and pole out into the current. They waved to each other. Colquhoun sat down and pulled on his soggy boots. Briefly, he contemplated whether to attempt to clean himself up before walking into Nantes and as swiftly discarded the idea. He looked and smelt like a boatman. As such, he would probably attract no attention. He pulled the boots off again. Best to remain barefoot. His feet were hard enough for any surface. He put the pistol in the right hand pocket of his overcoat and its powder flask and shot wrapped in a rag in the left hand pocket. He checked the flint and the priming. He felt the purse tied round his waist under his shirt. He threw the saddle bags and his boots into the river.

He stood up and set off towards Nantes.

Chapter 11

NANTES

A sixth sense had followed him so often.

It would, Colquhoun realised, take some time to find one's way around Nantes.

This was a big city, acres and acres of buildings, many of them very fine, on the North bank of the Loire. The river divided, forming an island of some size which appeared to be part of the city, connected by several bridges which continued on over to the South bank. So far as he could see the far bank was similarly built over.

There were wharves and jetties, boatyards, dry docks, canals, inlets all along the river banks of both the main stream and the island. There were hundreds, if not thousands, of ships of every size tied up or anchored in the river. Most, to his unnautical eye, appeared to be Loire boats loading or unloading, but there were two masted and three masted ships, many of them obviously ocean-going and probably, from the fast, businesslike look of them, blockade runners.

The waterfront was crowded with humanity, horses, wagons and goods of every description. There were inns every few yards, bustling and noisy with clerks and labourers, warehousemen, boatmen and sailors, smoke filled and stinking of food and stale wine. There were a fair number of women, prostitutes mostly, Colquhoun supposed, many ragged and lank haired with sharply lined faces grown old before their time, but some well-dressed and attractive.

There was also a noticeably heavy presence of men in uniform strolling or standing watching, always in twos or threes, granite faced customs officers, tough looking police, National Guardsmen, a few soldiers. There were groups of police apparently doing nothing, but, he had no doubt, they were just waiting for trouble to move in with the long bâtons they carried.

Colquhoun bought himself a meal and a jug of wine in the quietest inn he could find and sat in the window gazing out, wondering what to do next. He had, rather naively, imagined that it would be easy to find a fishing boat or something similar and to pay or bribe the boatman to row him out to one of the blockading English ships which must be on station somewhere close off the coast.

But how, in this mass of shipping and humanity, was he going to find such a boat? If he asked the wrong boatman the chances looked high that with such a heavy police presence he would be arrested on the spot.

To have got so far, to be one step from freedom and to feel thwarted at this stage was more than frustrating. He cursed the sea and all its shipping. He cursed the necessity of having to get involved with it.

He was out of his element.

He dared not approach anyone for help or advice. He wondered how long it would be before he attracted attention from the watching police. He might easily be picked up as a vagabond or, more likely, as a suspected deserter. The only good thing was that in his tattered state he blended in well with his crowded surroundings.

He ate morosely and drank sparingly. The serving girl came demanding payment. Having nothing else, he paid her with a *Napoleon*. She looked at the coin in surprise, then suspiciously at him.

He winked at her conspiratorially.

She shrugged her shoulders, raised her eyebrows, and went for change. The meal had cost only a few francs, and she counted several coins back and put them down on the table. He picked them up and was slipping them into a pocket when he was aware of someone standing beside him. He looked up.

A woman dressed in little better than rags was standing holding out her cupped hands to him. He looked up at her ravaged face. The bone structure was delicate. Once she must have been good looking. He felt a pang of pity for her.

Her dark eyes were dead, the eyes of someone who has seen and suffered more than the spirit can stand. But there was something in them, some message. He put most of the coins into the cupped hands. Fleetingly, as she looked down at them and then back at Colquhoun her eyes were surprised, then her face went dead again.

Her hands closed over the coins.

"Monsieur is very kind," she said.

Her voice was cultured. Then, almost inaudibly, she said: "You are a stranger here, Monsieur? You should not pay for a meal here with a *Napoleon d'or*. There are eyes everywhere. A man such as you paying with such a coin will not last long. Be careful, Monsieur. If the police do not get you, others will. There are still many such as I in Nantes. Not all have tried to keep their honesty."

Colquhoun said: "What do you mean?" but she had turned away and was gone.

He got up and went to the door of the inn, undecided which way to go.

To his left, upstream, was a group of the uniformed police.

He turned to the right, downstream, and walked on along the quay. The ships tied up here were all ocean-going. One in particular caught his eye. Its size, its three tall masts and mass of rigging and furled sails which even to Colquhoun's eye meant speed, its strong, clean rakish lines and lack of superstructure marked it out as a blockade runner.

A painted sign on its side proclaimed it as the 'Wayfarer.' It was flying the Stars and Stripes of the United States from a small flagpole at its stern.

The Stars and Stripes of the United States?

Colquhoun stopped.

The United States?

Why not?

This ship could get him out of France. It might fall foul of the blockading English Men of War. All the better if it did. If it was captured he would be free. It might get back to America, but to be imprisoned there would be far preferable to a bullet or rope here.

It would take some time, but once Lord Wellington knew he was in America he would surely arrange an exchange.

There was a gangplank from the ship's deck to the quayside. Colquhoun walked up it. A sailor sitting on a hatch in front of him got up, slightly menacingly.

"This here's a private ship. Get your butt off it."

"I want to see your Captain."

He emphasised what he hoped was a good American accent. He had been speaking French for so long that he was not sure how the words sounded. Neither, apparently, was the sailor. He looked puzzled.

"Do you now. Well, he don't want to see the likes of you. Get your butt off it."

Colquhoun stood his ground.

"Tell him I have a business proposition that I need to discuss with him."

The sailor eyed him contemptuously, much as had Jean when they first met at Flora's house in Beaulieu.

"Huh," he said. "What's a one bit bum like you got to offer anyone?"

A voice said "Well, let's hear what he's got to say before we throw him in the Loire."

A tall, athletic young man had appeared from the doorway at the back of the ship under the raised decking of the stern.

"Aye, aye sir." The sailor shrugged.

The man came forward.

"Well, I'm the Captain. What's your business proposition?"

"I want to buy passage to the States."

"You an American?"

The Captain was equally unsure of Colquhoun's accent and appearance.

"Yes. Jonathan Buck, from Boston."

"Jonathan Buck?" The Captain sounded surprised. "Johnathan Buck? Is that a fact?"

"Yes."

The Captain gave a snort of laughter.

"Jonathan Buck? The Jonathan Buck who's a gentleman or a soldier? From Boston, U.S.A? You don't look much like either a gentleman or a soldier to me."

"I assure you, I am Jonathan Buck."

"Well, I be damned. I'll take your word for it. If that don't lick cock fighting."

He stepped to the side of the ship and looked up and down the quay.

"You'd better come with me, Jonathan Buck."

Mystified, not a little suspicious, Colquhoun followed the Captain back to the doorway, which led down several steps to what Colquhoun took to be his cabin. Could it be that at last he was going to find out who Jonathan Buck had been and what he had been doing in France? But why had the Captain called him 'gentleman or soldier'?

The Captain sat down at a chart strewn table. He waved Colquhoun to a chair with a great grin on his face.

"Well, Major Grant," he said. "You could make me a rich man."

Major Grant?

For a moment Colquhoun did not react. It was like a heavy blow which for a second is numb.

Major Grant!

It was like a bucket of icy water.

It was impossible that the American Captain could know who he was.

Had he misheard? The Captain was still grinning delightedly at him.

There was no mistaking the mischief in his face.

"What did you call me?"

"Major Grant, of the Eleventh Regiment of English Infantry, if I'm not mistaken."

Colquhoun's heart seemed to stop, then to thump violently. His stomach turned over. He sat very still, staring at the Captain. He had walked into a trap.

At any second the door must burst open, armed men would crowd in: he would be taken prisoner. But it was impossible that this could have happened.

He reached into his pocket for the pistol.

The Captain seemed to think this a great joke. He laughed uproariously, pointed at the pistol, bent forward, clutching his stomach.

"Put that toy away, Major. Here, look at this."

The Captain opened a drawer in the table, rummaged in it for a second, and produced a paper which he passed over to Colquhoun. It was a handbill. It read:

WANTED. DEAD OR ALIVE.

A substantial reward of 100 NAPOLEONS D'OR will be paid for information leading to the arrest, DEAD OR ALIVE, of THE NOTORIOUS SPY MAJOR COLQUHOUN GRANT OF THE 11TH REGIMENT OF ENGLISH INFANTRY masquerading either as an AMERICAN GENTLEMAN, MR JONATHAN BUCK OF BOSTON or as MAJOR JONATHAN BUCK OF THE AMERICAN INFANTRY. MAJOR GRANT was last seen in ORLÉANS at the beginning of FEBRUARY 1813. He is believed to be attempting to flee the country. MAJOR GRANT, alias JONATHAN BUCK, is well built, about thirty to thirty five years of age, somewhat above medium height with dark hair. Any person with any knowledge of the whereabouts of the above NOTORIOUS SPY must contact the nearest POLICE

OR MILITARY AUTHORITY IMMEDIATELY. FAILURE TO DO SO WILL RESULT IN IMPRISONMENT. Any person found aiding or abetting this NOTORIOUS SPY will be PUNISHED BY DEATH.

Signed GENERAL SAVARY
MINISTRY OF POLICE
FEBRUARY 1813

Colquhoun looked up at the Captain, ashen faced.

The Captain laughed again. He had a devil-may-care face and reckless, feral eyes.

"Now ain't that the best joke of the season. 100 god damned *Napoleons d'or* to turn you in. A notorious spy. Never met one before, but sure glad to make the acquaintance of one. Put that peashooter away, Major. I ain't going to turn you in."

Colquhoun put the pistol down on the table.

"Why not?"

"It's the French we should be fighting, not the god damned British. That tinpot Napoleon boxed us into this war. Independence for the States, that was one thing. That was worth fighting you for. But this war is god damned stupid. It makes no sense for the States and none for you. We should be trading partners, not enemies. Mark you, though, it suits me well enough. There's no ship afloat can catch the Wayfarer. Give me a fair wind and an open sea and she'll outrun any god damned chaser. I'll be out of a job when the blockade ends. I'll have to go back to privateering.

Or maybe I'll take up spying. Become a notorious spy."

He laughed again, showing strong white teeth.

"Will you take me, then?" Colquhoun's heart had leapt.

"Ah, well now.... That ain't so easy. I'll not put to sea this dark quarter. Maybe even not next and as things stand I'll not try it by moonlight. There's a god damned seventy four out there right now. He'll get bored and sail off some other place sooner or later, but he could be difficult to get past."

Colquhoun's heart sank again. His disappointment must have shown on his face.

The Captain laughed. "Cheer up Major. It ain't the end of the world. There's always a solution for the resolute and the wicked. Let's think... You can't leave this ship as Jonathan Buck. They'll nab you before the day's out. On the other hand... you can't stay on board... So... Yeah... yeah, that's it. Amos Rostyn. You'll go ashore as Amos Rostyn, as big a god damned rogue as ever cheated the hangman - mark you, a dollar to a cent, they'll have hanged him by now. Now, here's the crib."

He leaned forward across the table.

"Amos Rostyn was - or is - a god damned drunken sot I signed on in Charleston the start of this trip. Couldn't get a cent's worth of work out of him. Useless son of a whore, he jumped ship when we put into New York. I'd have hanged him if he hadn't, sure enough. But by rights he was bound to the ship till we put back into Charleston. The men sign on for the round trip, see. The god damned Froggies know this, of course. They'd pick you up if you said I'd discharged you here. That can't be done.

"What can be done, though, is you can go to the American Consul here and lay a complaint that I've mistreated you. Which I would have done if you'd been Amos. I'd have flogged you to death and back. Lodge forty dollars with the god damned Consul and swear you'll prosecute me for ill-treatment when you get back to the States. No one'll know you ain't the real Amos Rostyn and the Consul'll give you a discharge certificate that'll let you move about free as air to look for another god damned ship and to the devil with the god damned police."

"I haven't got forty dollars."

"Pish, man, what's forty dollars among friends? I'll lend it you. You can pay me back some other time."

He was, Colquhoun reflected, accumulating some interesting debts. But what hope the Captain had given him. When the game had stalled fortune's wheel had suddenly turned.

"Why should you do that? I don't even know your name."

"Penhaligon. Captain Penhaligon, owner and master of the Wayfarer, at your service, Major."

"Penhaligon? That's a Cornish name."

"My folks came from Cornwell back awhile. Wreckers, they were. And pirates, of course. Cornwall got a bit god damned hot so we took ourselves to the States. Means I've more sympathy for you god dammed British than I have for these *sacré* French."

"Why should you risk yourself for me? I'm a complete stranger to you."

Captain Penhaligon sat back in his chair. He smiled, a smile of pure mischief.

"No risk. I ain't no lover of authority. Any chance comes along to poke a stick in the eye of authority and Dick Penhaligon's your man: 'specially if it's French authority. And if you're what they say you are, you're a man after my own god damned heart."

Colquhoun was silent

The Captain raised his eyebrows.

"Well, you are, ain't you?"

"I suppose I must be."

"Well, I reckon so."

He pointed to one of the charts on the table in front of him.

"Come and look here," he said. "Don't go looking for a god damned ship here in Nantes. You won't find one and there's too many *sacré* police around likely to ask questions. Here's the mouth of the Loire... This here's Saint Nazaire on the North bank...A good anchorage, no doubt of it, but when you god damned British get bored out here" - he indicated the open sea on the chart - " you think it a fine thing to come in and put a few shots into anything that's there. So you'll not find a ship there. No, your best bet, I reckon, is to go on along the coast a whiles. There's fishing villages all along the coast."

He drew a finger Westwards across the chart along the coast line.

"Pornichet, see? Try there. You'll find a boat there'll take you out to the blockaders. They're all god damned smugglers or wreckers out there anyway."

Colquhoun stared at the chart, trying to memorize it.

The Captain went to an inner door and shouted for someone. An elderly sailor appeared as if by magic.

"See this lubber?" the Captain indicated Colquhoun. "Fix him up as a sailor. Get him some warm stuff. He's got some walking to do."

The sailor sized up Colquhoun without speaking, nodded, knuckled his forehead, and disappeared. The Captain strolled across to the windows at the back of the cabin.

"Rum place, this," he said. "The terror was worse here than anywhere in France, Paris maybe excepted. Man called Carrier, Jean Baptiste Carrier. A real charmer he was.

France's number one sadistic bastard. He rounded up anyone he could lay his god damned hands on. Aristos, of course. Business people, tradesmen, lawyers, priests of course wherever he could find them. Men or women. Children too. The god damned guillotine was too quick for him. He wanted the poor devils to suffer.

"He put boatloads of them onto barges, took them out midstream here and threw them overboard. He'd tie a man and woman together - Republican marriage, he called it - naked, of course, before heaving them overboard. He hated the clergy most of all. God knows what he did to them..."

"Mark you, I'm not too keen on them myself. A long drop and no priests when it comes to my turn, says I... But to kill them like he did..." He shook his head.

"Not god damned sporting. Or he'd line them up and have them shot one by one down the line. Or starve them to death. Things like that. By the hundreds, thousands maybe. It's left a deep scar that's not forgotten, not by a long chalk."

The woman in the inn, Colquhoun thought. She was probably a victim of that terrible time. What had she said? 'There are still many such as I.' How many years ago had it happened? Fifteen? Eighteen, perhaps. And still the surviving victims were suffering.

"They guillotined him in the end, of course. Too good a way to go for the likes of an all fired bastard like that. They should have paid him in his own god damned coin. But there..."

The Captain pointed South across the river.

"Over there's the Vendée. D'you know about the Vendée?"

Colquhoun shook his head. Father O'Shea had mentioned something about the Vendée being Royalist still.

But the sudden change in his fortune and identity were enough to be thinking about.

There was a brief knock on the door. The old sailor came in with an armful of clothes. He dumped them on the desk.

"Ah ha. Take your pick."

Colquhoun chose a pair of baggy striped trousers, under vest, a greyish none-too-clean shirt, a thick wool pea jacket and roped soled shoes. While he put them on he half listened as the Captain returned to the subject of the Vendée.

"The Revolution didn't interest the Vendée. They went on being staunch Catholics - which of course the god damned Republicans hated - and, worse for them, Royalists. The fighting was cruel, real cruel. On both sides, that's true enough. All of them did things to each other you'd never credit, not in your worst god damned nightmares.

"It ended up the Republicans trying to kill the lot of them when they got the upper hand. Every man, woman and god damned child they could lay their hands on. It left one hell of a lot of unhappy folk over there. They say they'll rebel again, and I shouldn't wonder if that's right, with all this talk of Napoleon getting a god damned thrashing in Russia. I don't know whether the half of it's true but it'll be enough spark to explode the Vendée again. They don't like him, no sir, not one little bit.

"So, how're you doing? Yeah, you look quite the thing. As big a rogue as Amos himself. Amos Rostyn, remember? Here, get him a blanket to take with him... And take this bag. Don't forget your popgun. Now then, forty dollars you'll need... Here... Pay me when the war's over. It's worth forty dollars anyways to pull a trick like this."

He went over to the rear windows as he spoke and peered out onto the quay. He laughed again.

"Hah! This'll lick cock fighting. If we haven't the god damned police just right down there on the quayside. We'll have us some fun … Ill treatment, remember."

He flung open the door to the deck, grinned, and pushed Colquhoun up the steps.

"Get off my ship then, you son of a whore."

Colquhoun stumbled up the stairs onto the deck, unprepared for the Captain's sudden action. The Captain seized him by the scruff of the neck and planted a hefty kick on his bottom, propelling him off balance into the hatch by the gangplank. He fell over it awkwardly, barking his shins painfully.

The sailor who had barred his path aboard was still sitting on the hatch. He jumped up with an oath, clenching his fists.

The Captain stood over Colquhoun, hands on hips, and loosed a torrent of foul tongued abuse at him. The pain of the fall sparked Colquhoun into reaction. He scrambled to his feet

"You bastard. You god damned bastard."

"I'll give you bastard, you worthless sot."

The Captain advanced on him again.

The sailor raised his fists.

Colquhoun headed for the gangplank.

"I'll get you in jail for this."

Below him, on the quayside, the startled faces of three gendarmes were staring up at them.

"You god damned bastard. You can't treat your crew like animals. I'm not a dog to be kicked around. I'll see you in jail."

"Like hell you will."

The Captain was holding the sailor back. The man's face was alight with sadistic pleasure.

"You jump ship here you're the one'll land in jail. A Froggy jail. You'll see a god damned bit about god damned ill treatment then. You'll rot in hell where you belong and good riddance to you, you bum."

"That's what you think, you slave driver. That's all you are, a slave driver. I've forty dollars in my pocket says I'll see you in Court back in the States."

The Captain took a run at Colquhoun. He stepped smartly onto the gang plank and ran down onto the quay. He turned and they shook their fists at each other, shouting obscenities.

The gendarmes had stopped at the bottom of the gangway. They were looking interested. Colquhoun turned to them. He said, in English,

"See that bastard there? He ain't no better than a slave driver. I ain't no slave. He can't treat his crew like he does. Where's the American Consul? I'll see him in jail, I will, so help me God."

The gendarmes looked at him and up at the Captain. Their eyes were bright with malice: men who enjoyed violence.

One of them called up to the Captain:

"Are you having trouble, Monsieur. Do you want us to deal with this one?"

"No. Leave him be," the Captain called back. "Let him alone. Let him go to the American Consul with his god damned forty dollars. Much good will it do him, the god damned skunk. You're wasting your money, Amos. You'll never see me in court. Let him be and to hell with him."

The men nodded, disappointed. One of them jerked his head in the direction of the town. He spat at Colquhoun's feet.

"Centre," he said. They strolled off.

Captain Penhaligon was leaning casually over the ship's side.

"On your way, Amos Rostyn." He grinned down at Colquhoun. "And good luck to you."

Nobody looked twice at the sailor asking directions to the American Consulate.

Colquhoun found it quite easily, guided by the Stars and Stripes flag that flew from a flagpole on the front of the building. The Consul, if indeed it was the Consul he saw, was interested only in the forty dollars that Colquhoun produced. It crossed his mind, Colquhoun was pretty certain, to accuse him of stealing it and to pocket the money himself, but for whatever reason it might have been he thought better of it, recorded Colquhoun's complaint of ill treatment against Captain Penhaligon of the Wayfarer and wrote out and handed Colquhoun a discharge in the name of Amos Rostyn, stamped with the authority of the United States of America.

Colquhoun draped the rolled blanket over his shoulder, slung the bag across his body and set off immediately, walking out of the town on the road running West to Saint Nazaire and the coast.

The day was already dying as he cleared the city. He had stopped to fill his bag with provisions - enough to last a couple of days. He would sleep rough. He had hardened up so well since leaving Paris that the prospect of wrapping himself in the blanket and sleeping on the ground held no qualms for him now.

He left the road for the shelter of some pine trees, scooped himself a shallow bed in the sandy soil and was soon asleep.

It was raining when he rejoined the road in a gloomy dawn light. The country looked infinitely depressing, flat, wild with scrub and pine trees, a swampy wilderness in which a few small farmers had carved out miserable looking patches of sterile looking sand on which to build their hovels. Their emaciated dogs barked at him as he passed. Were it not for the hope of getting out of France Colquhoun would have found it a forbiddingly forlorn place.

The river had widened into a great tidal estuary long before Saint Nazaire came into view. The road led into the town without any apparent branches off that would keep him away from civilization. The land around him, the swampy low spots, the endless scrub and trees, looked featureless and uninviting. There had been very little traffic during the morning's walk. The rain was still pouring sullenly. He decided to risk it and keep to the road.

It was a fair sized town, big enough to have side streets and back streets through which he could pass unnoticed. Then curiosity overcame him.

Who knows? The day might come when a knowledge of the layout of the town could be of value to Lord Wellington. He walked cautiously towards the harbour. The town was heavily garrisoned. He could see gun emplacements thickly sited on the sea walls and a fort and barracks large enough for a formidable garrison.

He could see what must be a boat building yard, but it looked forlorn and unused. There were fishing boats just visible on the shore and a jumble of masts in the harbour. Apart from the wet and huddled figures of a few sentries gazing out to sea no one was about. There was little visible from where he stood that would not be seen just as well from the sea.

Thankfully he melted into the back streets and found the road leading on Westwards. It led away from the sea, a rutted cart track, across an empty land of scrub and sand.

In the dark, sodden afternoon he was again alone in the miserable landscape.

He slept that night in the dubious shelter of a low sand dune. The rain stopped sometime in the evening and the sky became bright with stars. The temperature dropped quickly, an uncomfortable reminder that he was soaking wet. He dug deeper into the sand to get below the cold wind that had driven away the clouds.

He was not far from the sea. He could hear it somewhere ahead breaking rhythmically on the beach. Perhaps this time tomorrow he would be safe on one of His Majesty's Men of War. The thought was enough to warm him.

Pornichet was a huddle of fisherman's cottages set close to the tide line above a tiny natural harbour.

Colquhoun studied it from the shelter of a pine covered dune in the early light. There was no visible activity in the village. There were some boats at anchor in the harbour. Others were drawn up on the wide sandy beach among the usual seagull haunted debris of nets and floats that were part of every fishing village he had ever seen.

It seemed to be fairly low tide. Probably the men would have put out to sea before it had got light.

As the morning brightened smoke began to climb from cottage chimneys. Women appeared from time to time. He thought one of the cottages must be a bakery as they all headed for it before disappearing back indoors.

The tide was still going out. Presumably the fishermen would come back ashore in the late morning when the tide was well on its way in again.

A man came out of one of the cottages and headed for the boats on the beach. Colquhoun watched him for a while. He sat down pipe in mouth and began working at a pile of nets.

The tide had turned. The breakers were creeping up the shore.

Colquhoun skirted the village and drifted onto the beach.

The man was old, his dark face deeply lined. He looked as though he had once been powerful but now had shrunk with age so that his clothes hung loose on him.

"Good day, Monsieur."

The man scarcely looked up.

"Monsieur, could I hire a boat here for a day?"

The man looked up and studied him without speaking.

"Would it be possible, Monsieur?"

"Maybe." He returned his gaze to the nets.

"How would I do it?"

The man looked out to sea and pointed with his chin. Colquhoun had not noticed. There was a boat half a mile or so from shore. It was under sail, heading in towards them.

Further conversation seemed useless. Colquhoun sat down and waited.

The boat headed into the harbour. There were two men on it, busy first with berthing the boat and then with unloading their cargo. Two or three women appeared and helped carry away some baskets of fish.

The old man got up and plodded across to the boat. The two fishermen looked across to where Colquhoun waited. One of them shrugged his shoulders. The old man plodded back. He jerked his head in the direction of the boat.

Colquhoun got up and strolled across.

The two fishermen did not look overjoyed to see him. They stared at him suspiciously.

"Good day, Messieurs."

No reply.

"Can you help me? I want to hire a boat."

"What for?"

'Here goes,' Colquhoun said to himself. 'Neck or nothing.' And aloud: "To get to the English ship on station out there."

Silence. Automatically, the two men raised their eyes and looked out to sea. They looked back at him and out to sea again. Had suspicion changed to hostility? They certainly did not look happy.

"Why?"

"That's my business."

"How much'll you pay?"

"Ten *Napoleons d'or* for the hire of the boat. Fifty more when you deliver me safely to the ship."

"Huh. Not worth it. It's agin the law, that."

Mildly encouraging. The man's first reaction had been mercenary.

"Fifty five then. Sixty. That's my limit."

The men looked at each other. One raised his eyebrows and shrugged. The other said:

"When d'you want to go?"

"Today."

"Let's see your money."

In anticipation of this, Colquhoun had put ten *Napoleons* in his pocket. He produced them and held them out in his hand. The men gazed at them.

There was a long silence. One of the men swallowed noisily

"Where's the sixty *Napoleons*, then?"

"You'll get them when we reach the ship. You have my word for it."

"Huh. What's that worth?"

"Take it or leave it."

They looked at each other again, and all round the bleak shore line and village as though to ensure that no one overheard them. Colquhoun wondered what was going through their minds. The second man shrugged again.

"All right. Come back here this afternoon when the tide's near onto full."

Colquhoun nodded. "I'll be here."

Not that he felt in the least bit happy about it.

The men were altogether too surly. The looks that they had exchanged had been heavy with unspoken messages.

Every instinct warned him not to trust them.

He retreated to his vantage point overlooking the village.

Should the men have agreed so readily to take him that afternoon? There was no Man of War in sight. But maybe they knew exactly where it was. Would they be able to locate it before it got dark? Would the men risk approaching an English ship at night? And would they want to sail back in darkness?

To add to his unease it was not long before a man and woman - not, so far as he could tell one of the fishermen he had spoken with - left the village in what seemed like a hurry on the road to Saint Nazaire leading a donkey loaded with two wicker panniers. Without a doubt the panniers would be full of fish, for sale at the Saint Nazaire market, but even so...

He watched them clear the village. They stopped. They looked back and all around. He kept very still. They talked for a moment. Then the man left the donkey and hurried on ahead by himself.

Suppose the two men had already talked about the stranger's request. Word would have spread quickly. Suppose they had decided it would be more profitable to alert the Authorities. No doubt there would be a reward from the police for turning in someone asking for passage to an English ship. The man with the donkey had gone on ahead with what looked like great purpose. It must be his imagination, now that he was so close. Nevertheless…

He checked the priming of the pistol. The powder was dry. He put it back into his pocket, wishing that he had a pair to it. If it came to an emergency he would shoot the man who had done most of the talking. The other would probably not give much trouble on his own.

Colquhoun watched the tide coming in again.

One of the men reappeared at the harbour. Colquhoun left his vantage point, skirted the village and went to meet him. The man was definitely uneasy. He did not look at Colquhoun as he said:

"There's not time today to get out there and back. Tomorrow. Before it gets light. It's dangerous work. Give me the ten *Napoleons* now if you still want to go."

There was no doubting the shiftiness in the man's voice and manner.

"Tomorrow."

"Now."

"Not one."

The man would not look him in the eye.

Colquhoun said: "All right. Forget it. I'll be on my way and find someone else."

"No. No. Alright. Tomorrow. I'll take you tomorrow. Be on the beach from midnight on. Give me the money then."

Colquhoun nodded. The delay was frustrating but as the

reasoning echoed his own doubts it was slightly reassuring.

He said, "All right. I'll be here."

"You can come in the village. Wait there. Get a meal. That'd be best."

"No. I'll be here at midnight."

"Where you going now, then?"

Colquhoun did not reply. He set off back along the beach feeling the man's eyes following him.

He did not look back.

A meal would have been welcome. His food was getting short, though water, after the recent rain, was no problem. It tasted no worse, drunk from a pool, than the water that had kept him going a thousand times in Spain and Portugal. But his instinct was shouting at him, the sixth sense that he had followed so often and which so often had saved him from capture or maybe death.

He walked back two or three miles towards Saint Nazaire, well clear of the fishing village, and found a vantage spot hidden in the scrub overlooking the road. He would have liked to go further but if the man with the donkey had raised the alarm it would not be long before they came looking for him.

He lay and waited.

He heard them before he saw them.

Snatches of a marching song, then a tiny tremor in the ground, then the clink of metal on metal. There were two companies of them. Colquhoun counted them as they passed him. Ninety two blue coated soldiers in the first company: eighty five in the second.

He could not be sure, but he thought the civilian hurrying along with them was the man he had seen that morning leaving the village with the donkey.

They were led by a mounted officer with a pinned up

sleeve and an eye patch. There were two other officers on foot, sub-lieutenants probably. The soldiers were little more than boys, herded by their non-commissioned officers, struggling with the step, the pace, the packs and the muskets they carried.

A single platoon of Lord Wellington's army would have seen them off in a second. Be that as it may, though, nearly two hundred men, however ill trained, would be more than enough to run him to ground.

The light was beginning to fade. Colquhoun waited until they were out of sight, then set off on the road back to Saint Nazaire and Nantes.

He thought there might have been a road block at Saint Nazaire. It was dark well before he reached the town, but there was no sound, no sign or smell of a fire as he approached. He was pretty certain a road picket would have some sort of fire to ward off the February cold. He waited. Nothing. Cautiously, he went into the town then fast through it and back onto the empty road.

He walked all night, a hard, driving pace to put as much distance as he could between himself and Pornichet.

In the early light, dog tired and ravenous, he was back in Nantes.

Chapter 12

PORNIC

Yet another turn of fortune's wheel.

In a way Colquhoun had been lucky. There had been no roadblocks, no random police demands to produce his papers and justify his identity. Although they were looking for Jonathan Buck no one, presumably, would yet be suspicious that Jonathan Buck and Amos Rostyn were one and the same.

That happy state of affairs would not last for long, though. When they failed to find him at Pornichet they would alert the whole area, Nantes certainly included. If the police were now looking for an escaping sailor trying to get out to the blockading English ships they would surely soon put two and two together.

No one would dare take him out now. Even if he could find someone who was potentially willing he could not even match the reward money offered for his capture. It would be far simpler and safer to turn him in. The situation was getting deadly serious. He was running out of options.

He wondered whether to try to find a ship that would take him to America as Amos Rostyn, but dismissed the possibility immediately. He did not even know the language of the sea - the names of the masts and sails and ropes and all the paraphernalia of a ship's equipment, let alone have any idea of what his duties would be as a sailor or how to carry them out. He would not last a minute.

He wondered whether to go back to Captain Penhaligon and the Wayfarer, but pride forbade it. The Captain would be contemptuous of a man who could not look after himself and came running back for help. It would be too painful if the Captain laughed at him, as Colquhoun suspected he would. Capture and even death would be preferable to such ignominy. And anyway, what more could Captain Penhaligon do? No, he could not go near the Wayfarer again.

In honour, too, perhaps he should get rid of Amos Rostyn's discharge certificate. If he was arrested with it, it would lead straight back to the American Consul and the Wayfarer. Captain Penhaligon would be in deep trouble. It would probably be safe enough to use it for a day or so more - perhaps only this very morning. After that he would have to get rid of it.

The only remaining option, so far as he could see, would be to steal a rowing boat and to row himself out to the English man of war on station somewhere out at sea. He had messed around in rowing boats as a boy - albeit without any great enthusiasm as his dream had always been to join the army - and surely his recent experience on the Loire should help.

Assuming he could do it, how long would it take? Days, presumably. It should be relatively easy in the estuary as the river would carry him downstream. The open sea would be another matter. Even assuming the weather held calm. Maybe he would never find the ship. Well, it was a chance he would just have to take.

Where, then, to steal a boat? That, Colquhoun reckoned, should be easy on the jumbled and clustered waterfront here in Nantes. Pick a boat and take it confidently as though he owned it. Probably no one would give him a second glance.

Absorbed with his dilemma Colquhoun had drifted back to the quayside, and found himself near the tavern where he had eaten two days ago. He was starving. He went inside and ordered food and drink.

Immediately, but too late, he realised his mistake. Should anyone recognize him, they might remember how he had been dressed last time.

"Monsieur is a sailor now?"

A woman's voice. He cursed himself for an idiotic fool. It was the beggar woman to whom he had given his change. Her dead eyes were expressionless. He looked past her and round the room, fearing she might be overheard.

She nodded. "I think Monsieur is in trouble? A fugitive, perhaps?"

What was going on behind those blank eyes? Whatever it was, surely she would hate and fear the police. Surely she would hate the State that had brought her so low.

"Yes."

She nodded again.

"Perhaps I can help you, Monsieur. Not here. There are eyes and ears here. Follow me out. It is not safe here."

She turned away, and moved slowly among the customers, hands held out, pausing until she saw whether they would ignore her or reach into their pockets for a few *sous*.

Dare he trust her? What was the alternative? She could be a police spy. But if she was would she not have left him and hurried off to alert them while he was still eating? All she had to do was point him out to the police. No. Surely not. She had the same sort of aura as the Spanish guerrillas, the same pent up hatred, the same simmering fury.

Colquhoun got up and paid his bill. He sauntered to the door. She came past him, holding out her hands to him as she went. He gave her the change from his meal. She bobbed a tiny curtsy, not looking at him, and set off along the quay.

The woman turned into a street running at right angles to the quay, and then into a side street and on into a narrow lane of closely packed low houses, unpainted, tumbledown, broken shuttered with ill fitting doors. The lane was foul with rubbish and sewage. Some filthy, ragged children, thin as lathes, stared at him with hostile eyes as he passed.

He wondered whether she was leading him into a trap. Such things were common enough. A woman luring a - usually drunken - sailor or stranger into the slums, usually on the promise of a quick coupling, her partner in crime waiting with a knife or a cudgel as the victim undid his breeches, and the body thrown that night into the river. Hardly an eyebrow would be raised by the floating corpse of an unknown sailor. He felt for the reassuring butt of the pistol in his pocket.

She did not stop, but led him backwards and forwards, he

was pretty sure, round the side streets and narrow lanes. She stopped briefly at the corners, ostensibly looking round about for alms givers. Wherever they were going, she wanted no witnesses.

She must have been satisfied that they were not being followed or watched. She stopped in one of the streets that he was sure they had been into before. She looked about her and vanished into one of the rickety doorways. He waited a minute, and followed.

It was dark inside and he stepped back into the light.

She said, "Don't be afraid. Come in and shut the door. Quick."

Reluctantly, he did as she said, the pistol in his hand. He cocked it as he pulled it out of his pocket.

She laughed, a cynical snort in the gloom.

"Monsieur does not trust me."

His eyes were getting used to the dark. There were a table and chair, a bed in the corner, not much besides. There was no one else in the room. There were no internal doors. It must have been a one room lodging. She was standing by the table.

She said: "Who is after you, Monsieur?"

"Your pardon, Madame. One has heard stories."

He eased the hammer of the pistol forward to uncock it and put it back into his pocket.

"Of course."

"Every one, I fear, is after me, as you put it."

"Why? You do not look a criminal."

"I am an escaped prisoner of war. My life is forfeit if I am taken."

"Ah. An English soldier, then?"

"Yes."

"An officer, of course. Why should they shoot you?"

"They call me a spy. It is a long story."

She nodded. "What are doing in Nantes?"

"I am trying to find a boat to take me out to the English blockade ships."

"I guessed as much. You are not the first."

"No, I am sure not."

"Have you tried already to find a boat?"

"Yes. At Pornichet, yesterday. They alerted the authorities. They sent two hundred soldiers to find me, from Saint Nazaire, I imagine."

She shook her head.

"Ah. That is bad. The alarm will be raised all along the coast, but they will probably take some time searching Pornichet for you before they do so. You have moved quickly to be back here again. But they work quickly also. They are very efficient when they want to be. You must be gone today."

"I know. But how? It seems it is not so easy to find a boat."

"You are the wrong side of the river, Monsieur. Do you not know that across the river is the Vendée? The Vendée that has never accepted this wicked regime, nor ever shall. You must cross the river to find a boat."

"Will I find one there? How?"

"Because over there any enemy of the State is a friend to the people of the Vendée. You must cross the Loire and take the road that leaves the river and runs west across country. When you reach the sea you will come to a village called Pornic. It is about fifty kilometres from Nantes. A full day's march for you, I think. Go to the house of Pierre Gillet in the Rue de la Marine. It is just back from the quay, number sixteen. Tell him that Amalie Moreau sent you. You can trust him. Talk openly to him. He will take you."

Colquhoun was silent, digesting yet another turn of fortune's wheel.

"Do you doubt me, Monsieur?" There was anger in her voice.

"No, Madame. I counted myself almost lost half an hour ago. I cannot believe my good fortune. Why should you do this for me? Why should Monsieur Gillet take me? Why should he help me escape?"

"I have told you already, Monsieur. We will do anything to destroy that little Corsican who sits on the throne of France. I come from the Vendée, Monsieur. When I was a girl - no more than a girl - the soldiers of the Revolution killed my family. They raped me. Not one. Five of them. They took turns to rape me. Pitilessly. A child. Their officers looked on and laughed as I wept and screamed for their mercy. They burned our house. They burned our whole village. They killed everyone they could find. They left me for dead. On that day my childhood ended. I live for the day that the Vendée will rise again. Nor shall it be long in coming."

Again Colquhoun was silent. What could he say? She must be younger than him: she looked twenty years older. What could her life have been compared to his? He wondered if she had known a day's happiness since the massacre of her family.

She said: "You do not speak, Monsieur."

"Madame, what can I say that can atone for what you have suffered. I am ashamed for my sex."

She laughed, the same mirthless snort.

"Oh, I have taken my revenge over the years. Many times. See here."

She lifted her ragged skirt to her knees. Strapped to her - shapely, Colquhoun could not help noticing - right calf was a leather holster carrying on the outside a useful looking pistol and on the inside a thin bladed dagger

"I learned to look after myself, Monsieur, believe me."

Colquhoun looked into the dead eyes.

"I believe you, Madame. I should not wish to cross you, I think."

For the first time a faint smile lightened her face and sparked momentarily in her eyes. It was the smile of the predator that sees its prey.

"You are a wise man, Monsieur."

"And Monsieur Gillet. Who is he?"

"A fisherman - now. He has no cause to love Napoleon. You may trust him."

"How much will he need to take me?"

"I do not understand you."

"I will have to pay him."

"He will take you for the honour of France, Monsieur. He will take you because his doing so is a blow struck for our liberty and the liberty of France. He will not take your money." There was scorn in her voice.

"Once again, I must beg your pardon, Madame. Please forgive me. I did not realise… Would it also be an insult if I begged you to take some money to thank you for coming to my assistance?"

She shrugged. "It is not necessary, but if you wish, I will not refuse. A professional beggar earns more than you would imagine. But, if you wish… You must not delay here, Monsieur. You have very little time before Nantes is alerted. Perhaps we are already too late. The police are formidable here. They have spies everywhere. They fear that the people have not forgotten the horrors of the Revolution and the Vendée war. And they are right to do so. Our day is fast approaching…"

She broke off. The thin smile that again briefly brought her face to life was blood chilling.

"You must cross the river immediately. I will show you the road to the bridge. You must cross at three or four minutes to midday. There is always a police guard on the bridge whose job it is to check the identities of those they do not know. The guard changes at midday. For a few minutes the old guard are thinking of nothing but their relief and their *déjeuner*. For a few minutes they do not want trouble nor anything that might detain them on the bridge. When the new guard comes on duty they will be alert and aggressive. Do not be late. And let us pray that word of your escape at Pornichet has not yet reached Nantes."

Colquhoun gave her the ten *Napoleons d'or* that he had shown the fishermen at Pornichet. She held the coins in her hand for a long time, looking intently at them, her face expressionless. He would have liked to have given her more, but Scottish prudence told him that he might still have need of every *sou* that he had. He wondered if he had insulted her. It was impossible to know what she was thinking as she gazed at the gold coins. Abruptly, she closed her hand over them.

"Come on," she said.

She left the hovel first, signalled to him to follow her and led him back into a main street which he could see led directly to a bridge over the Loire onto the mid stream island.

Without a backward glance she vanished into the throng of people and traffic.

There was a clockmaker's shop in the street with several clocks in its window. All told the same time. He had to assume that they were correct. He judged it would take him two or three minutes to reach the bridge and one or two to get to the middle. While he waited he took the opportunity to refill his bag with bread and some cheese and dried meat.

At six minutes to midday he set off.

He walked with a confidence that he was far from feeling. He saw the police guard immediately, half a dozen of them, in the middle of the bridge. They had stopped somebody and were examining his papers.

At the same moment out of the corner of his eye he saw, still some way off, a squad of six police marching along the quay towards the bridge.

The relief guard. Almost certainly. Whoever they were, they would be behind him when he reached the centre of the bridge

There would be no escape. If the police on the bridge stopped him there could be no retreat, no dash back the way he had come to lose himself in the streets behind the quay. He could only pray that no one was yet interested in Amos Rostyn.

Heart in mouth, Colquhoun strode onto the bridge. He saw one of the policemen there pull a large watch out of his pocket. He said something to his comrades. They gave the man back his papers, waved him on, and, as Colquhoun approached, they turned their backs on the passers-by and stood looking out over the river.

Colquhoun walked past them. They did not look at him.

There was, of course, a further bridge to take him off the island back onto the mainland, but the woman had not mentioned a guard on it. There were far less people there and the river bank had far less shipping . Probably a guard was thought unnecessary. He crossed to the Southern mainland without challenge.

He had no trouble finding the road to Pornic. At an obvious road junction the word 'Pornic' with an arrow pointing westwards was beautifully carved into the stonework of one of the houses. For the second time Colquhoun walked out of Nantes.

Fifty kilometres. Thirty miles, more or less. He might have reached Pornic that night, but exhaustion overcame him once the tension of possible arrest in Nantes had left him. He forced himself on until the light began to fade. The country seemed deserted. Several times he passed the overgrown ruins of what must have been farms or hamlets. They still bore the scars of their torching by the Revolutionary army in crumbling walls and mouldering blackened timbers that lay forlornly among the weeds.

He found a stone barn that was still partially roofed. He wondered whether it would be safe to make a fire. The smoke just might be seen, and he needed to sleep without one ear and eye open. Eating restored his strength somewhat, and, he had to admit it, his morale. Being a hunted fugitive on the run on his feet dressed as a sailor in a country where potentially every man's hand was against him was a far cry from the excitement of his life in Spain.

He wished he had the companionship of León. Two brains, two pairs of eyes and someone to talk to would have made things a lot easier.

He made himself as comfortable as he could and rolled himself up in the blanket.

Exhausted as he was, he slept uneasily. Amalie Moreau haunted his dreams. Who was she, anyway? He kept seeing her dead eyes and the flicker of her smile. She had the thin bladed dagger in her hand. It dripped blood.

His instinct had been right as he had stood on the threshold of her lodging. She was no helpless beggar. She was a merciless cut throat. How many men had she murdered? Like the Spanish guerrillas, her revenge would probably include some ghastly form of torture. Yet he could not condemn her and in his dreams she was seductively attractive to him. He kept jerking awake, alternating between hope that Pierre Gillet would take him to safety and fear that his luck must run out.

And as at Idanha a Nova, he eventually fell into a deep coma and overslept. He had intended to move before it was light, but the sound of fast moving hooves mingled with his dreams and he came awake aware that they were no dream, that the day had dawned and that there were horsemen passing his hiding place.

He lay absolutely still. The horses clattered past. Cautiously he raised his head.

They were gendarmes. Four of them. Going at a determined gallop on the road towards Pornic.

For long minutes Colquhoun did not move. There was only one likely reason for their urgency. They were on their way to raise the alarm. Not only that. Had he woken and gone on as he had intended they would almost certainly have seen him and demanded his papers. The game would have been up.

Well, it wasn't. His luck had held.

He had, he reckoned, walked about ten miles from Nantes yesterday. Twenty to go. Seven hours walking, probably. The morning was sunless so it was impossible to tell exactly what time it was. Fairly early, from the feel of it. Say eight o'clock. If he set out now he should reach Pornic about three o'clock. If he waited a couple of hours before starting he should reach the village just before it got dark.

He would have time to find the Rue de la Marine. There should not be too many people about at that time. Time enough here, then, for a leisurely breakfast.

He had expected Pornic to be like Pornichet - little more than a cluster of hovels.

He was wrong.

It was a substantial village rising up a steep hill on the north side of a long natural sea inlet. The inlet was crowded with fishing boats along a wide quay beyond the sea end of which, on a rocky promontory, he could see the towers of a chateau behind walls loop holed for musketry with a battery of gun emplacements covering the entrance to the inlet. Across the inlet the land, tree covered, rose again. Past the chateau the inlet widened for some distance between craggy rocks, almost low cliffs. Colquhoun could just see the grey sea beyond.

There was a heavy military presence. There were too many blue coated infantrymen for comfort in the square by the church at the top of the hill and in the cafés and streets running steeply down to the waterfront. They appeared to be middle-aged or elderly men at the end of their service life, third rate soldiers fit only for garrison duty. They did not appear to be popular. They stood apart from the villagers who passed them by without greeting, more like an army of occupation than the fellow countrymen of the inhabitants. They were badly turned out and slack looking. From their demeanour they could not yet be on the look out for an escaped prisoner. He supposed that these men were off duty and had not yet been informed of the alert.

Whatever the reason, thank God.

Colquhoun had decided that boldness would be his best

bet. He had walked resolutely into the village as the light was beginning to fade, head held high as though familiar with it and its people. It would, he reckoned, have drawn far more attention to himself to do anything else.

The Rue de la Marine was one street back from the quay, an unbroken row of one storey fishermens' cottages facing towards the inlet. He noted the position of number sixteen, a low terraced cottage with one door and a window either side. He walked back out of the village.

Some of the villagers had glanced curiously at him. The soldiers had ignored him.

He waited until it was well dark before venturing back into Pornic.

He felt sure there must be a patrol either on the quay or visiting it regularly. He waited in the darkness of a doorway. Sure enough, after perhaps twenty minutes a lantern appeared from the direction of the fortified chateau. By its dim swinging light he could glimpse the uniforms and weapons of an armed patrol, six or eight men. They marched almost the length of the quay then turned about and vanished into the village.

Colquhoun waited a minute longer, then slipped into the Rue de la Marine. His knock at the door of number sixteen was at first unanswered. He knocked again.

There was movement behind the door and a voice: -
"Who's there?"
"I am come from Amalie Moreau."
Silence.
"Monsieur Gillet? Amalie Moreau sent me."

The sound of a bolt being drawn. The door opened a few inches. Pale light silhouetted a face.

"Amalie?"

"Yes. She told me to come to you."

The door opened.

"Come in, then."

The man stood aside to let him in, then stepped past Colquhoun to peer up and down the street. He stepped back, closed the door and bolted it.

The cottage reeked of fish.

A bright fire burned in the hearth. The only other light was a single candle. The remains of a meal were on the table. A second man sat by the fire, his face turned towards Colquhoun and the door. He did not speak.

The man who had opened the door said:

"I am Pierre Gillet. What business of Amalie's brings you here?"

The man was probably in his fifties. The room was too dark to see clearly, but he was strongly built and Colquhoun thought the weather beaten face peering at him was hard and determined.

"Amalie Moreau told me to come to you and that you would be able to help me. I am an English army officer. My name is Colquhoun Grant. I am an officer of Lord Wellington's army in Spain."

He stopped and waited for Gillet's reaction. Nothing.

"I was captured by your army in Portugal and sent back to France on parole. I was already in France when I learned from intercepted dispatches that I was to be handed over to your secret police. I believe I was to have been shot. So I escaped. Whether or not I should have been executed then my life is forfeit now if I am taken. My only hope of escape is by boat out to an English blockader."

"Ah. Has anyone seen you come here?"

"I do not think so. I have been as careful as possible. I

waited for the patrol to pass before coming. I do not think anyone has seen me."

Gillet nodded, studying Colquhoun, weighing him up.

"In what way did Amalie say I might help you?"

"She said you would be able to help me get out to the English blockaders."

Gillet nodded again, unsurprised, as though he had known that Colquhoun would say this.

"You are, presumably, a fugitive? By which I mean, the authorities are actively searching for you?"

"Yes, and I fear that your garrison has been alerted to my escape. Some gendarmes came past me on the road from Nantes early this morning - Oh, don't worry on that score. They did not see me - I imagine they were on their way here to raise the alarm."

Gillet contemplated this for a while.

"Hum. I have heard nothing of this. There has been no alarm in the village today. Perhaps you are mistaken. But it is true that the garrison commander here is old. He is idle and stupid. He is incapable of moving quickly - luckily for us."

Colquhoun's heart rose. If Gillet was already thinking of them as allies against the garrison it augured well. Gillet went on:

"The Customs and the Marine are a different matter, though. They are far more alert. They are efficient when they want to be and they have a fast cutter."

He relapsed into a silence that Colquhoun was reluctant to break.

At length Gillet said:

"This is my son, Pierre also."

The man sitting by the fire did not move. He sat looking at Colquhoun without speaking. He was youngish, probably rising thirty, strongly built like his father. His face was expressionless.

Colquhoun said, "How do you do?"

The young Pierre did not answer.

His father said. "So Amalie sent you? How do you know her?"

"She came to my aid in Nantes. She saw that I was in trouble and came and offered to help me."

"Ah, Amalie." There was affection, a tenderness, in Gillet's voice. Colquhoun wondered why.

"Normally this would not carry any great risk. If you are right, though…" Gillet left the sentence unfinished. "But we must not lose the opportunity. If the risk is increased we will nevertheless have to take it. There is a seventy-four on station taking on water at Noirmoutier at the moment. She will be there for a day or so yet."

"May I understand then that you will take me?"

"Of course, Monsieur. If Amalie has sent you I will take you. Do not worry. When the authorities are not looking - which means when they are bribed sufficiently - there is always a certain amount of traffic with the English." He smiled. " Sadly, an escaping English officer is too large a fish for them to turn a blind eye to. So we will have to be careful. But I do not think it will be too difficult. Noirmoutier is not far. We will be fishing tomorrow. You shall come with us, that is all."

Just like that! Colquhoun could hardly believe his ears.

"You make it sound easy, Monsieur Gillet."

"It will be, Monsieur. No, do not thank me. It is not necessary. Amalie told you our story?"

"No. No, she told me nothing about you other than that I can trust you and that you are no lover of Napoleon."

Gillet's laugh was as bitter as had been Amalie's.

"I am no lover of the Revolution, nor Napoleon, nor his Empire. I was a landowner when the Vendée rose against the Revolution in '93. Young Pierre here was a boy of ten. I left my home and family to fight with the Whites, as we called ourselves. As opposed to the Blues - the Revolutionaries. We did well to start with. But of course they were too strong for us. It soon degenerated into the most horrible of what is now called guerrilla warfare. It went on until '96.

"We were finished then, utterly worn out. Starving. Exhausted. You see young Pierre there? That he does not speak. I will tell you why. He was my courier. He brought me food and information. One day when he returned to his mother the Blues had been there. Our house had been burned to the ground. The heads of his mother and all his brothers and sisters were stuck on stakes at the gates. He has never recovered from the sight."

Colquhoun looked at young Pierre.

The man's face was blank as he stared back at Colquhoun.

Gillet said: "That is why I am a fisherman. If I had not changed my identity they would have hunted me down. So I disappeared, and we reappeared here as Pierre Gillet father and son."

"I see." There seemed nothing else he could say.

Gillet shrugged. "Then you will also see why I will do anything I can to hasten Napoleon's downfall."

"Amalie Moreau said almost the same."

"Of course. She is my niece."

It was cold and dark when they left the house. Young Pierre had gone on ahead. He reappeared at the cottage door and nodded.

"Good lad." His father patted him on the shoulder. "Coast's clear. Come on."

They did not speak as they crossed the quay. There were other men dimly glimpsed moving about in the darkness but no one took any notice of them.

Gillet's boat was fair sized with two masts. So far as Colquhoun could tell, it looked a sturdy sea going craft.

Whatever young Pierre's disability might have been he came to life on the boat, wordlessly casting off, poling the boat out into the inlet and hurrying to hoist the stern sail. Colquhoun sensed and heard, rather than saw, that there were other boats similarly preparing for sea and moving out into the tide.

Gillet said. "Come, Monsieur. Stand close up to the main mast. If the alarm has been raised they will certainly stop and search us on our way out. I am going to wrap the main sail round the mast with you inside it. Make yourself as small as you can and do not move a muscle until I give you the word."

Wrapped up and swathed in the heavy wet canvas Colquhoun could hardly breathe.

After some minutes he could hear shouting and then raised, muffled voices. He thought the boat had stopped moving. They seemed to be waiting for something.

They seemed to be waiting for a very long time.

He heard something bump against the side of the boat, more muffled voices, booted feet on the deck, more voices, a laugh, and he sensed that whoever had come aboard had gone. There was another bump on the side, and he thought the boat was moving again, rocking very gently as it went.

Breathing was difficult. He must have used up all the air. He felt hot, started sweating and felt panic rising in him. He pushed against the canvas. It was unyielding, like a shroud or a winding sheet pressing on him, suffocating him. His head began to pound. Sweat was pouring off him. He was fighting now for every breath.

He was going to die wrapped up like an Egyptian mummy.

The claustrophobia was terrifying.

He tried to call out but the sound was inchoate and muffled. His lungs were bursting. Part of his mind was wondering if Gillet could have done this deliberately, that perhaps after all it was a trap to rob him, kill him and pitch him into the sea.

Then, abruptly, the movement of the boat changed. It was rolling and pitching.

They must have cleared the inlet and reached open water. And simultaneously the sail was being unwrapped, and he could breathe again. He slumped to the bottom of the mast, the sweat suddenly icy cold in the sea air.

"Forgive me, Monsieur, but it was a very necessary precaution. We are safe now. Are you alright?"

"I will be in a minute. Dear God. To be wrapped up like that is not amusing."

He gulped in the clean sea air and gradually his heart stopped its wild thumping.

"Who came aboard?"

"Soldiers from the chateau. They are looking for a notorious escaping spy. They say he was seen at Pornichet some days ago trying to hire a boat to take him out to the English blockaders. He is armed to the teeth and very dangerous. He has already killed a dozen or more of our brave soldiers who are searching for him. You are to be congratulated. You have stirred up a hornets' nest. The whole coast has been alerted."

He chuckled. "They warned me to keep well away from

the warship taking on water at Noirmoutier."

"What did you say?"

He chuckled again. "I told them that I know these waters so well that I can escape from any *sacré* English ship and that if I don't go where the fish are I will starve. I said I'd bring them back some fish to prove it. In the circumstances I think we are fortunate to have got past them. We will have to be very careful. They will have their cutter out, that's for sure."

The day dawned darkly. Sea and sky were uniformly grey and merged into one on the horizon. The boat pitched and rolled in the swell. Gillet warned again that they must not do anything to attract attention from the shore. There were always watchers with spyglasses and the fast cutter standing by all the time to investigate anything suspicious. They would just have to hope that the mere fact of approaching the English ship would not catch anyone's eye. Colquhoun kept well down out of casual sight in the bottom of the boat as father and son went about their daily business, all the time heading imperceptibly farther out to sea.

When the boat rose on the swell Colquhoun could sometimes see a low contour of land to the south west of them. It was, Gillet explained, the Ile de Noirmoutier, a long narrow strip of land reaching out into the sea at the head of which the English warship was anchored as its crew ferried fresh water from the shore.

The day wore on slowly. At first they could see other similarly occupied fishing boats, but as they went further out to sea they found themselves alone. Father and son were busy all the while, line fishing with multiple lines. The fish must have been plentiful. The pile of fish flapping about in the bottom of the boat grew steadily and father and son were both occupied baiting and casting, checking and pulling in the lines, Gillet all the time with a glance at the single sail hoist on the stern mast, a hand on the tiller and an eye on the sky.

And then Colquhoun saw it.

The outline of Noirmoutier was clear now, a great stretch of deserted scrub covered sand dune, and there, where the land ended, some hundred yards or so from the shore he could see the warship. It was at anchor, its sails furled. At this distance it looked little more than a child's toy. Even so, he could sense its size and power. His heart leaped.

He clambered to the bows and stood straining to catch every glimpse of the ship as the boat rose to the waves.

Slowly, slowly, the ship was getting bigger.

Gillet called out "Here, Monsieur, take this. Hold this up so that they will see it. It is the flag of the Vendée. It is the signal to the English that we wish to communicate."

Colquhoun scrambled aft and took the flag that Gillet was holding out for him. He went back to the bows and shook it out. It was white with a cross surmounting a sacred heart embroidered in red in the centre. He held it aloft, letting it stream out in the wind.

Behind him the younger Pierre spoke for the first time.

"Cutter," he said.

He pointed behind them.

Gillet said urgently:

"Get the mainsail up. Quick. Haul in the lines."

"God damn it," Colquhoun swore.

Distance was impossible to judge over the water, but there, just visible a long way behind them, appearing and disappearing in the swell, he could see the sails of a ship that undoubtedly was heading towards them.

Young Pierre sprang into action. The sail rose on the mast, billowed out and the ship gave a sort of lurch and plunged forward. Colquhoun stuffed the flag into his pocket and scrambled back to pull in the fishing lines. He began hauling at the first one, hand over hand.

"Too slow. Take this. Cut them." Gillet had pulled his knife from its sheath on his belt. He held it out to Colquhoun. "Quick, as you value our lives. Then get back to the bow and keep waving that flag."

It was an uneven race.

The sturdy fishing boat was not built for speed. It was no match for the cutter. Colquhoun watched in an agony as the French boat drew nearer, more menacing every moment. There could be no doubt now that they were its quarry.

It was heading straight for them, growing bigger by the minute, slicing up and down through the waves, white water streaming from its bows. He scrambled back to the bow and held up the flag, waving it so they would see it on the warship.

That, too, was getting bigger all the time. He could plainly see its masts and yards, its furled sails, the forest of ropes, the open gun ports, even little figures on the deck.

They had seen Gillet's boat, he was sure of it. Men were studying them through spyglasses. He could not be certain, but a knot of men at the ship's side looked like a gun crew clustered round a long barrelled gun.

But equally he could see the blue coats of French soldiers on the deck of the cutter.

They were out of range, but the soldiers on the cutter were firing on them now. There were little puffs of dirty smoke that vanished almost immediately in the wind, followed seconds later by the familiar rattle of musketry.

Colquhoun turned back to judge the distance to the warship.

Four hundred yards?

Five hundred?

Six, maybe. Impossible to tell looking over the featureless water.

How far was the cutter? Much closer, and narrowing the gap so quickly. They would be overhauled before they could reach the warship.

He could even hear their loud hailer: "Lower your sails. Heave to. Lower your sails. Heave to immediately in the name of the law."

They would not hear him on the warship - they could not hear, but Colquhoun was shouting: "Fire on them! Open fire on them, for the love of God!"

And, as though his plea had been heard, there was a flash and a burst of smoke on the warship's deck. Seconds later he heard the faint whistle of shot and the report of the gun. A spout of water rose briefly fifty yards behind them.

They were in range - extreme range, maybe, but if the gunner knew his business...

The tension was almost unbearable.

As he watched the cutter, praying it would sheer off, another shot whistled overhead. This time the spout of water was eighty yards behind them, only two hundred yards in front of the cutter.

A third shot was even closer to it.

Suddenly the cutter was no longer head on. She had turned sharply showing the beauty of her lines and the majesty of her crowded sails. A great tricolour flag streamed from her mast. The soldiers were lining her deck, shaking their fists, shouting, but she fell away behind them.

Gillet was looking resolutely ahead, jaw set, willing his craft forward, steering straight for the warship.

"Thank God. Thank God."

Gillet half turned and looked over his shoulder.

"That was close," he said.

The warship loomed massive above them. Young Pierre lowered the mainsail. They bobbed slowly towards the huge bulk of the ship.

A voice shouted down to them:

" Steady as you go. Declare yourself."

Colquhoun stood in the bow waving the flag.

He shouted: "I am Major Grant, 11th Regiment of Foot. Escaping from France. Can I come aboard?"

Several officers and a crowd of sailors were lining the ship's rail, gazing down at them as they came alongside.

A ladder was tossed down.

Gillet indicated for Colquhoun to climb up first.

Just touching the ladder was like sanctuary.

He climbed up onto the deck. Hands reached over the side to help him aboard. The decking under his feet felt unbelievably solid and safe. He looked all round, at the young, dependable English faces of the sailors, at the smart blue uniforms of the officers, at the masts and the crowded deck, at the long barrelled gun where the gun crew were standing grinning at him, at the sea and the sky, at the Union flag flying at the ship's stern.

He had never before known such relief. It was like a burst of glorious sunshine.

Life had never been so beautiful.

The officers were looking at him with amused curiosity. One said: "You cut that a trifle fine, sir. Two or three hundred yards, that's all, and they'd have had you. Near run thing, sir, near run thing. Who did you say you are?"

" Major Grant, sir. 11th Regiment of Foot. I was taken prisoner in Portugal"

"You're a long way off course from there, sir."

"Yes. It's a long story. I had no option but to escape."

The officer was reassuringly stout and red faced.

"Escaped, eh? Well, we must hear all about it. You look as though you could do with a wash and a shave, Major. And a tot of rum, I've no doubt."

He held out his hand. "Welcome aboard, sir. Welcome aboard."

Colquhoun took the proffered hand and shook it hard. "Thank you, sir. From the bottom of my heart, thank you."

EPILOGUE

There was no going back for the Gillets. They were taken back to England where they were interned as prisoners of war. Colquhoun eventually managed to get them released and gave them enough money to buy another boat. History does not record when, or indeed if, they returned to France. Presumably it would have been suicide to have done so before Napoleon's abdication in 1814.

The Vendée did rise again in revolt. Napoleon had to leave twelve thousand soldiers there when he marched to Belgium to take on the armies of Wellington and Blücher. Had he had those men the result of the Battle of Waterloo might well have been different.

Colquhoun was probably still uneasy about breaking his parole. Whatever the reason, parole was a matter of honour, and to break it was a dishonourable act. To honour his undertaking not to serve against the French army until he had been exchanged rank for rank he arranged for a French major to be exchanged for him when he reached England.

Colquhoun rejoined Wellington's army in France probably in September 1813. He served as Wellington's chief intelligence officer during the Waterloo campaign. Information which he had gained about Napoleon's troop movements and which might have altered the site of the final battlefield of Napoleon's Empire failed to reach Wellington due to the stupidity of a General Dornberg who judged it unimportant.

Colquhoun was taken off the active list and put onto half

pay after Waterloo. He retired to Scotland where, on 1st March 1820, he married Margaret Brodie, who bore him one son.

He was recalled to the colours in November 1820, and joined the 33rd Foot - Wellington's old regiment - as a Major where he served for a year until he was promoted to lieutenant colonel and transferred to the 54th Foot who were then serving in India. Colquhoun, accompanied by his wife, joined the regiment as its commanding officer in the summer of 1822. In 1824, under his enlightened command, the 54th were described as being 'as near perfect as can be looked for in this country, ... a fine body, well drilled and steady, healthy and cleanly, well conducted in quarters.'

In 1824 the regiment was ordered to Burma. War had broken out there in a country that was virtually unknown and with an appalling disease ridden climate that decimated the English troops and broke Colquhoun's health. He returned to India in 1825 a very sick man.

Worse was to come. In 1828 his wife Margaret became ill, a virtual death warrant in the Indian climate. She set off with their son to return to Scotland in March that year, but died on board ship within sight of Saint Helena. She was buried there - close to Napoleon's grave.

Perhaps the news broke Colquhoun's heart. In 1829 he was declared unfit for service and was invalided home.

In the hope of curing him Colquhoun's doctors sent him to Aix la Chapelle to take the waters there. In vain. He died at Aix on 28th September 1829, aged forty eight.

As to this story, matters of historical fact are:
Colquhoun was taken prisoner at Idanha a Nova on 16th April 1812.

General de la Martinière's letter to General Clarke of 28 April 1812 and the copy of Colquhoun's parole agreement were intercepted by the Spanish guerrillas, and passed to Wellington.

From inspired research by my friend François Milleron at Vincennes French military records it is almost certain that Colquhoun was sent back to France under escort of the 4e Léger regiment under the command of Major Magaud.

There is a letter at Vincennes dated 26th May 1812 from the commandant at Bayonne stating that Colquhoun left the town on 25th May on route to Verdun under parole of honour.

This was our most exciting find. The accounts that I had previously read of Colquhoun's escape had him jumping parole at Bayonne and hitching a lift to Paris as companion to General Souham. It had seemed an unlikely story, and here was as near proof as possible that Colquhoun had continued his journey northwards at least ostensibly as a paroled officer.

But there the factual trail ends and the rest of the story relies on the accounts of Colquhoun's adventures related by his brother-in-law, Sir James Mcgrigor, Wellington's Chief Medical Officer in the Peninsular, as presumably told to him by Colquhoun.

Despite searching the log books of ships which I believed might have been on blockade off the Nantes coast at the time when I think Colquhoun must have escaped from France, my wife, Sue and I were unable to find any record of his being picked up. Mcgrigor relates that it was a seventy four that rescued him, but I was amazed at the vast amount of ships that the Royal Navy boasted at that time and there must have been many warships of all sizes watching the French coast. I think such record must be there, somewhere.

Taking Colquhoun on board must surely have been noted in the log of whatever ship it was.

Neil McEachen was the father of Marshal Macdonald and Jean Grant was supposed to have danced and diverted the English soldiers from their hunt for Bonnie Prince Charlie. Unlikely as it may seem, Colquhoun told the story of going to the house of a French Marshal and of obtaining his help. He does not say who the Marshal was but Macdonald is the only French Marshal who fits this story.

Marshal Macdonald was not the brightest of Napoleon's Marshals, but his reputation is one of loyalty and honour. He fought valiantly, if not necessarily successfully, for his Emperor in the campaigns of 1813 and 1814. At the battle of Leipzig he escaped capture by swimming the river Elster to safety after the sole bridge had been prematurely blown up cutting off Napoleon's rearguard on the wrong side of the river.

He was one of the four Marshals who, on 6 April 1814, urged Napoleon that further resistance was useless and that he must abdicate. With Ney and Caulincourt, he was charged with negotiating terms with the Allies. Touched by his loyalty Napoleon observed that while many of those he had loaded with honours had deserted him, Macdonald, for whom he had done little, remained faithful to him.

Accepting the Bourbon restoration, Macdonald took no part in Napoleon's 1815 campaign. He eventually retired to Courcelles le Roi, where he spent the last ten years of his life, dying there in 1840.

It is an amusing, salacious, and entirely irrelevant story that in his earlier days Marshal Macdonald had achieved a seventy-two hour sex marathon with Pauline, Napoleon's nymphomaniac sister, the young lady having prudently laid in a stock of food and drink to last the course.

Marshal Marmont, Duke of Ragusa, went on to give a new word to the French language - *raguser*, to betray,- when he changed sides in 1814 and ensured the abdication of Napoleon.

Major Magaud was the tough much wounded veteran that I have described. He was promoted colonel in February 1813 and given command of the *29ᵉ Régiment d'Infanterie Légère* . He died, in November 1813, of wounds received at the battle of Leipzig the previous month.

I have perhaps been unfair to General de la Martinière, though the personal violence with which I have discredited him was not unknown in senior officers. He had been a prisoner of war of the English for a short time during the revolution and is said to have loathed them. He was, however, a very brave and determined fighting soldier. He distinguished himself at the battle of Salamanca, was promoted General of Division in 1813, commanded the right wing of the French army as it retreated across Spain, and died in September that year of wounds received at the crossing of the river Bidassoa.

Doctor Curtis, the Irish priest in Salamanca, was appointed Bishop of Armagh in 1819 at the age of seventy nine, partly, probably, in recognition of his invaluable services in the Peninsular and partly, probably, because of his acquaintance with Wellington. He died of cholera in 1832, aged ninety two. A tough old boy!

And Claudette d'Yves? She is a figment of my imagination... but! Mcgrigor tells us that when he was in

Paris Colquhoun 'frequently met a gentleman with whom he contacted some degree of intimacy. These two gentlemen, as acquaintances, became most acceptable to each other and Grant gained much very valuable information from him.'

Was it indeed a 'gentleman'?

Or was Mcgrigor, writing for Victorian readers, being coy?

My thanks to Madame Simon, the owner of the chateau at Courcelles le Roi, for letting me walk round the old house, now sadly unoccupied and in need of much repair.

My daughter Fiona painted the cover as I particularly wanted to show an officer of the 11th Foot on horseback but had failed to find one anywhere. Many thanks to her and to Sue and Anna for their support and encouragement throughout.

And finally my enormous thanks to Vee Bellers and Sue Duke for putting this book into print and for all their hard work in doing so.

Printed in Great Britain
by Amazon